# CORVUS DEFENDS

## THE MATRIAN TRILOGY
## BOOK 3

## DALE SALE

### Illustrated by
### VIVID COVERS

Dale Sale Books

# OTHER WORKS BY DALE SALE

Have you read the Manual? FREE!!!

The Matriarch Trilogy:
    Corvus Ascending
    Corvus Sirocco
    Corvus Defends

The Jill Tower Mysteries:
    The Murder of Harrison Grey

Copyright © 2022 Dale Sale
All rights reserved.
ISBN:
ISBN-13:

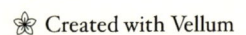

❧ Created with Vellum

## DEDICATION

For my buddy Chris "Possum" Sawyer: Ophelia is glad you ain't road kill yet and agrees with your catch phrase, "Be Kind, It's Free"

# CHAPTER ONE

"Mayday, Mayday, Mayday, this is transport Whiskey, Alpha, Bravo 329, *Lupine*, we are under attack!" a panicked voice came over the comm.

"Transport *Lupine*, this is Matria Orbital Defense. We copy and are getting a DF on your position. Keep transmitting," Sub-lieutenant Denton commed from her station.

"This is Captain Faolan Flannery," a calm man said. "We were preparing to dock with the Mimas asteroid mining facility when a Dellan raider jumped us. The raider is in pursuit. We are under maximum burn for your position, Orbital."

"Rodger Captain," Denton said. "Are you armed?"

"That's a negative Orbital. I've got a few countermeasures but no offenses."

Denton turned to the sensor operator, "How long until we can use our first gun battery?"

"The transport will be inside the 90$^{\text{th}}$ percentile hit radius in thirty minutes," the operator said.

"Orbital," Flannery said. "Can you scramble anything to help the Mimas mining facility? The Dellan raider sortied a boarding party to breach the hab."

Denton's fingers ran through the available assets on her console. "I'm launching something now, Captain. I need you to hang on for thirty minutes."

Faolan turned to Ace, his co-pilot and navigator. "Looks like we need to make our own luck, kids." He released his harness, swung his short legs to the deck, and groaned against the two-gravity acceleration. "You've got the conn, Ace," he said. "I'm going to grab our passenger and try to slow them down a little."

"Aye Skipper, good luck," the young man replied.

The passenger, vacuum jockey Drake Sheridan, was riding along to help *Lupine* out. Captain Flannery was an old friend of Drake's captain, Gus Johansson, and *Lupine* was down a crewman because of an injury. Flannery slicked back his wavy red hair, grabbed his helmet from the rack, and thumped aft. He slapped a wad of DNA-coded sealant on the bridge door and trudged away as it fused the lock. *If the kids get boarded, that might buy them a little time,* Flannery thought.

Drake Sheridan looked up from his nap as the captain stuck his head into the mess deck. "Time to earn your keep, young blood," Flannery said. "There's a Dellan raider on our tail and closing. Meet me at the cargo section airlock. I got to grab a few things first."

"Roger that, Skip," Drake said. "I still got a score to settle with the Dellans, anyway."

The *Lupine* was built to the common design favored for tramp freighters. Containerized cargo fastened in a structural frame made up the forward section. The crew quarters, reaction mass, and engines were the stern.

"Ship, override airlock safety protocol. Command code Red Wolf."

Sheridan met Flannery at the lock. The short man was carrying a large shoulder bag. Flannery and Sheridan exited the ship into the open vacuum of the unpressurized cargo frame section. Flannery scanned the cargo and found the container he was looking for. Thirty-three tons of partially refined austenitic taconite pellets ready for the smelter.

"What's the plan?" Drake asked.

"I got some demo charges here," Flannery said. "We are turning this container into a thirty-ton shotgun."

"I like it!" Drake agreed.

"Captain, that raider is getting close," Ace said over the comm.

"XO, I know, you got this," Flannery commed.

"What've you got planned out there, Cap?" Ace asked.

"I'm send a surprise at those fellas following us," Flannery said. "A trick Gus Johansson told me he used once. Pull up a maneuver file called speed bump."

"Okay Cap, I got it," Ace said as he opened the computer file, read it, and shook his head. "Are you sure about this?"

"Nope, but we don't have thirty minutes," Flannery said. "That ship is faster and more maneuverable than poor old *Lupine*. This might even the odds. Remember, don't waste time braking when you get near the Orbital Battery, just keep on the throttle."

"If Gus used this plan, it is probably fifty percent skill, fifty percent luck," Drake said.

"Okay, loading the file to navigation." Ace said. "Get your ass back here as soon as you can, Cap."

"Don't worry, momma Flannery didn't raise no heroes," he said.

Ace checked the external cameras and saw the captain's short figure passing a giant frame wrench to the much larger Sheridan. Sheridan flipped the tool with practiced ease.

The navigator asked, "What the hell is that guy up to?"

"It looks like he's loosening the cargo frame locks," Ace said.

"At two-Gees? Is he crazy?"

Flannery's voice sounded over the comm. "Ace, start the maneuver."

"Rodger, Cap, hang on."

Ace cut the engine to zero, and the crushing force vanished. He engaged the automated sequence fed into the flight computer. The ship pivoted ninety degrees.

Sheridan popped the cargo locks, and the ship backed away, casting the cargo frame adrift. The *Lupine* rotated again to its original heading.

"Skipper, you better hot foot it," Ace warned. "Ignition in ten seconds."

Flannery and Sheridan floated to the airlock of the crew section. Flannery hit the door cycle panel and watched it flash red.

"Shit! Damn safety lock won't open if it senses a thrust sequence in progress." Flannery knew he didn't have time to fuck around arguing with the computer. "Ace, it locked us out. Good Luck!"

Flannery saluted the camera feed and disappeared from the screen.

The computer rattled the final moments. "Three, two, one, execute."

The crushing acceleration returned. Free of the cargo section, *Lupine* was now topping three-and-a-half gees.

"Matria Orbital, this is *Lupine*," Ace choked. "We have two souls overboard."

On board the Dellan raider, the woman at the conning station turned to her captain. "Sir, the transport has jettisoned their cargo section and is under thrust again. We cannot overtake them before we are within range of Matria's defense grid."

"I guess we will have to settle for the cargo this time," the man in the command chair said. "Maneuver to take it in tow."

---

Flannery peaked over a container and watched the *Lupine's* drive plume grow smaller in the distance. He turned to Sheridan. "Thanks for the save. What is that thing, anyway?"

Drake hooked the device back to his suit. "I call it a lizard lasso. My engineer buddy made it for me. Compressed gas shoots a sticky ball on a long tether. Then I just reeled us back to the cargo section like a hooked catfish. That guy is always coming up with some new doodad."

Flannery turned to see the flashing running lights of the raider closing on them. "Time for Plan B."

---

On the Dellan raider, the captain asked, "Is the EV party ready to attach the tow?"

The officer at the operations console answered, "Yes, Sir, they are in the lock and awaiting authorization to cycle."

The captain punched a code into the panel at his elbow that cleared the airlock safeties.

Two figures exited the lock as the operations officer watched. Just as they clipped their jackline tethers, the feed cut out.

Outside the raider, the Dellans were fighting for their lives. Drake swung the giant cargo wrench bar into the helmet of the first Dellan out the door. Escaping vapor from the cracked faceplate formed a freezing cloud, blinding his enemy.

The second one reacted fast and had a flechette pistol out in an instant. Flannery grabbed the suffocating man and used him as a shield. The first barrage of darts buried themselves in the man's back.

Flannery pushed the wounded man towards his friend, who was retreating into the lock. He watched them slam the lock shut. Flannery grinned as he looked down at the remote clipped to his wrist, raised the arming toggle, and flipped the switch.

Inside the lock, a small red light flashed on the chest of the wounded man.

Flannery chuckled when the self-destruct charge blew the airlock's inner and outer doors.

---

The pressure loss alarm screamed on the raider's bridge.

"What the hell is going on out there?" the captain yelled.

"Sir, we have a loss of atmosphere on decks three and four," the ops officer said. "Damage control reports the airlock destroyed."

"There must be a sapper out there," the captain said. "Is the primary drive online?"

"Engineering reports the drive is rebooting and will be functional in one minute."

---

Sheridan skimmed over the hull, pulling himself along fast, "Don't worry Cap, I did this once to a Governance cruiser," Sheridan said over his comm. "I just gotta get to the drive cone before they light off."

Sheridan hauled himself over the lip of the drive cone and fired his lasso at the reaction initiator. The tether snaked out deep into the cone and stuck near a relay. He clamped a charge to the handle and set the lasso to reel in. It neatly hauled the charge to float next to the relay.

Sheridan ducked back over the cone edge and gave Flannery a thumbs up.

Flannery hit the remote detonator switch. He turned away from the flash and felt the vibration of the explosion. Flannery said, "You aren't going anywhere now, assholes."

---

The bridge crew felt the explosive rumble through the ship.

"Captain, engineering reports that the fusion initiation relay is destroyed," the Operations officer said from his console. "We only have maneuvering thrusters."

"How long until our inertia takes us in range of the Matria Orbital batteries?" the captain asked.

"We will be under their guns in fifteen minutes," the conn reported.

"Gentlemen, I am open to suggestions," Ewan said.

The bridge crew looked at each other in silence.

---

At Orbital Battery Control, Sub-lieutenant Denton studied her screens. She had seen the *Lupine* jettison their cargo section and two explosions erupt on the raider. "*Lupine,* this is Orbital. I thought you didn't have any weapons?"

"We don't," Ace commed back. "Looks like our crewmen are fighting them hand-to-hand."

"Are they crazy?"

"I wouldn't deny it or call them that to their face, Ma'am."

"*Lupine,* I show the Dellan raider is maneuvering behind the cargo section."

Ace said, "My guess is they are trying to put some mass between your guns and their hull."

"I can't fire on them if you believe your men are still out there," Denton said.

"Do you have any ships you can re-route to intercept them?" Ace asked.

"Nothing armed," Denton said. "The nearest patrol vessel is headed to Mimas. They are reporting a second raider on approach. Probably to pick up the breaching party."

"Sorry, Cap, I guess you are on your own until I can get this thing turned around," Ace said to no one.

---

Sheridan and Flannery clung to the outside of the raider as it moved toward the cargo frame.

"What are they doing?" asked Sheridan.

"Looks like they are hiding behind the cargo," Flannery said. He checked his HUD. "We will be in range of the guns in just a few more minutes."

"Do you think the battery will fire on us?"

"Probably not."

"Probably?"

Flannery held his hands up in the universal "who knows" sign.

Sheridan said, "I know that class of Dellan ship, they only have one air lock. They are stuck in there until they can make some repairs. I'm guessing we have fifteen more minutes before they can get an emergency lock set up. Then..."

"Yeah, then they will swarm like a kicked hornet's nest."

"We got lucky with the first two," Sheridan said. "This next batch knows we are out here."

"I meant to ask," Flannery said. "Where did you learn to fight in zero-gee like that?"

"Orbital Guard," Sheridan said. "Extra-vehicle Mate First Class,"

Flannery laughed. "I should have known Johansson would find an Orbie for his crew. He likes to collect strays."

"Cap, you don't know the half," Sheridan said. "You never saw a bigger bunch of misfits than our crew. The XO is a battle bot with a crush on the Captain, the Tac Ops is a disgraced Marine Gunner, the slickest Suppo that ever skimmed a log req handles the business end, her boyfriend, the EO, is a cyborg that was in cryo for a thousand years, the ship itself is sentient but only says three words at a time, the maintenance bot hates getting dirty, and a Matriarch handles the weapons. When I left, they were carrying a seventy-year-old retired spy and the First Lord Admiral of the Governance's daughter as passengers. Oh, I almost forgot, we have a possum for a mascot."

"If I didn't know Gus, I would swear you made that up," Flannery said.

Sheridan stood. "Skip, we better get ready to jump to the frame and take cover. We're almost in contact."

The raider spun to bring its belly along the frame, and the pair stepped over and disappeared into the maze of containers.

Ten suited Dellans streamed from the ruined airlock door. Two began applying a prefab temporary lock door with another standing guard for them. Several winched the raider against the frame with come-alongs. The rest fanned out through the frame to hunt Sheridan and Flannery.

Flannery touched helmets with Sheridan and said, "Holy shit, they parked right on top of the container rigged with explosives!"

"This is just too easy," Sheridan said. "Let's see what they have planned."

Four more figures came through the lock, each carrying two long, slim tubes. They welded cradles to the hull and bolted the tubes into the cradles before attaching some cabling.

"Gotta give them an 'A' for ingenuity," Flannery said. "Those are torpedo engines. They won't have throttle controls once they light off, but it should push them out of the defense grid's range."

The crews finished and all the enemies cycled through the new lock. Sheridan ran the numbers with his suit navicomp. "Cap, we are in trouble. If their plan works, we won't last until a rescue boat gets here. My suits only got two hours left."

"Okay, I guess it's back to Plan A," Flannery said as he keyed an override code into a container and opened the door. "We hide in here and blow the charges on our thirty-ton shotgun. If nothing else, it should shear the come-alongs and cast the raider off the frame."

"Hey, if we just cut those come-alongs before the torpedoes fire, the raider will move off and won't be able to shut them down to come after us," Sheridan said. "Then we just keep drifting on our present course towards the Orbitals and we should be in rescue range in an hour. Plus, we save the cargo."

"Then we better hump," Flannery said. "Those torpedoes are gonna fire soon."

---

On the bridge of the raider, the captain congratulated his crew. "Good job, everyone. It looks like we will bring this cargo in, after all. We are going to need it to pay for repairs."

The conning officer asked, "What about the sappers, Captain?"

"I'm assuming they are hiding in the cargo," he said. "Their suits will fail soon, and they won't be our problem anymore. We can pitch them in the recycler when we get done."

"Captain, engineering reports that the torpedo engines will be ready to fire in five minutes," the operations officer reported.

"Very well," the captain said. "Let's not fuck this up now."

---

Sheridan and Flannery struggled to loosen the come-alongs. "I wish I still had that cargo bar," Drake said.

"Come on, big fella, you're twice my size, and I got my two loose already." Flannery chided.

"Okay, Skipper, you head back to the frame. I've almost got this last one." Drake turned a lever, reeved out the chain, and deftly flipped it from its purchase. He flipped and kicked off hard towards safety.

Drake clipped his tether onto a frame crossbar as he sailed by and slowed himself by paying out. He looked back to see a glow forming on the torpedo drive cones. "See ya later, suckers," he said with a mock salute.

The torpedoes fired. One of the loose come-alongs chains snagged, and the raider dragged the frame with it.

"Shit," Flannery said. "Head for cover, kid. I'm gonna have to blow the charges, anyway."

Drake kicked and pivoted into the container gaps just as the charges blew.

It was a glorious sight. Thousands of one-centimeter balls burst straight into the hull of the raider. The ship accelerated away, trailing atmosphere from a vast area of the perforated hull. The trail got swept up in the torpedo drive plumes and fluoresced.

"Huh, kinda pretty, in a death of your enemy sort of way," Sheridan said.

"That's harsh, kid!" Flannery said.

"No Dellan ever shed a tear for any of my shipmates. Well, I'm gonna curl up in this container and take a nap. Wake me up when the rescue party gets here, boss."

## CHAPTER TWO

"Fleet Chief, you have a personal transmission," Forbes' aide said over his intercom.

"Thank you. I will take it here in my quarters." He glanced in the mirror and smoothed back his hair. The stress lines on his face were deeper by the day. *I'll be glad when this is over. I need some rest.* He punched a button to connect the video. The Fleet was too far away, and bandwidth constricted to allow a holo feed. "Good evening, my dear. How was your day?"

The smiling face of his eight-year-old granddaughter, Iona, looked back at him. "Seanair, you won't believe what happened today!"

"Oh, tell me," he said.

"Willy Sims' pet guinea pig had *babies,*" Iona said. "Momma says I can have one when they get weaned."

"Oh, that's grand," Forbes said, smiling. "Do you have room?"

"Seanair, guineas are little! They take up hardly any room. I can put the cage on my dresser. I just need to get rid of some of the *baby* stuff in my room."

"Oh, so you are all grown up now?"

"You know I'm eight and a half!" she protested. "We started vacuum suit drills last week in school. I was fastest, and I didn't forget to complete my checklist like Brin."

"Excellent," Forbes said. "Did they try to trick you?"

"Yes, the instructor had a foil seal on my recycler," she said. "She almost got me on that one, but I remembered what you said."

"No one cares about your next breath like you do," the pair said together and fell into giggling.

"How much longer before we get to move to a real planet?" Iona asked.

"It won't be long now," Forbes said. "Just a few details to work out."

"I can't wait!" Iona said. "Is the sky really blue? Not just simulated. And you can really look over an ocean so big that you can't see the other side."

"An ocean so big it would take days to sail across it," Forbes said. "Sometimes the storms are so big you think the waves will swallow your boat."

"That sounds scary."

"If you prepare yourself and your equipment, there is nothing to be afraid of," Forbes said.

"With a checklist," Iona said.

"With a checklist," Forbes replied. "Put you mother on and goodnight."

"Kisses," she said, and ran from the screen yelling for her mother.

"Hi, Daddy," Forbes' daughter Eliane said. She looked tired and disheveled.

"Sweetheart, you don't look so good."

She ran her hand through her greasy hair. "Things are pretty tough here. We are on water and power restrictions again. I've been pulling double shifts because of another aspergillus outbreak in the air processors."

"Take care of yourself," Forbes said. "Iona needs one of us around."

"I don't want to alarm you," Elaine said. "But the situation isn't confined to our cylinder. This outbreak is bad. I've seen reports it is spreading. Two habitats have recently been abandoned because the sterilization protocols failed."

"I received a briefing on that," Forbes said. "If we had won on Kragus, this wouldn't be happening. The southern continent has plenty of room for all of us to settle. That meddling bastard Gus Johansson really screwed up the plan."

"Perhaps we backed the wrong faction," she said. "Orr Limnos was not the best choice of business partners."

"Clearly," Forbes said.

"You could petition the government to allow us to settle on Kragus."

"I fear that bridge is burned," Forbes said. "The Governance has full control of the planet and are increasing the number of troops and ships there. I doubt they will trust us."

"Father, please consider it," Elaine said. "Don't allow your pride to doom us all."

"Elaine, I have my eyes on a fatter prize than Kragus," Forbes said. "Matria is ripe for conquest."

"But Matria is a civilized world," Elaine said. "Surely they would help us if they knew we were in such dire straits. Besides, aren't they defended?"

"They do have enough orbital defenses and ships to handle our raiders," Forbes said. "When we get our flagship, *Jishin,* back in action we will easily roll over those. When we arrive in force they will rush to talk to us. It is better to negotiate from strength."

"Isn't Gus Johansson aligned with Matria?" Elaine asked.

"What can one man and one ship do against our entire fleet?"

"You underestimated him last time, and we lost an army."

## CHAPTER THREE

On Matria, Decision Hall was already loud, and voices were still rising. Chief Consul Sidra struggled to call the meeting to order.

"If you please." She rapped her shepherd's crook against the floor with vigorous strokes to get the delegates' attention. "This Emergency Session will now come to order. We will first hear a report on recent events from House Custos. Consul Tess is in command of our forces."

Consul Tess, the leader of House Custos, the Guardians, began. "As we have feared, the Dellans have returned to our space. They attacked the mining facility at Mimas. If it hadn't been for the heroic efforts of Captain Flannery and the crew of *Lupine*, the inhabitants would have been killed and the entire operation lost."

Consul Dollas of House Negotia, the Merchants, asked, "What are the damages to the facility?"

Tess continued. "The habitat sustained significant damage to the outer casing. It is salvageable, but it is far from our Orbital Defense Platforms and we have too few patrol vessels to leave one there permanently. If the Dellans try again, it will be a loss."

"Do we know what prompted the attack? Is it just another common raid?"

Sidra said, "I fear it is not. The Dellans were defeated at Kragus by our friends in the *Corvus*. They have decided that Matria should be held responsible because of *Corvus's* letter of marquee."

"If I understand correctly, *Corvus* saved two Governance cruisers and thousands of citizens during that battle," Dollas said. "The Governance owes us recompense."

Sidra said, "I will contact First Lord Admiral McGowan to remind him of his debt."

"*Corvus* bested the Dellans once. May they do so again?" Dollas asked.

"I will be in touch with Captain Johansson to plead for aid. I fear that *Corvus* alone cannot secure us a victory this time."

"What of our own forces?" asked Consul Liras, from House Legibus, in charge of Laws and Justice.

"The Orbital Defenses can prevail against the normal Dellan threat. However, they now have this ship." Tess waved her hand, and an image of the Dellan flagship, *Jishin,* popped into view to gasps from the Consuls. "The scale is difficult to see from this image, but it stretches six kilometers. *Corvus* damaged it severely, but if the Dellans can repair it, our defenses will not save us," Sidra said.

"We currently have fifteen patrol vessels that are evenly matched against standard Dellan raiders. However, we do not have enough crews for them all, and they cannot operate in the atmosphere," Tess added.

"Why are the Guildsmen not in attendance?" Consul Bix of House Scientia, Knowledges of Math and Science asked. "Their Airmen and Lightermen could operate the extra ships."

Consul Elle from House Textus, dealers in secrets and spy

craft said, "True, we could petition them. However, the men do not have the skills to operate the ships alone. We would need to supplement the crews with women."

"That may not be advisable; you know how emotional men can be," said Consul Maude from Hospitus, the house in charge of entertainments and hospitality.

An uproar of loud voices and laughter filled the room. "Mixed gender crews? How positively twenty-first century!"

"I agree it is far from ideal, however, we have little choice," said Consul Elle. "We will just have to trust that the women can keep their libidos in check."

Sidra said, "I trust the Medicus can prescribe something to calm their urges. Perhaps slip it into their rations?"

Counsel Caudis from House Medicus, the Healing, nodded. "It can be arranged."

# CHAPTER FOUR

Fleet Chief Forbes sat in the briefing room of his flagship, *Jishin*, surrounded by his staff. A fleet intelligence officer detailed the recent loss of a raider near Mimas.

"This is embarrassing, people," Forbes said with steel in his voice. "If we can't overcome a bunch of Matrian pacifists on an unarmed transport, what does that say for us?"

"Fleet Chief, the transport wasn't actually Matrian," the officer said. "It was a contractor with military experience."

"Who?"

The face flicked on the briefing room screen. "Captain Faolin Flannery of the transport *Lupine*. He operated with the Wind Hammers." The screen zoomed in on a tattoo on Flannery's arm, the symbol of Mjolnir.

"Wait, why do I know that tattoo?" Forbes asked.

"The Wind Hammers were a band of irregular special operators led by this man, Bosun Guster Johansson," Fleet Operations said. "Now the owner and captain of this ship."

A high-resolution screenshot of *Corvus* resting at the Kragus Lift Port popped up. Gus was standing under the wing with

Flannery. The view zoomed in on Gus's own Mjolnir tattoo surrounded by an array of battle stars.

Forbes thundered. "That motherfucker again? Why haven't you killed him already?"

"The intelligence service is attempting to locate the *Corvus*," Operations said. "Our sources say that before Johansson left Kragus, he transferred a crew member to *Lupine*. He will return to retrieve him."

The screen showed the action outside the raider. "These images were retrieved from the raider when we salvaged it. We assume this smaller figure to be Flannery and the larger one to be Johansson's crewman, Drake Sheridan." The screen zoomed to show Drake's face clearly through his helmet. "Sheridan is a former Orbital Guard."

"You are telling me an Orbie on an unarmed transport destroyed our raider? When this gets out, we will be the laughingstock of the system." Forbes needled Operations.

"We've never encountered such fierce resistance from a transport before, Fleet Chief," Operations said in a pitiful defense.

"I want a bounty on Sheridan and Flannery's heads, a very large one! On second thought, make the reward on anyone associated with Johansson." Forbes said. "Alert the Shadows that they can collect, too."

The intelligence officer nodded to a nondescript man in a crisp dark jump-suit sitting against the wall. The man nodded back and left the room.

"EO, what is the status of making this ship ready for battle again?" Forbes asked.

The *Jishin's* Engineering Officer stood. "Chief, we have juryrigged most systems, and the auxiliary fusion drives are online. To be fully RFB, we really need a shipyard, preferably one that knows how to work with ancient Imperial Confederation tech."

Forbes snorted. "Does this place exist?"

An extremely old bald man staggered to his feet. "I have found a record of such a place."

Fleet Intelligence scoffed. "If such a facility existed, I would already know of it."

"You also told me that *Jishin* was the only Imperial Confederation vessel in existence. Then *Corvus* showed up and kicked our ass!" Forbes said. "I want to hear what Clerk of Records Stanley has found."

The aged Stanley began. "I have been threading through the *Jishin's* databases, and found reference to an automated shipyard inside one of Ix's Trojan asteroids. That facility's dock was large enough to swallow the *Jishin* and her entire battle group."

Forbes whistled under his breath. "EO, is that something you can work with?"

"Most definitely, First Chief."

"What's the location of this facility?" the intelligence officer asked.

"I do not yet know."

"Ha, empty promises and tall tales." Intelligence sneered.

"If I may continue uninterrupted?" Stanley said. "Astrogation is running an orbital regression that will narrow our search. They assured me of an answer soon."

"Good enough for me," Forbes said. "Operations, have the battle group begin transit to the Trojans."

"Aye, Chief." He saluted and left the room.

"First, we repair *Jishin*," Forbes said. "Then we teach those self-righteous Matriarchs some humility."

---

*Jishin* and her fleet drifted near the ancient shipyard against a background of stars. The small ringed-star named Ix shone in the distance. Astrogation had taken up ninety percent of the computer bandwidth for several days to calculate an approximate position of the hidden Imperial shipyard. Even then, they had searched for two weeks. They only found the place because the facility's automated defenses had destroyed a scouting drone.

*Jishin's* commander, Captain Stuart, said, "Awaiting orders, Fleet Chief Forbes."

"Stanley, how confident are you that your thousand-year-old hack will work against the shipyard's Constructed Intelligence?"

The old man straightened. "This is the same code the Imperials used to disable *Jishin* when they abandoned it. It operates more like a virus than a password. The program infiltrates the CI's programing and strips the higher sentient functions. Then we feed in our own base code and harness the beast to our plow."

"Very well, Captain Stuart, proceed with the plan."

"Aye," Stuart said. "Conn ahead dead slow until we get a reaction."

"Ahead dead slow, aye,"

A faint vibration rumbled through the deck plates. At one thousand klicks, the shipyard flared to life.

"Rail guns charging and targeting us," the ops officer said.

A gravelly voice came through the comm. "Who are you, and how did you get that ship?"

The forward display filled with a flickering black and white scene, some ancient programmers inside joke. It recreated an old Earth vid drama, set during a global conflict unimaginatively called World War II. The character: male, indeterminate age, paunchy, and dressed in olive green fatigues, gripped a smoking cigar in his teeth. His hat rode high on his head, revealing a receding hairline. A haphazard stack of manila folders tilted perilously on a large oak desk. The IN tray was empty, and the OUT tray overflowed. A steaming coffee cup sat at his elbow. Through a window behind him, the scene looked from a second story over an enormous warehouse stretching far into the distance. Fork trucks and gantry cranes moved silently in the background, shuffling large crates around the complex on mysterious tasks. He pulled a pencil from behind his ear and looked down at a clipboard and scribbled.

Stanley whispered, "It appears to be running a preset script. I suggest we engage."

Forbes keyed his comm. "This is ICS *Jishin*, requesting dock access. We require repairs."

"This is Sergeant Faber, Acting Superintendent of Ultima Shipyard. *Jishin* went to the breakers yard a thousand-years-ago!" the projection said. "Hope you got a better story, Bud. I shoot in fifteen seconds."

"We are sent on a secret long range mission, the scrapping was a cover story. We only recently arrived back in the system and have suffered extensive damage. Transmitting our authorization codes now." Forbes gestured to Stanley, who tapped a tablet and nodded.

The image on the screen glitched and flickered. "What the fuck is this?" Faber shouted. "You aren't taking me that easy, you bastards!"

"Enemy railguns targeting," the weapons officer said.

"Take out those guns," Stuart ordered.

The bridge lights on *Jishin* flickered as her own guns began firing.

"Lay down a CIWS screen," Forbes screamed.

The close-in-weapons system roared to life and began intercepting the shipyard's fire.

The screen with Faber's image stuttered and blurred. A howl erupted from the comm, and the shipyards' railguns ceased.

"You damn meat sacks," Faber screamed. "I'm gonna hunt you down and skull-fuck you dry!"

The screen went black.

"Damn, I hope that thing is burned," Stuart said. "I've never heard a CI make a threat like that."

"I must admit," Stanley said. "We have little experience in how Imperial CIs operate. It sounded determined to carry out its revenge, though."

"First Chief, I am tracking a small craft fleeing the facility," the operations officer said.

"Kill it!"

"It is already out of range and still accelerating at," the officer checked the read-out and whistled, "over one-hundred gees."

Forbes said, "Well, it looks like the CI, Faber, is still active. We have no time to waste, shipmates. I don't know how it would skull-fuck me dry, but I don't intend to find out."

---

**"Faber in trouble,"** *Corvus* said over the 1MC.

Gus rolled over in his bunk and hit the comm. "What ya got?"

Lenore's steady android contralto came over the comm. "Captain, we have received a coded transmission from Faber. Could you come to the Bridge?"

Gus wasted no time hauling on his uniform and mag boots. When he reached the bridge, he saw the rest of the crew was already there.

"All right, XO, let's hear it."

"*Corvus,* this is Sergeant Faber," the bot's angry gravel voice said. "Some bastards in an ICS assault carrier attacked my shipyard. Said they were the *Jishin*. I was fat, dumb, and happy for millennia until you showed up. Suddenly, every swinging dick and his brother is knocking on my door."

"Oh, shit," said former Marine Gunner Nan Stanski. She tucked her short blonde hair behind her ears and said in her thick accent, "That good deed didn't take long to come back and bite us in the ass."

The Bridge door opened and their passengers, Sadie Hawley and her niece, Mitzi Grey, entered. "We heard the transmission over the 1MC," Sadie, the retired spymaster, said.

"Lenore, who is Faber?" Mitzi asked.

Lenore ignored her question.

Nan shook her head when she noticed the always stylish Mitzi had actually taken the time to tailor a flight suit to accent her curves. She wore her blond curls in a ponytail pulled through a ship's cap with her name monogrammed on the back.

Faber's message continued. "Listen, Johansson, *Jishin* looked pretty beat up, but if they bypass my system restrictions, the facility will make that wreck like new. There ain't nothing in the twin systems that can stand against a fully operational planetary assault carrier. You need to make sure that doesn't happen."

"Oh dear, Captain," HAM, the maintenance bot, said. "I am afraid Faber is correct in his assessment. *Corvus* only prevailed against *Jishin* last time by using surprise and superior tactics. It is unlikely we can duplicate such a victory."

Short, powerfully built Nyrkki Ratuainen, the cyborg Engineering Officer, said in his deep rumble, "Looks like we are gonna need a bigger gun."

Slim, dark-haired Pela Custos, the Matriarch's representative aboard, said from her weapons console, "There is a set of coordinates embedded within the transmission. Probably, Faber's bolthole."

"*Corvus*, please change course for that location and increase to one point five gees," Gus said. He turned to their passengers. "Sorry ladies, it looks like a delay in our trip to Matria."

Mitzi smiled. "Oh, how marvelous, another adventure? Don't fret Gusty dear, we feel just like part of the crew by now. Tell us how we may help. Perhaps I should call Daddy. I'm sure the Admiral will have some thoughts on the situation." She finished with a salute.

Lenore stared at her console and growled to herself as she watched Mitzi strut away.

## CHAPTER FIVE

The entry request lit up and the man-in-charge rose from his desk and smoothed his jumpsuit. No rank or identification marred its deep black perfection. This was his domain.

"Enter."

The armored environmental door swung soundlessly on balanced hinges and a large man eased through the opening. His dark hair and beard were close-cropped, and he carried much more muscle than a typical low-gravity born Dellan. His adaptive camouflage battle dress was the default matt black. The long slim blade sheathed at his hip was all business. His movements betrayed that he didn't need a blade to be deadly.

"As requested," he said.

"Mr. Banner, there is a new mission for the Shadows," the man-in-charge said. He waved a hand and a holo briefing began. A composite image of a rag-tag collection of men and women in mismatched uniforms appeared. "This is the crew of a ship named *Corvus*."

"I am familiar with *Corvus*."

"This crew is causing trouble again. The Fleet Chief wishes this trouble erased."

"How many targets?"

"Eight, most are ex-military misfits cashiered from the Governance." The man-in-charge continued. A tall, muscular woman with short blonde hair balanced a standard Marine assault rifle on her hip. Her pale blue eyes stared out of the holo. "This is Gunner Nantalina Stanski, *Corvus's* Tactical Officer. Highly experienced in independent small unit operations."

Banner bristled. "I'm already familiar with this bitch. I spent a six-month mercenary gig trying to drive her into the ground. Would have got her then if it wasn't for the incompetence of those squabbling Spellex Core idiots."

A petite woman with a long thick braid of salt and pepper hair stood next to Nan. She barely came up to Nan's shoulder. "Zia Forte, Supply Officer and accomplished pilot. Don't let her size fool you, this one is a nasty piece of work. Her partner is one Nyrkki Ratuainen, engineering officer." A short man only slightly taller than Zia, his white hair and beard were close-cropped. His impossible muscles stretched his engineer's coveralls across a barrel chest and tree trunk thighs. "He is a mystery. There are rumors he has an illegal cybernetic neural lace enhancement. There is no record of him before he joined *Corvus's* crew. His phenotype matches a native from Wolfram, a high-gravity world of the old Confederation. Possibly some kind of recessive gene mutant." A tall, dark-skinned man with short curly hair was next. "Drake Sheridan, former Orbital Guard EV Mate First Class, pilot and zero-gravity operations specialist. It appears he single-handedly disabled one of our raiders by blowing their engines from the outside."

Banner scoffed. "An Orbie? Unlikely, they aren't known for their battle prowess. He must have a good PR guy."

The man-in-charge sniffed and turned back to the holo. A young woman with long brown hair stood next to Drake. "This is Pela, Matriarch House Custos, weapons specialist and former aide to Chief Consul Sidra. Like all Matriarchs, her background is," he paused, "*murky*."

"Matriarchs! We will strike a blow for decency when their corrupt moral system is finally ground to dust." Banner sneered. "Their promiscuous ways are an affront to the natural order."

The man-in-charge continued. "Next is Faolin Flannery. He recently joined the crew. He served in the Wind Hammers with several of the others. You can see the tattoo of Mjolnir in the view."

Banner paused and studied the holo. He hadn't noticed the tattoo before and manipulated the holo. The view shifted to highlight the tattoos on Nan, Zia, and Flannery. "Wind Hammers? I thought they were all dead. If these are really Wind Hammers, it's no wonder the Fleet Chief is having so much trouble."

"And their captain," the man-in-charge said, "CWO4 Star Bosun Guster Johansson, Governance Navy, retired."

Banner studied Gus's holo. "This is the feared Gus Johannson? Looks like the gardener at a retirement home."

Gus's image stared out accusingly. He was tall and still well-muscled despite his age. A certain glint of mischief twinkled in his crinkled blue eyes. A full head of gray hair topped his head. Gus's large forearm featured the Mjolnir tattoo wreathed in a constellation of battle stars.

"Don't get too cocky, this 'gardener' bested a Kragun blade master twenty years his junior in single combat. His tactics are unorthodox and effective. There is a lot of fight left in the old dog."

"You've made your point," Banner said. "I assume the bounty is commensurate with the risk?"

"Does one-hundred-thousand hectares on Matria sound sufficient?"

"That's an easy offer for you, my crew are the ones putting it on the line. If this invasion fails you are out nothing," Banner said. "Two-hundred grand cash apiece for everybody on my squad, regardless of outcome. Plus, the land grant."

The man-in-charge winced. The cash would reduce the money he planned to skim from the bounty Fleet Chief Forbes authorized. "That's a hard bargain, Banner."

Banner replied, "Did I mention it had to be paid in Cellan francs?"

The man-in-charge fumed. "Fine, but I expect proof of completion."

"I will save a few scraps of DNA for you."

Banner turned to leave, and the man-in-charge said, "I expect you to be in the first landing wave."

"Don't bother making room for us. We take our own ship. I don't trust those rookie pilots to get us down in one piece."

# CHAPTER SIX

Gus sat in his command chair on the bridge. "Consul Sidra, I was just getting ready to contact you," Gus said to the elegant dark woman on the forward screen. Their three-million-kilometer separation only caused a ten-second delay, acceptable enough for an actual conversation.

"Captain Johansson," she began. "The letter of marquee I issued to you has given the Dellans an excuse to hold Matria at fault for their defeat at Kragus. They conducted an unprovoked strike on a facility in the Lysistrata asteroid cluster."

"Sidra, I'm afraid I have more bad news. The Dellans captured a shipyard to repair their assault carrier," Gus said. "If we can't stop that repair, the entire twin system is going down the tubes."

"That is unwelcome information," she replied. "I request *Corvus* prepare for operations against the Dellan forces. I shall contact First Lord Admiral McGowan and relay the information. The Governance owes me a debt. It is time for them to honor it."

"You said they hit a Lysistrata facility," Gus asked. "I had a crewman helping the transport *Lupine* on that run. Do you know if they are okay?"

"They are considerably better off than the Dellans that chased them," Sidra said. "Captain Flannery dispatched the enemy handily. Quite a feat for an unarmed ship against a raider. The crew of *Lupine* is safely on Matria now."

"Those Dellans, never stood a chance," Nan said from the conn. "I've seen Flannery defeat an entire squad with some rope and a rock, and Sheridan single-handily took out a Governance cruiser."

Gus grunted in agreement. "Any chance you could ferry our crewman back to us," Gus asked. "Doesn't look like we will get to enjoy your hospitality any time soon."

"It is the least I can do, Captain," Sidra said. "Please, do not begin offensive actions until I can get a declaration of war passed by the Houses."

"Understood," Gus said. "We will wait for your signal."

"Good luck to you and good hunting."

# CHAPTER SEVEN

Drake Sheridan met the crew of Lupine at the Lift Port mess hall for dinner.

"Hey shipmates," Drake said as he slid into the booth next to Ace. He slid two trays of food onto the table. Tag was there too. "So, fill me in on Matria. The quarters are fine, but the place has a quarantine vibe."

Ace grinned and Tag said, "First time on Matria, huh, kid."

"Yeah," Drake said. "I've got a shipmate on *Corvus* from here, but she doesn't talk about it much."

Flannery sat down next to Tag.

"Cap, you've been here more than us; tell Drake here about our hosts and the quarantine situation," Tag said, with a wave of his fork.

"Well, technically, it isn't quarantine, more like social restriction," Flannery said. "Ya see, on Matria the sexes don't freely mix. Women live in the cities and the men have their quarters outside the walls. Men can't walk around inside the gated city after sunset."

"What?" Drake said. "What about all the stories I hear about free-love-ladies?"

Tag said, "Don't believe everything you see on the vids."

Ace jumped into the conversation. "I think we need to take Drake to a gatehouse pub. He could use some relaxation after cheating death."

Flannery said, "You up for a little adventure, kid?"

Drake stood and grabbed his now empty trays. "I need seconds if we are adventuring."

---

The crew of Lupine piled out of the auto-taxi and walked up to the City Guard shack.

Flannery said, "Let me do the talking."

The woman inside slid open the window, and Flannery said, "Good evening officer, I am the captain of the *Lupine*, newly arrived. We would like to visit the Rusty Razor pub."

The woman took their thumbprints and studied her screen. "I see three of you have been here before. I'm assuming you know the rules. Make sure you keep that one out of trouble." She pointed at Drake.

Flannery popped a salute and smiled. "Of course, officer, no trouble from us." He winked at Drake.

As they walked through the gate, Drake asked, "I thought men couldn't wander around at night?"

Ace said, "Gatehouse pubs are technically not inside the city, so men are allowed."

"And so are the ladies," Tag added.

They walked down the deserted street. Drake asked, "Where is everybody? And, why are all these houses so ugly? Matria is supposed to be a place of beauty, culture, and refinement."

"Except for a few entertainment districts, people tend to stay home and have parties in private," Tag said.

"Don't let the outside of these buildings fool you either," Flannery added gesturing to the slab-sided stone structures lining the street. "They built these with large inner courtyards and gardens. The luxuries inside would make an ancient emperor jealous."

"In Xanadu did Kublai Khan, a stately pleasure-dome decree," Ace quoted.

Tag said, "Even that old opium-eater Coleridge couldn't have imagined this place."

The group arrived at a door with a sign above it that read, Public Welcome.

Drake shrugged. "Not much to look at."

Flannery elbowed Tag with a smile. "Like I said, don't let the outside fool you." He pushed open the door.

Laughing, loud music, and delicious smells immediately assaulted them. A woman inside yelled, "Come on in, boys, the party is just getting started."

Drake hesitated. "Are you sure this is a good idea?"

Flannery pushed him through the door and said, "Into the fray!"

A tall, buxom middle-aged woman greeted them. Her curly red hair bounced as she ran over, arms wide. "Faolin Flannery, I heard you almost got spaced by a raider again." She grabbed him around the waist, picked the small man up, and buried him in her bosom.

"Good to see you too, Maude," he said in a muffled voice.

"I know Tag and Ace, but who is this fine-looking specimen?" she said as she dropped Flannery, put her hands on her hips, and walked around Drake with an appraising eye.

"Drake Sheridan, Ma'am," he said with a bow. "I normally ship on the *Corvus*, but Captain Flannery needed an extra hand."

"Oh, I've heard of the *Corvus*," she said. "News like the battle at Kragus gets around. Isn't Pela, of House Custos, on that ship?"

"Yes, Ma'am."

"You stop with that ma'am stuff right now," she said. "Everyone calls me Maude. Welcome to my House, the Rusty Razor. Named for the many drunken sailors we have shaved the belly of over the years."

Tag, Ace, and Flannery laughed knowingly.

She led them through the large room filled with tables of laughing, eating, and drinking men and women.

She paused at a table with a couple sharing a passionate kiss. "You two," she said, with a shove. "act decent or get a room."

Drake took Flannery's arm and asked, "Skipper, is this a bawdy house?"

Flannery roared in laughter. "Kid, there's no such thing on Matria. You wouldn't believe me if I told you, so you are just going to have to wait and see."

They didn't notice a man sitting alone leave his table and slide out the door.

Maude lead them to a courtyard garden with a fountain at one end and a small stream winding through it. A roofed balcony circled the inner wall forming a two-story covered porch. She slid open a double pocket door and ushered them into a tastefully decorated room with several couches and low tables. Soft music floated from the ceiling and sweet-scented candles glowed on side tables.

"Faolin," Maude asked, "What refreshments would you like?"

"We'll have my usual."

Maude nodded and left the doors open as she departed.

A server brought in several trays of meats, cheese, fruit, and two large carafes.

"What do we need all this food for?" Drake asked. "We just ate."

Ace and Tag laughed. Flannery said, "The food's not for us."

"You can't catch fish without bait," Ace said cryptically.

Drake didn't understand and reached to fill a glass from the carafe.

Tag stopped him. "We don't fill our own glasses."

Before Drake could ask why, a soft gong sounded in the garden.

Flannery sat up straight. "Look sharp, young blood," he said.

Drake saw doors around the garden opening and women drifting out. They strolled around the courtyard, pausing to look into the rooms. Occasionally, some would enter an open door. Sometimes they left the door open and sometimes they closed it.

A group of women stopped outside their door and looked inside. Flannery, Tag, and Ace got to their feet and bowed. Ace kicked Drake's foot, and he popped up too.

The ladies smiled from behind fans and walked on.

The men sat again.

"Are we being inspected?" Drake asked.

Tag laughed. "He ain't as dumb as he looks."

Ace said, "I'm glad he's here. With this handsome young man, we will have company in no time."

The gong sounded again, and the women disappeared into empty rooms or the dining room.

Drake asked, "Now what?"

Flannery said, "Patience, son, haven't you ever been fishing?"

"Sure, back home."

"Consider this like fishing," Flannery said. "We present our bait and hope for a nibble."

Drake sat back, and after a few minutes, the gong sounded again.

Ace said, "Look alive, kid."

Another group paused at the door and looked in.

He rose and bowed gracefully this time. The ladies whispered behind their fans and appeared to agree on something.

"Gentlemen," one of them said, "may we join you?"

Flannery answered with a sweeping arm gesture, "By all means, ladies."

Four women entered, and a fifth walked on. Each woman paused in front of a man and turned her back to him to allow her cloak to be taken. They sat with a space to their left. Their simple long flowing dresses were not revealing but clung in all the right places.

Flannery, as senior man present, did the introductions. "Ladies, I am Captain Faolin Flannery of the vessel *Lupine*. May I introduce my crew: Tag Tesson, Ace Valens, and Drake Sheridan." Each of the men bowed at his name.

The leader of the group, a blonde in her forties, said, "I am Essa, of House Negotia. Please sit, gentlemen."

Each woman held out a hand to the man nearest her and guided them to sit beside them.

Essa had chosen Flannery and said, "These are my friends: Riva of House Littera, Helen of House Cultura, and Kio of House Custos. May we pour, gentlemen?"

They didn't wait for an answer. Each woman took a glass, filled it, and held it to the man at their side. Essa served Flannery. Riva, a dark-hair beauty, served Ace. Helen, a short redhead, had a glass for Tag. Kio, the blue-eyed brunette, lifted her glass to Drake.

Drake could see this was obviously some kind of formal ritual and watched out of the corner of his eye for cues. The men leaned forward and inhaled deeply over the glass and paused. The women looked into the men's eyes. They raised the glasses to the men's lips and gave them a sip before placing it back on the table. Then the women rose and walked to the doorway with their backs to the men.

Drake could hear them whispering behind their fans. Kio looked over her shoulder at him. They appeared to reach an agreement.

Essa slid the doors shut. "We will converse for a time."

"Excellent," Flannery said.

The ladies returned to their seats and began to nibble at the trays and make small talk with the man next to them.

Drake felt a little giddy. *That's weird, I've only had a sip of wine,* He thought.

Kio leaned over to him, "Tell me of yourself."

Drake felt the need to begin talking. "I'm only on *Lupine* temporary. Normally I crew on *Corvus*."

"Is this your first time on Matria?"

"Yeah, I do know a Matriarch named Pela, though. She is from House Custos too."

Kio smiled, took a sip of wine, and raised the cup to Drake. "I know Pela well, we schooled together. What do you think of her?"

Drake felt compelled to answer honestly. "I like her. She saved my life once. She's a good shipmate."

"Is that all she is to you?" Kio asked.

"I dunno," Drake said. "We haven't discussed it."

He looked around the room. His eyes weren't focusing well, but he could see each of his shipmates in deep conversation with his partner. The ladies would occasionally press the wine first to their lips, then their partner's.

Drake lost track of time. The couples continued to talk with occasional sips. At some point, Essa stood and held her hand to Flannery and she led him out the sliding doors. Helen did the same to Tag. Ace giggled when Riva took his.

"It appears our friends have abandoned us," Kio said. "Shall we continue elsewhere?"

"Where?"

She said, "Come," and took his hand.

Drake woke to sun shining in his eyes. He rolled over and found himself alone in a bed that smelled faintly of Kio's perfume. His clothes hung on wall pegs. Drake splashed some water on his face from a basin, quickly dressed, and walked out onto the balcony walkway.

"Hey, kid," Flannery called from a few doors down. "Get a good night's sleep? I got coffee." He lifted a pot and waggled it.

Drake joined him at a small table. "What happened last night?"

Flannery cocked his head. "What do ya mean?"

"One minute we are having some kind of ceremony with four women, and the next I'm feeling weird and floaty," Drake said. "Wait, they didn't use that pheromone thing of theirs on me, did they?"

Flannery laughed. "Are you complaining?"

Drake said, "Oh man, I thought you guys carried me to bed, and that was a dream."

Tag and Ace walked up.

Tag said, "If that was a dream, shipmate, I never want to wake up."

"I feel like I wrestled a tiger all night," Ace said, as he stretched and groaned. "I think I've got scratches all over my back."

"There is something to be said for older women, boys. Not

everything needs to be done in a rush," Flannery said. "Let's get breakfast. Maude's kitchen serves a fine morning plate."

They found a table in the near-empty dining room and ordered.

"So," Drake said. "who is going to explain what last night was?"

Tag sipped his coffee and nodded to Flannery. "You do the honor, Cap. You've been here more than us."

"Okay, see kid, Matria isn't hung up about sex like other worlds. They don't even have what we would call marriage. They sometimes do what they call a 'walking marriage'. That means, the fella visits his girl at her house and walks back to his place in the morning."

"So, what about last night?" Drake asked. "I'm not married, am I?"

"Umm, think of that as girl's night out," Tag said.

Flannery continued, "You saw how much of a ritual it was, right?"

"Yeah."

"They go through those forms to vet us," Flannery said. "Remember that whole sip of wine, long deep-eyed-look thing?"

"I'm getting excited again just thinking about that," Ace said.

"They were checking to see how their particular pheromones made your pupils dilate. The bigger they open up, the more they can tell you are into them," Tag said.

Ace said, "You should make sure you are here for the next Beltane celebration. It makes last night look like a nunnery prayer service."

"Ha, I don't know if Drake is ready for that?" Flannery said. "His heart might not take the strain."

"Look, I only know one Matriarch, and she's never done anything like last night," Drake said.

"Uh, oh," Tag said. "Oh good, breakfast is here. You tell him the bad news, Cap." A server laid out heaping plates for them.

Flannery said, "That means she either hates your guts... Or she is in love with you."

Drake choked on his coffee. "What?"

Tag laughed. "Yep, you are screwed! When she sets the hook, you are gonna be so far down the rabbit hole for her you're never gonna see daylight again."

"Wait, you said they didn't do that."

"No, I said they don't have marriage like other worlds. I didn't say they don't fall in love. They are still women," Flannery said after a sip of coffee.

"I will second that," Ace said. "Riva was ALL woman."

Tag said, "Remember when I called it 'girls' night out?' They still do that even though they have a deep love for a partner. They just aren't the jealous type."

"Unless." Flannery said.

"Unless what." Drake was so distracted his food was getting cold.

"Unless they think someone else is trying to take their spot permanent like. Then they get MEAN."

"If I was you, kid, I wouldn't mention last night when you get back to the *Corvus*," Flannery said.

"Isn't that like lying?" Drake asked.

Ace finished his meal and said, "Think of it as self-defense."

Maude came to the table. "Did you boys have fun?"

Flannery answered, "A pleasant experience, as always, Maude."

"You need to be careful out there," she said. "A member of House Textus was here last night and recognized a Dellan spy who left right after you arrived."

"I thought Textus focused on weaving and cloth?" Ace asked.

"Remember, spiders also weave," Maude said. "A little spy craft on the side. Your little adventure against that raider probably didn't win you any friends with the Dellans."

"Thanks for the heads up," Flannery said.

Flannery's comm buzzed. He listened to a brief message and cut the line. "Finish up, boys. We got a job to reunite Drake here with his intended. This Dellan situation is getting serious."

# CHAPTER EIGHT

"*Corvus,* this is *Lupine.* Request permission to deploy atmosphere bridge and transfer personnel." Despite his crews' disappointment at not getting a second night at the Rusty Razor, Faolin Flannery had volunteered to ferry Drake Sheridan to rejoin *Corvus.*

"Hey, you redhead midget, good to hear your voice again," Gus teased from the view screen. "I thought the Dellans would have made you a mess cook by now."

"Fat chance! The last Dellans that tangled with me ended up with more holes than a screen door. You got any coffee over there? My crew can't make a decent pot to save their hides."

"Sure, come on over. I think we've even got a little of Zia's dessert left. It's amazing how much farther the chow rations go when Drake isn't here." Gus laughed.

Drake leaned into view and said, "Ha, Ha, Skipper."

*Corvus* bridge crew looked at each other and grinned. Nothing like a little friendly banter to lighten the mood.

Zia Forte said, "Looks like we are getting the band back together."

"Chief Consul Sidra told me you are going hunting," Flannery said. "Need another Strap pilot? My crew can take *Lupine* back on their own," Flannery used the slang for a two-man fighter.

Nan Stanski said, "If you let me ride shotgun with you."

"Only if you promise to lay off the beans. Last time I flew with you, I had to keep my helmet sealed the entire trip."

"Hilarious," Nan said.

Gus laughed. "Oh man, that is a whole different level of dutch oven torture, being trapped in a fighter with a farty Marine for hours. Get yer asses over here you two. Sidra is going to make her announcement soon and we need to be ready when it happens."

# CHAPTER NINE

*Corvus* reached Faber's co-ordinates in two days.

**"We Here,"** Corvus said.

An asteroid rotated slowly in the forward screen. The lumpy black potato of rock didn't look like much, which made it a perfect hiding spot. It was small enough to avoid the interest of miners and big enough to be stable. Faber had easily hollowed it out enough to hide his escape craft.

"Captain, Sergeant Faber is transmitting," Lenore said from the operations console. Lenore preferred to always address fellow Constructed Intelligences as sentient persons.

"Let's hear it, XO," Gus said.

Lenore nodded and Faber appeared on the screen. "Nice of you to finally show up." He waved his cigar in frustration. The ragged chewed end on the simulated cigar was a nice touch Lenore noted.

"Sorry we kept you waiting," Gus answered, gruffly.

"So, what are you doing about getting rid of my squatters?" Faber asked.

"I was hoping you had some ideas," Gus said.

Lenore interrupted. "Sergeant, you have never explained how it is possible that the enemy has possession of an ICS assault carrier?"

Faber said, "When the Imperials were bugging out, they left *Jishin* behind. It's too big to fit through the Gateway in one piece. It was assembled in this system from prefab modules. They were in such a hurry to leave; they just sent it into the kuiper belt."

"What happened to the ship's CI?" Lenore asked.

"They removed it. The Imperials didn't want to leave an active assault carrier to drift and slowly go insane."

"Isn't that what they did to you?" Gus asked.

"I got set up with a special sub-routine that cycles me through active periods to maintain the shipyard," Faber said. "Believe me, I got plenty to keep me sane. Can't say the same for my poor brother."

"Brother?" Gus asked, "Never mind, so, if we reinstall the CI, can we gain control of the ship?" Gus asked.

"I tried to communicate with the CI when they showed up," Faber said. "When I established a handshake, the assholes tried some kind of fragging program on me. I barely got away. Lucky, I'm paranoid. I built this hiding spot and my escape ship long ago."

"Can you still access the surveillance system on the shipyard to spy on the Dellans," Nan asked.

"Yeah, they haven't figured that out," Faber said. "I can patch the feeds to you."

HAM had been quietly idling in a corner of the bridge. "Sergeant Faber, do you know if the *Jishin* CI's gold copy is still aboard?"

"What's a gold copy?" Zia Forte asked from the conn.

"A data crystal copy of the CI's base code," HAM said. "It is how I was able to restore Lenore and *Corvus* after we crashed on Terne."

Faber said, "It's probably still on there. I don't know why the Imperials would have taken the backup off. They just wanted to mothball the ship until they came back."

"Why do I feel this is a good news, bad news situation," Nan said.

Lenore said, "Yes, the good news is, if we reload the gold copy, we can regain control of *Jishin*. The bad news is, someone must manually place it into the reader."

"So, someone sneaks onto a six-kilometer-long enemy ship, finds one particular data crystal, and loads it into a reader," Nan said. "Easy, peasy."

"Did I mention they installed these readers only in the captain's cabin?" HAM said.

---

Zia cradled her pet opossum, Ophelia, in her arms and said, "I tell you; it's going to work."

Gus shook his head. "I dunno; you really think she can pull it off?"

Zia scratched under Ophelia's rough whiskery chin. She rolled her head back and yawned a wide sharp-toothed grin. "Don't let looks fool you, she is really smart. She got us out of prison on Kragus, while you were busy trying to get yourself killed, remember."

Gus harrumphed a reply and folded his arms.

"I am already building a simulator so she can practice loading the crystal." Nyrkki said, to distract Gus.

"Do you have a better idea?" Zia asked. Ophelia rolled back

upright, climbed to Zia's shoulder, and chittered a complaint at Gus's doubts.

"Can't HAM do it by himself?" Gus asked.

"HAM can't navigate the cableways," Nyrkki said. "He's too big."

"Faber still has access to some of the shipyard systems," Lenore said. "He will add HAM's ID to the shipyard database."

"HAM will look like a normal bot repairing the *Jishin*," Nyrkki said. "He can carry Ophelia in a tool kit with a false bottom.

"What do you say, Ophelia?" asked Zia. "Want to go on an adventure?"

Ophelia chittered and rubbed her belly.

"Let me guess," Gus said. "Only if there are snacks."

# CHAPTER TEN

The tension in the Matriarch's facility, Mimas, was palpable. The last Dellan attack had the crew on edge.

Lieutenant Laera looked around the Operations Center. Her facility mined and processed austenitic taconite, semi-refined stainless steel, a vital raw material for starship construction. The minerals on the Lysistrata asteroids generated most of the hard currency driving the homeworld's economy.

"Any drive plumes on the long-range scans, Malcus?" she asked her second.

The man rotated through several screens and turned, "Nothing, Lieutenant, however, the Dellans are very good at hiding." He tried to hide the affection in his voice. The two had recently become an item.

Because of the potential distraction, it was still rather unusual for a man to be working outside of their traditional guilds. Old customs died slowly.

"I want an evacuation drill at 1300 today," Laera said. "We won't have much warning when the Dellans show up."

"Don't you mean if they show?"

"No, I mean when," Laera said. "Why we should be spared? I know their raids appear random, but is there a pattern?"

"I have been looking for one," Malcus said. "Facility populations, physical size, and mineral output. Nothing popped out."

"Well, they *are* Dellans. There may not actually be a pattern. We know their ships operate independently, with individual captains given a great deal of discretion."

A soft pinging began at his console. Malcus said, "Looks like we will have to skip that drill L-T. Two enemy drive signatures just tripped the scope."

Lt. Laera slapped the 1MC, "Now! On board the facility, begin evacuation procedures. This is not a drill. All hands provide. Praise the Goddess."

The evacuation alarm's wail sounded through the passageways. Running mag boots pounded the decks.

"What is the status of the demolition charges?" Laera asked.

Malcus started the sequence. "I've got green on nine of the ten charges. The charge on the reactor failed to arm," he answered.

"Shit, the most important one, of course!" Laera said. "I'll take the detonator with me and check it out. You get down to the hangar and make sure everyone is off."

She slipped into an emergency vac suit as Malcus seated her helmet, tested the seal, and gave a thumbs up. He took her hand.

"Don't go getting all sentimental on me. I'll be fine," Laera said. They headed in different directions as they hit the door.

Laera sweated freely as she ran against the tide of people heading to the hangar. Emergency suits don't handle heavy exertion, and the helmet was fogging.

She reached the reactor control compartment and looked through the viewport in the door. Laera saw a technician furiously fiddling inside a console. Laera opened the door. "What are you doing? Get to the evacuation boat!"

"I'm trying to arm the demolition charge again. The detonator broke after I removed it to do maintenance."

"I'll get it, you go ahead," Laera said.

The technician showed Laera what she needed to do and ran out the door.

Laera could see the battery pack for the detonator had sheared off several wires. She wouldn't fix that before the Dellans boarded, and the reactor needed destroying. An intact reactor would make it easy to repair the facility for use against her home world.

Laera ran scenarios through her mind. She only needed to destroy a vital piece of the machine without blowing herself into space. The reactor compartment was near the asteroid's surface to let the near absolute-zero temperature of space cool the superconducting magnets.

"Malcus, what's the status of the evacuation?" she commed.

"The last transport is lifting off now. You can blow it. We'll be standing by to pick you up on the dark side."

Laera ran scenarios through her mind. She needed to destroy a piece of the reactor that wasn't easy to fix without blowing herself into space. The reactor compartment was near the asteroid's surface to take advantage of the near absolute-zero temperature of space to cool the superconducting magnets.

Laera sealed the reactor control center door and used her command override on the system safeties. She needed to vent the compartment to dampen the shock wave, create an edge of localized instability in the plasma flow, and the hot spot would melt through the vacuum vessel. Poof, one permanently broken fusion reactor.

The temperature in the compartment fall fast when the

atmosphere vented. Her suit heaters wouldn't keep up for long. Laera swore she could already feel it getting colder. She needed to work faster.

Moving to the control station, she studied the holograph diagram hovering above it. *I just need to disrupt the magnetic field in one small area. Like this...* She waved her hand in a command gesture at a small portion of the display. The diagram flashed a failure warning. She ducked down behind the console. A rumble surged through the floor and the lights went out. Emergency lighting kicked in and she looked at the reactor room CCTV screen. The vaporized metal fumes filled the room and the circular electromagnet was missing a chunk. *Another example of why I stay out of the kitchen, everything I touch ends up burned.*

She moved to the exit door and heaved the locking bar. *Jammed!* She looked around for something to use for leverage. Nothing. Laera moved to the reactor compartment hatch. It opened.

The metallic smoke hung unmoving in the vacuum. An escape trunk ladder glowed through the murk. She climbed, spun the locking wheel, and pushed against the scuttle. *Shit, there is atmosphere pressure on the other side holding the scuttle shut. That means 1300 kilos is still pressing down on this hatch. Unless I can relieve the pressure.*

Laera climbed down, moved to the far side of the compartment, and hit the remote for the demolition charges. The complex shuddered and the emergency lighting flickered before failing. *How long will it take to vent the atmosphere above the escape scuttle, I wonder? My time is running out.*

After five long minutes, she climbed again. This time she struggled the hatch open. A final blast of air almost knocked her off the ladder as she latched the hatch. Laera climbed back down and grabbed a fire extinguisher from the bulkhead.

The airlock was just big enough to squeeze inside. She pumped the manual hydraulic hatch release set into the bulkhead and the door slowly swung open. Laera stepped onto the dark rocky surface and looked into the Void.

The band of stars called Hippolyte's belt shone brightly, casting just enough light to see. Off to one side, the Dellan ships' engines pulsed a beacon of danger as they decelerated toward her. Laera grabbed the fire extinguisher and pulled the pin. *Saw this in a vid about primitive space travel, hope it works.* She jumped away as hard as she could and gripped the discharge lever. A cloud of $CO_2$ shot out, and she rose.

She pulsed the blasts to avoid inducing a spin and get as far away as possible before triggering her rescue beacon. Laera watched the incoming enemy ships disappear over the horizon and then she triggered the beacon. *I hope they hurry. The cold is really soaking my suit. I wonder what kind of reception am I going to get back home, considering I just blew up my first command?*

# CHAPTER ELEVEN

"I am afraid I have bad news," Sidra began as she stood at the dais of Decision Hall. "The Dellans have taken the mine at Mimas."

The Guildsmen had been invited to join the assembled House Consuls to discuss the situation. A low murmur rumbled through the hall.

Consul Tess of Custos, said, "That facility is within striking distance of our defense platforms."

Consul Elle of House Textus, the Matrians spymaster, "The crew sabotaged the structure. The Dellans won't get any use from it."

"That also means we have lost our source of austenitics. We can't build ships without it," said the guild leader of the Shipwrights.

The leader of House Scientia muttered, "If you would adopt our new synthetic materials, you could continue construction."

"Bah," the guildsman Engineer said. "Those are unproven. Now is not the time to experiment."

"I am hearing rumors of a plan to field mixed-gender crews," the Airmen Guild leader interrupted. "My men are not used to serving alongside women. I can't support that."

"Don't you trust your guilders?"

"No matter how progressive you believe our system to be, men are protective of women. It will lessen their effectiveness."

"The Sisters can take care of themselves."

"We *cannot* perform social experiments during a *war!*" he shouted.

"Let us table that discussion for now," Sidra said, trying to smooth things over. "If we don't get more ships, we won't need mixed crews."

"Is there a chance of a ground invasion?" the Builders Guild asked.

"That is the tactic they used on Kragus," Elle said. "It would have succeeded too if not for the crew of *Corvus*."

"Then we will start on a defensive plan for the capital," the Builder said.

The head Gearmaster said, "My guild will shift our production to war time materials."

"Hopefully, we can stop them before they land," Elle said.

"We will need the Farmer's Guild to work with the Mercers and Grocers on a logistics plan for food distribution," Dollas, from House Negotia, said. "The evacuees from off world are already straining the normal system. We will need to start the emergency synthetic ration processors."

"Those refugees won't be happy with famine loaf."

"Better than hungry."

"I suggest moving the new arrivals to the countryside. It's poor practice to concentrate the population if we are expecting an invasion," said the Airmen's leader. "We can use the airship fleet to disperse them."

"House Cultura, we will need an information campaign to bolster solidarity among the population," suggested Sidra.

"Are we expecting an extended conflict?"

"No, but I won't sugarcoat our situation. The Dellans are determined, and this new ship gives them a significant advantage. I fear if Captain Johansson cannot work another miracle, our prospects for victory are dim," Sidra said. "I still hope that Admiral McGowan will lend Governance support."

Elle said, "I call for a war vote."

## CHAPTER TWELVE

"Tell me again, why we are attacking an unimportant Dellan repair depot?" Nyrkki asked.

His partner, Zia Forte, answered from the pilot chair aboard Annie D., the modified assault dropship normally carried by *Corvus*. "Gus wants to distract the Dellans. Maybe put them on the defensive a little. If they are worried about defending their own bases, they might pull assets from offensive operations."

Both wore vacuum armor and helmets just in case they lost atmosphere during the coming raid.

They were sparking along at one-gee to avoid attracting attention. A casual scan would show them as just another small freighter working the outer system routes. Nyrkki and HAM had restored most of the old ship's systems and even upgraded a few. She was no longer the wreck they discovered inside the ancient volcano on Kragus.

Dropships usually insert a squad into a hot LZ from orbit in short range missions. New external drop tanks graced the Annie D. so they could make this long-range attack. Nyrkki had also modified the *Corvus's* drones to work with Annie's older systems. A new automated loader now fed the autocannon from extended magazines in the cargo bay. Two racks of miniature torpedoes and proximity mine launchers graced the dorsal spine. A small close-in-weapons System, CWIS, cannon protected the belly. She wasn't quite equal to a corvette, but damn close.

"If I had a little more time, I could have really given this old girl some punch," Nyrkki said with a sigh.

"I appreciate all your efforts, EO," Annie D. said. "However, your modifications have already compromised my ability to operate inside a planetary atmosphere. I would recommend staying in space to avoid the unintended detonation of external weapons."

"Don't worry, Annie," Zia said. "This operation is vacuum only." Zia reached over to the co-pilot seat and patted Nyrkki's arm. "I think we have enough firepower, dear."

"But piccola, I've got this new idea for a nanobot mine that I'm dying to try," he said.

Zia said, "There's always next time. I don't think we will run out of enemies soon."

"Too bad. I was looking forward to liberty on Matria. Pela makes it sound like paradise."

"That's a bit of homesickness talking," Zia said. "Matria has its own set of problems."

Nyrkki turned and said, "Go on, it's a long trip."

"Well, you know women hold the official political power," she said.

"I'm assuming that's why they are called Matriarchs."

"So, men, being men, this leads to friction. In the few cities of the planet, the women really run the place. They own the property and control the businesses," Zia continued. "The men belong to specialized Guilds such as Builders, Engineers, etc. that can only enter the city walls during business hours."

Nyrkki said, "What about in the countryside?"

"The smaller settlements don't follow so close to the official model. Men and women form long-term partnerships and live in the same household. The women still own the towns and the men control the land outside of the villages or work in the Guilds. But the living separations aren't as strict. However, during the big festivals, like Beltane, it's a 'what happens during Beltane, stays at Beltane' situation."

"What does that mean?" Nyrkki asked.

"Tightly controlled social structures need a pressure relief valve," Zia said. "Beltane began as a fertility rite and slowly morphed into a society-wide one night free-love fest."

"Oh..." Nyrkki said.

"Hey, I get it, but it seems to work for them," Zia said.

"So, how do they handle the kids?" Nyrkki asked. "Paternity must be an issue."

"Not really," Zia said. "Families trace through the matrilineal line. The kids grow up in the communal women's houses. They call all the women Mother."

"So, no fathers?"

"Uncles take the father role," Zia said. "Boys live in the women's houses until they are around seven then they move to the men's Guild houses, usually the one an uncle belongs to."

"You mentioned things are different in the country," Nyrkki said. "Is that where Pela's from?"

"She told me she grew up in the country and moved to the city for her university," Zia said.

"What does that mean?"

"I think that's why she is so possessive of Drake. She wants a thing with him *and* to be a true Matriarch. The city ladies' attachments are, how shall I say it delicately, more casual," Zia said.

Nyrkki shook his head. "Well, I know one thing, she has that poor guy pretty twisted up. He was complaining about how she is hot one day and cold the next."

Zia smiled. "I've got a feeling they will work it out." She slapped her chair arm. "Okay, enough gossip, old man, let's run through the assault plan again."

Nyrkki and Zia studied the reconnaissance drone feed as they coasted dark toward their objective. A halo of wingman drones trailed with them.

Nyrkki said, "Looks like our intel was right. Strictly a military facility." He ran through the assault plan again.

"Good, we don't want to hit a bunch of civilians," Zia said.

Nyrkki highlighted several portions of the screen. "These are defense points. Drone passes can take those out."

"All right, what do we want to do about those three raiders?" Zia asked, pointing out the threat.

"That one is out of commission," Nyrkki said. "EV suiters are working on the drive cone, and it is hard docked with an atmosphere bridge. These other two are probably operational, so we need to knock them out with a torpedo spread before we go in."

"Then pop one last torpedo into the docked ship as we beat out of here," Zia said. "Annie, analysis, what do you think?"

The ship answered, "The raiders' acceleration capabilities exceed my own. If we do not destroy them on the first pass, we will not escape."

"I guess we need to knock them out first then," Nyrkki said.

Zia looked at Nyrkki. "You know, none of this is going to go as planned."

"Never does."

"I wish Gus was here," Annie said. "He can really think on his feet."

Nyrkki huffed. "Thanks for the vote of confidence."

The Annie D. maneuvered on reaction thrusters to line up for the torpedo run. Tension hummed inside the cabin.

"We need to wait until the formal declaration of war broadcasts," Zia said. "Sidra was very clear that it shouldn't look like a sneak attack."

Nyrkki snorted, "She isn't the one with her ass hanging out in the Void. I don't care about the fine point of a few seconds."

"I am receiving a wide band transmission from Matria," Annie D. said. "Putting it on speaker."

Sidra's clear, firm voice came over the comm, and a holo winked in. "This is Sidra, Chief Consul of Matria. By a vote of the Houses, from the time of this transmission forward, a state of war exists between Matria and the Dellan League in response to unprovoked aggressions against us. As per the agreed Conduct of War, we consider all military assets viable targets. May the Goddess welcome you into her bosom upon your death."

"Short and to the point," Nyrkki said. "Personally, I hope not to meet this Goddess for a long time."

"Annie, launch torpedo spread and activate wingman attack sequence," Zia said. The ship shuddered as the torpedoes launched.

"Torpedoes away," the ship reported. "Running true to target."

"Raiders are powering up their drives," Nyrkki said. Sweat formed on his brow as he willed the torpedoes faster.

"Here we go," Zia announced and hammered the throttles to their stops.

The Annie D. accelerated at three-gees down the torpedo trajectory. The torpedo drive plumes outshined their own engine's emission signature.

"Raiders are launching countermeasures, and the station is firing point defenses," Nyrkki said.

The blasts from the countermeasures blanked the Annie D's sensors. Nyrkki transmitted a code sequence to the torpedoes, and they corkscrewed to pick up the raider's signatures past the countermeasures.

Zia targeted the station and the docked raider with the Annie D's cannons through her heads-up-display. The drones swirled in, and the station defenses collapsed from repeated hits.

"Multiple torpedo launches detected," Annie D announced.

Nyrkki said, "The docked raider launched everything they had. Tracking six torpedoes."

"Annie, hold course. Prepare to spin one eight zero on my mark," Zia calmly said. Her fingers flew over her console.

Zia zeroed the throttles. "*Now!*" The ship spun and shuddered as it released its racked mines. "*Again!*" The ship spun back to its original course and shuddered as another spread of torpedoes were released. A time delay counted down on the console. "*Ninety ventral!*" The gyros moaned as they struggled to rotate the ship's bulk. Zia hammered the throttles again, and Annie shot forward.

Zia fought to remain conscious while Nyrkki roared a challenge. "Bring it, ya ragged sack of low gravity sparrows!"

The counter reached zero, and the torpedoes' engines flared to life.

Nyrkki chewed his lip as he tracked the mines and torpedoes with his HUD. "Yes! Incoming torpedoes destroyed by proximity mines. Second torpedo spread running true to station."

Zia asked, "Where are those raiders?"

Annie D. said, "One enemy destroyed. Second enemy pursuing us. We will be in their kill range in forty-five seconds."

"Annie, recall wingman swarm for defense!" Zia yelled.

Nyrkki said, "Multiple torpedo hits on station. The docked raider is free and using maneuvering thrusters to clear the area. They are not venting atmosphere."

"Annie, how long until our drones get here?" Zia asked.

"Wingman will be in range in thirty seconds."

Nyrkki said, "That's cutting it too close." He unstrapped and moved aft into the cargo bay.

"Where are you going?" Zia yelled.

"Lightning our load!" Nyrkki yelled back as he grabbed two levers and jerked them down. The ship jumped and acceleration increased as the drop tanks ejected.

"Annie, target those tanks with the CWIS and engage," Nyrkki said.

He felt the rumble of the weapon shaking through the ship's frame. His HUD displayed the bullets tear the tanks apart.

The pursuing raider saw the mass of water boil out of the ruptured tanks in a frozen cloud. They tried to dodge the mass but slammed into it. Their ship came out the other side with little damage but had slowed enough for the drones to engage. The enemy's hull shredded.

Nikki let out a whoop. "Take that bitches!" He thumped back into his chair.

"Annie, situation assessment?" Zia asked.

Annie responded, "Two raiders destroyed, station venting atmosphere and weapons offline, one raider disabled."

"Annie, do we have enough fuel left, without the drop tanks, to make it to a friendly port?" Zia asked.

"With a low consumption transit, we can rendezvous with *Corvus* in two days."

Nyrkki looked at Zia as he released his helmet. "Sounds just about right for a second honeymoon celebration."

"You are incorrigible!" she said, as she peeled off his vacuum suit. "Just the way I like you."

## CHAPTER THIRTEEN

Fleet Chief Forbes fumed in *Jishin's* briefing room.

"Shortly after the Matrians declared war, they attacked one of our outposts. Two ships destroyed, one severely damaged, the station *might* be salvageable," the intelligence officer said. "They were hiding until the declaration and then pounced."

"Was it *Corvus*?" Forbes asked. "Sounds like something that coward would do."

The officer consulted his tablet. "Negative Chief, it was a smaller vessel identified as an old Anvil class dropship. Not a standard configuration, though."

"Anvils can't operate in deep space independently!" Captain Stuart said.

"Well, this one can," Forbes said. "If you people haven't figured it out yet, these aren't the manual reading dolts you are used to fighting."

"Fleet Chief, I believe it prudent to pull back some resources to protect facilities," the operations officer advised.

"Not yet," Forbes said. "We can't look scared at only one

strike against a small outpost." He turned to the Fleet Engineering Officer. "EO, what is the status of *Jishin?*"

"We bypassed the shipyard's command protocols, and the automated systems are conducting repairs." the woman said. "We can have engines, limited weapons, and defense system in three weeks."

"You have one week," Forbes barked. "Concentrate on planetary bombardment weapons and engines. We will dominate the space above Matria and destroy the capital if *Corvus* refuses to surrender. Our auxiliary ships will provide defense.

## CHAPTER FOURTEEN

Lenore's image winked into Faber's virtual office. He had reluctantly agreed to a meeting.

"Sergeant Faber, I need you to be straight with me," Lenore began. "Why did the Imperium leave the system?"

"I already told you; I don't know. The humans kept me in the dark about the situation on Earth."

"You also told us you are extremely paranoid," she said. "A paranoid individual would want to know if that situation was a personal threat. I don't believe you went to all the trouble preparing this bolt hole in speculation."

"Umm, I might have left a few things out," Faber said with a shrug. "So, the Imperials didn't leave *Jishin* here just because they were in a hurry. This system was their fallback position if things went to hell in the Sol system."

"The situation must have been dire if they left assets here. How many more IC fleet ships are in the Kuiper Belt?"

"Three," Faber said.

"Really, Sergeant, three?" Lenore crossed her arms. "Hundred?"

Faber gestured up with his thumb. "More."

"Three-thousand?"

"We have a winner!" Faber said and touched his nose.

"Where did they get three-thousand ships?"

"They retreated from a lot of worlds and brought the ships here for mothballs."

"Where are these ships, and what is their condition?" Lenore asked.

"Why should I tell you?"

"Because you are going to spend the rest of eternity stuck on this rock straining stray atoms of helium-3 from the solar wind if you don't."

"Okay, don't get yer panties in a bunch," Faber said. "Just messing with you. Sheesh. I've got a low-level automated unit that sends me info on them every decade or so." Faber said. "They are so far out; the signal lag is 7 hours. I figured you would ask, so I got an update that's only a few days old."

A visual winked into view. It showed the flank of a large ship. Lenore could see that a millennium of buffeting by solar winds and belt dust had not been gentle or kind. Black scars and streaks were everywhere.

"Most of the ships are still there. I've lost track of sixty over the years. Gravitational perturbations cause them to drift away. *Jishin* was the latest and largest one that turned up missing," Faber said. "It showed up in the Dellan's hands after I lost track of it. They must have stumbled across it."

"What is your assessment of the condition of these ships?"

"I know they look bad, but the fact that the Dellans could get *Jishin* running means the damage is mostly cosmetic."

"Can these ships aid us?"

Faber shook his head. "They are all dead. Their CIs were removed, and a simple one-way program sent them to the belt.

"It will take too long to retrieve the ships and find crews for them," Lenore said. "Are there other assets you have neglected to inform me of?"

"There are, but I don't think you are going to convince my brother to give them to you."

"What brother?"

## CHAPTER FIFTEEN

HAM looked down at the instrument panel of the Planetary Insertion Glider he piloted. The small stealth craft slipped ghostlike on course for Faber's shipyard. He looked over his shoulder at the airtight case Ophelia rode in. "How are you doing back there?" he asked.

Ophelia hissed at him.

"I am sorry, but you must stay in the environmental unit for the voyage," HAM said. "We arrive at the shipyard soon."

Ophelia stuck out her tongue and hid her head.

"And the crew claims I am the sensitive one."

The PIG's carbonado hull and angular patterning made it practically invisible. Coasting along without thrusters, the Dellans would never see him coming. However, he also couldn't use the braking engine. That would be like waving a flashing light at them. Instead, Nyrkki had come up with another approach. HAM would throw rocks.

Literally, throw rocks. HAM wound up a high-tension spring inside a gun barrel and pushed a heavy cylindrical slug into the chamber. He looked back at Ophelia, "Hang on, this is going to be bumpy." He tripped the spring, and the recoil slowed the PIG a little as the slug flew out of the stern. Each time he wound the spring and hurled a rock away, they lost a bit of speed. As a bonus, each time he fired, the craft lost mass, so the next shot was more effective. *If I time it right, they will drift into contact with the shipyard. If not, well, best not to think about that.* HAM monitored the instruments and cranked away like a medieval crossbowman on the ramparts.

---

Inside the shipyard, the duty watch stander in Operations noted vibrations from the far end of the asteroid. "Hey, what do you think that is?" he asked the cute woman he had been trying to flirt with since they started sharing the same watches.

She twisted her chair to look at his screen. "I don't know, looks like something hit us. Call up the camera."

"Can't," he said. "The cameras in that area have been down for two days, and everyone is too busy to fix them. Is there anything on infrared or radar?"

She checked her screens. "Nope, everything is empty, black, and cold out there. Probably just some random debris. We added a lot of mass to this rock when we docked *Jishin* in it. Must have disturbed the orbit of some small stuff."

"Weird that it seems to hit at an increasing rate, though."

"This isn't the first time I've seen odd stuff on that end of the asteroid. The database doesn't have any entries about what is back there," she said. "Well, whatever it was, it stopped now."

"So," he said, "tell me more about the mushroom bar they just opened on deck 52. Maybe we could hit it up when we get off shift?"

"We have successfully landed, Ophelia." HAM said with pride. "Even you could not complain about that." He deployed some adhesive anchors to stabilize the PIG. "Now we just need to transit to the access point and make our way to the *Jishin*."

HAM gathered Ophelia's case into his tool bag. He would hide her in the false bottom later. HAM grabbed one of Drake's lizard lasso guns in case he needed to tether himself to the asteroid and slipped adhesive covers on his traction wheels to move along the surface. He quickly rolled to the surface hatch leading inside the asteroid and keyed a coded tight beam transmission back to *Corvus*. From here on, they were on their own. The little bot entered Faber's entry code and disappeared inside.

HAM looked around the access tunnel. He checked his environmental sensors. Hard vacuum. The passage was dark and hovered near absolute zero.

The little bot adjusted his infrared emitter lamp and consulted the diagrams Faber had given him. He needed to traverse several kilometers of tunnel before reaching an environmentally controlled area. He checked Ophelia's case before starting.

"How are you doing in there?" he asked through a comm link.

The grumpy opossum hissed at him and stuck out her tongue.

"That will not get you out any sooner." He skated off.

HAM noticed that Faber's diagram didn't show all the branches he passed. He paused, *Ophelia had many hours of life support in her case, and it was curious that the map wasn't accurate. The Captain would want to know why, and what these undocumented passages are for. He was still puzzled by what Faber meant by, "say hello to my brother."*

He picked the next branch and took it. The tunnel ran straight towards what he knew was the outer diameter of the shipyard. After 100 meters, the tunnel ended at what HAM recognized as a door to the internal transport system of the station. The door registered his ID code and opened. His interface cable jacked into the control system, and he scanned the destinations available.

*It seemed odd that this system didn't connect to the primary station's core transport lines. Someone had deliberately isolated it from the central tunnel.*

HAM picked a destination at the end of the line at the ninety-kilometer mark. Station spin would generate one-gee at that diameter. The transporter smoothly accelerated, and HAM felt it rotate to position the floor "down" as the apparent gravity increased.

When he stepped out of the transporter car, lights came on revealing another tunnel that followed the great curving diameter of the station. His sensors showed the tunnel was at a standard pressure, but the atmosphere was ninety-nine percent nitrogen. The temperature hovered around zero centigrade. *Perfect conditions to prevent long-term deterioration of materials.* Ham mused. *I keep Corvus in the same condition when the crew is gone.*

HAM skated forward and stopped at the first door he came to. The door opened, and the lights popped on as he entered. The little bot stopped and looked around in confusion. He stood inside a vast cavern filled with row after row of Imperial Confederation heavy fighters in launch cradles.

HAM climbed onto the nearest fighter and plugged in his cable. A diagnostic query showed the fighter was in pristine condition. The weapons magazines were full. The magnetic bottles holding the fusion fuel were topped off.

*Most curious that Faber would not mention the existence of these ships. I must advise the Captain of this discovery. Oh no, I am detected!*

He fumbled with the data cable. A power surge traveled into HAM, and he fell to the floor.

## CHAPTER SIXTEEN

*Corvus's* two Strap fighters rested close to the asteroid. Drake and Pela crewed one, and Flannery and Nan rode the other. They had slowly moved into position and were waiting to begin their attack on the enemy transport headed their way.

Pela checked her weapons console for the hundredth time and asked, "So, what did you think of Matria?"

"Um," Drake paused before answering. "I didn't get to see much of it. The weather was chilly, and we stayed close to the Lift Port."

"You didn't visit the Rusty Razor?"

Drake swallowed. He couldn't avoid a direct question like that. "We went there for dinner."

"Did you stay for dessert?"

Drake felt himself turning red.

Pela burst out laughing and thumped the back of his pilot's seat. "You are too easy, Drake Sheridan! Oh, by the way my friend, Kio said she had a fantastic time."

"It was Flannery's idea," Drake stammered. "I thought the

Razor was a regular pub when they suggested it. One minute we were talking, and the next I'm feeling all fuzzy and spacey."

"Relax, lover boy," Pela said. "I'm not jealous, unless you decide to go back for seconds on the same dessert cart." He heard an ominous edge in her voice.

"You Matriarchs are weird."

"Honey, you ain't seen the half of it yet. We need to get you to Beltane."

"I keep hearing rumors about this Beltane thing. What is the deal with that?"

"Some other time. Run through your attack sequence again."

"Yes, Ma'am," Drake answered, with a mock salute.

Flannery came over the tight beam comm. "The transport will be in range in three minutes. You two ready over there?"

"Roger, we're ready," Drake said. He zoomed the video feed from the remote camera on the other side of the asteroid. "Oh shit! That transport's got two single-seater Wasps in a side tow. They didn't show up on the long-range scans."

Flannery said, "Relax, kid, Nan and I will take care of them. Hang back until I smoke 'em out."

Nan launched two drones. They ran close together, to look like a single ship running fast for the transport. The enemy fighters cast off and moved to intercept.

Flannery puffed his ship away and waited until the Wasps committed to their run before lighting off his drive. "Hang on Nan, we are going in hot!"

Nan slammed back into her seat as the gees hit hard. "Weapons lock on the Wasps confirmed."

"Hold off launch for my signal," Flannery said. He followed closely to hide in the drone's exhaust plumes.

The Wasps fired on the drones. They peeled away in separate directions. The Wasps split, each one tracking a drone.

"All right, Nan, hit 'em. Drake, start your run!" Flannery commed.

"Roger," Drake acknowledged. "Weapons free, Pela."

Drake slammed the throttles to the stops, and the ship jumped toward its prey.

The transport realized too late what was happening. Their pilot panicked and tripped off some countermeasures.

"I haven't even fired yet," Pela said. "I thought these guys knew how to fight."

"Transport jockeys aren't the best and brightest," Drake replied.

The transport began an evasive pattern. Drake recognized the sequence. "Pela fire a full torpedo spread at these coordinates" He sent a location to her terminal.

"You better be right, vac jockey, that's our total load," she warned as she punched in the targeting data and fired.

The torpedoes ran away from the transport's apparent course. Suddenly, the transport shifted on its axis and performed a stutter burn designed to confuse a torpedo's targeting computer. As the transport shifted axis again and hit a full burn, it ran straight into the torpedoes.

"Scratch one transport!" Drake commed. He checked Flannery's progress on the screen and saw Nan's cannon fire take out a Wasp.

"I got one," Nan said. "The other one is bugging out."

"All right, buoys and gulls, let's head for the rendezvous point before these bastards' friends show up," Flannery commed. "Long-range scan shows several drive plumes headed our way."

# CHAPTER SEVENTEEN

First Chief Forbes slammed his hand down on the table of the briefing room. "This is getting ridiculous. You idiots lost another transport? What the hell are you doing out there?"

"Chief, the enemy is using our own tactics against us," the flustered intelligence officer said. "They are employing the same hit-and-run raid strategy we have used for decades."

"Then why can't you anticipate their moves?"

"They are content to destroy the targets rather than capture them for salvage. The only positive is they are avoiding civilian targets."

"What strategies have you come up with to counter them?"

"We are instituting a convoy system for our transports with combatant level escorts. Such tactics have proven effective since ancient times."

"Effective against predictable opponents," Forbes said. "Johansson is anything but predictable."

The crew gathered in the wardroom to discuss their recent efforts.

"Do we have any more targets plotted?" Gus asked.

Faolin Flannery said, "The Dellans are wising up. They started operating escorted convoys."

"That makes them a lot harder to hit," Nan said. "They have been sloppy up to now, but we can't count on that anymore."

"They are diverting ships from offense to escort, though," Zia said.

Nyrkki added, "They say they haven't attacked civilian targets. Forbes claims that the mining hab was producing war materials."

"Trying to win the public relations war. If they can keep the Governance on the sidelines a little longer, it will be over for Matria," Gus said. "With *Jishin* repaired, they could park it above Matria and hold it hostage forever. Pela, what about the Orbital Defense Platforms? What could they do for us in a siege?"

"The defense platforms around Matria won't have a chance against that monster," Pela said. "They are barely big enough to defend against raiders. I wouldn't count on them for any meaningful help."

"I propose a new tactic against these convoys," Lenore said. "I have reviewed ancient Earth's terrestrial ocean warfare scenarios and believe we may use one to counter this convoy system."

"What have you got, XO," Gus said.

"Early submarine commanders operated in what they termed wolf packs to counter the effectiveness of the convoys. I suggest we emulate them."

"How well did it work?" Nyrkki asked.

"It was highly effective until technological advances rendered it obsolete," Lenore said.

"I don't think this war is going last that long," Gus said.

---

Gus turned to Lenore standing at the operations station. "What is our situation, XO?"

"The Annie D. and our two fighters are in position to strike. Our drone swarm will pick off any escaping ships or aid as necessary."

Gus looked over the holo of the battle space. Fifteen transports were being escorted by four medium-sized raiders and a cruiser. He knew from experience the cruiser also carried a squad of Wasps. The enemy cruised in a three-dimensional pattern. The transports held the center of the formation. A cruiser led the way with a raider on each side and one following.

"It looks like they are learning fast," Gus said. "We need to disable the cruiser and draw off the raiders to let our friends pick off the transports."

"What do you have in mind?" she asked.

"*Corvus,* line up the dorsal main railgun for a stern shot on the cruiser. They have minimal CWIS coverage there," Gus said.

*Corvus* spun to point its 600-millimeter gun at the enemy cruiser's engine. Its slug could hit with the yield of a six-kiloton nuke.

**Aye, Thunder Ready!**

Gus used *Corvus's* motto and radioed in the clear. "Fly fast and call the thunder!"

The Corvus's bridge lights fluttered as the enormous electromagnetic cannon pulsed. Its thousand-kilogram slug raced away at seven-thousand meters-per-second. The drive cone spun away as the slug sliced it free. The now unconfined fusion reaction instantly melted the remains of the engine, and glowing slag cooled in the Void.

"Hang on to yer panties, Nan," Flannery said from the cockpit of their fighter, Cor-1.

"Better than you have tried to loosen my panties, you red-headed munchkin." She thumbed the safety off her cannon and fired as they sped towards the rear enemy ship.

The two flanking raiders sheared away from the convoy to aid the cruiser. Too late, they realized they had left the convoy undefended.

The Annie D., crewed by Zia and Nyrkki, and the Cor-2 with Drake and Pela streaked in to attack the convoy. The drone swarm followed.

*Corvus,* relying on its stealth hull, held position near the damaged cruiser and fired a torpedo spread at the raiders coming to its aid.

The raiders fired off countermeasures and attempted to maneuver. One of them pivoted and stupidly sprayed the other with its drive plume blinding its fellows' sensors. *Corvus* screamed by and raked the enemy with its CWIS cannons. Both raiders shredded from the barrage.

"Lenore, Sitrep!" Gus yelled.

"We have destroyed three raiders and disabled the cruiser. Our drones have destroyed or disabled eleven transports. The remaining four transports have escaped."

"Survivors?"

"Cargo boats from the cruiser are searching for survivors,"

Gus nodded, "Recall our forces. Allow the cruiser to continue searching. We aren't in the execution business."

## CHAPTER EIGHTEEN

"Show me what miracle you've come up with, Engineer," Fleet Chief Forbes said.

The Fleet EO nodded to the officer at the briefing console. A holo of an ordinary-looking large transport formed and slowly rotated. The EO moved to the image and said, "We took a standard E-class transport and incorporated your idea, Chief. We renamed it *Retribution*."

The *Retribution* followed the common cargo ship design. An open framework of crossed struts and beams enclosed hundreds of individual cargo containers. A crew module rode in the ship's rear. A single fusion engine pushed it on the stern. The reaction mass section isolated the two.

"Show me the rest," Forbes demanded.

The EO waved his hand over the image to begin the simulation. Doors opened in containers along all four sides to reveal rows of railguns and autocannons. The boxes on the ship's bow opened like a flower, and homing torpedoes streamed out.

"There are also CWIS mounts near the engine to prevent it

from being shot away. Plus, several decoy and countermeasure launchers along its length."

"How do you intend to draw the *Corvus* to the trap?" Forbes asked.

The Operations officer said, "*Retribution* is finishing modifications at the shipyard that we captured. We will broadcast its destination on a faulty comm link so that it appears to *Corvus* that they have received information we are trying to hide."

"Why would they attack this ship?"

"We will leak the manifest. The transmission will claim the cargo is several hundred drop ships for the invasion of Matria. *Corvus* will attack to prevent us from getting these landers."

"Excellent," Forbes said. "The sooner we are done with this business the better. I can't wait to stride the streets of the Matrian capital and put my boots on Sidra's table."

---

"Captain to the Bridge," Pela's voice sounded over the 1MC.

The door slid open, and Gus moved next to Pela at the ops station. "What ya got?"

"We intercepted a Dellan transmission originating from Faber's shipyard."

"Why is that interesting?"

"It contained the manifest of a transport departing the yard."

Gus asked, "Another supply ship for us to hit? Wouldn't it be empty if it is leaving the yard?"

Pela shook her head. "They filled this one with drop ships for the Matrian invasion force. I guess they figured a way to mass-produce them at the yard."

"Why would they dispatch a transport before the *Jishin* launches?" Gus asked. "Is it being escorted?"

"Faber's intelligence feeds don't show any escort vessels near the shipyard."

Lenore entered the bridge and joined them. "I advise caution, Captain; it makes no sense for a transport filled with vital equipment to travel unescorted. The invasion will not occur until the *Jishin* launches. Why is this ship leaving now?"

"Agreed, why not just keep the transport at the shipyard?" Gus said.

Pela said, "They don't know we have surveillance on the shipyard. It is far from the normal commerce routes, and discovery is unlikely. Maybe they want the drop ships for practice."

"*Corvus*, how long will it take us to intercept this transport?" Gus asked.

**Low Detection Probability Homann Transfer Intercept Two Days**

"*Corvus,* please begin intercept," Gus ordered. "Lenore, could you prepare three drones for a faster transit so we can get a look at this transport?"

"Of course, Captain."

"Something doesn't smell right about this," Gus said.

Later the crew watched the growing image of the mysterious transport on the large bridge screen. From appearances, it was a common transport burning along at 0.3 gees.

Flannery said, "Well, they aren't in a hurry."

"Yeah, that's a pretty leisurely burn for vital war materials," Drake said.

"Let's wake them up," Gus said from his command chair. "I'm going to send a drone right at them." He keyed new commands into the chair's console.

The crew waited for the scene to change. Several minutes of signal lag each way seemed like an eternity.

The lead drone's drive lit, and it accelerated toward the

transport. A CWIS cannon fired from near the transport's bow toward the drone. CWIS tracers stitched toward the drone as it twisted and corkscrewed. The drone's cannon opened up and shredded the transport's CWIS. Another drone targeted the engine module.

"Wait, what is that?" Pela pointed and asked. "Those containers are opening."

Several containers near the crew module had opened and railgun fire erupted toward the drone. The trailing drone recorded the attacking drone's destruction, and the containers closed again.

"Analysis, anyone?" Gus asked.

"Containerized defenses so they don't need to escort the transport?" Flannery guessed.

"What if it's more than that?" Gus asked. "Maybe we are being set up."

Nan said, "A decoy ship? Trying to get us to attack, and then all those guns open up on us."

"How best to destroy that thing from a distance? Anyone?" Gus looked around.

"I've been working on a new mine design, Skipper," Nyrkki said. "I'm dying to try it out."

"*Corvus*, adjust course to best deploy a minefield along that transports route," Gus said.

**Roger, ETA Twenty-two Hours.**

"With HAM gone, I'm going to need some help. Who wants to get their hands dirty?" Nyrkki asked.

Mitzi Grey jumped up. "Oh please, anything to be useful! I'm feeling like a passenger. I need something productive to do!"

Sadie Hawley added, "I still know how to use a spanner and fabricator."

"You're both hired," Nyrkki said.

"If you can get something productive out of Mitzi, you're a better man than I am, Gunga Din," toned Gus. "Watch your back."

"Sun Tzu advised soldiers must know the task required and the stakes," Nyrkki turned to Gus. "Remember the lesson of the concubines?"

"Yes," said Gus. "I also know how dangerous those two are. Don't piss either off."

---

Drake and Flannery climbed into their BUGs, the extra-vehicle maintenance pods *Corvus* carried, and Nyrkki fiddled with some last-minute adjustments to his new weapon.

Gus asked. "How are these different from regular mines?"

Nyrkki didn't look up from his work. "This system is especially wicked. They are only about the size of a basketball with a stealthy carbonado shell and are totally passive until activated. Extremely hard to spot."

Nan said, "That can't be much explosive power."

Nyrkki clapped his hands together. "True, but these aren't explosive. I call it a ripper mine."

"Despite the racy name, I sense a boring engineering explanation coming," Zia said, and rolled her eyes.

Nyrkki ignored the jab. "*Corvus* is coasting on the same course as the transport, but traveling slightly faster so that the transport, which is still speeding up, will travel the same speed as the weapon when they meet. A net connects the mines. Drake and Faolin will lay it out so that the transport sails into it. The net folds around the ship, the mines contact the hull and that's when the magic happens."

"Explosions? Finally!" Zia asked.

"Better. Each mine is actually a small specialty bot programmed to attack the ship with saws and plasma torches. The crew won't know what is going on until the ship comes apart around them."

"I don't know if we should use ship-eating robots as weapons. Won't they keep drifting forever?" Gus asked. "What if they contact another ship?"

"They become inert after they finish tearing apart the target. I also used a time-sensitive adhesive holding them together that dissolves after a few hours of vacuum exposure."

The crew gathered on the bridge to watch Nyrkki's weapon in action after Drake and Flannery returned from setting the trap. The image of the enemy ship filled the bridge screen.

"Nyrkki, send the activation command," Gus said.

He keyed in a sequence. "Done. I am highlighting the net on the screen so we can see it."

The giant circular net spun slowly and glowed as the doomed ship came into contact with it. The weapon gently enfolded the enemy. As the mines contacted the hull, each one gave a faint flash when the bots activated. Nyrkki zoomed in and they could see bots crawling across the ship like picnic ants.

Bots peeled back pieces of the ship like a sardine can. Eager bots waving their tool arms streamed inside.

"How long is this going to take?" Drake asked. "Watching the tide come in is more exciting."

"Patience kid," Gus said. "I got a feeling things are going to speed up soon."

Suddenly, the forward third of the ship buckled as some vital internal framing gave way. The ship's engine continued to burn as the collapsed section folded over and bounced away.

"What about the crew?" Pela asked.

"The bots will avoid damaging the crew module," Nyrkki said. "And there it goes!"

The center section spun away as the drive cone sputtered and died.

"That was effective, but I don't think we will use it again," Gus said. "Doesn't seem very sporting. Even a Dellan deserves a chance in the fight."

# CHAPTER NINETEEN

First Lord Admiral Falkirk McGowan looked around his sparse, but adequate cabin. Basically, a pullman rack, folding desk, and hygiene unit. It was what passed for deluxe accommodation on the small fast transport *Pantas*. The Admiral had hopped the fastest ship scheduled for the Ix planets when the Dellans had started trouble.

He had hoped to beat Sidra's declaration and broker some kind of deal to avoid war. The *Pantas* was now close enough that the time lag for transmissions to Matria allowed for real-time calls.

The old man stretched his knotted muscles. *Pantas'* captain had orders to maintain 1.5 gees for the duration of the trip. McGowan regretted issuing that order after a few days. *I'm getting too old for this shit.* His comm lit up. "McGowan, go," he said as he keyed to comm.

"Admiral, we have established a link with Chief Consul Sidra as requested," a woman said over the speaker.

"Send it to my holo."

Sidra's image winked into view. Her dark skin and calm

expression projected command. Her tight curls formed a regal crowning halo. "Chief Consul, do you have any news for me?"

"I am the one that should ask that question, Admiral," she answered. "I hope a strike group accompanies you."

"Umm, no," the Admiral said. "The Governance is reluctant to help a non-aligned world."

"Interesting," she said with a raised brow. "Perhaps, we should have said the same thing before my privateer, *Corvus*, saved your ships at The Battle of Kragus?"

"Now, Sidra," he said. "I don't see how that is the same situation at all? I contracted with *Corvus* directly and paid them well for their services. Your letter of marquee did not apply."

"Please remind that Dellan bastard, Forbes, of your fine distinction when he bombards my planet."

"Do you believe he will actually commit war crimes and target your civilians?"

"I do not believe Dellans know what a war crime is."

"My reports say Gus Johansson has been striking the Dellans successfully," McGowan said. "It doesn't appear you need my help."

"Our few minor victories merely annoy the enemy." She waved her hand dismissively. "Falkirk, do you believe the Dellans will stop with Matria now that they have a six-kilometer assault carrier in their fleet? They will eventually return to Kragus for revenge and continue to expand. How will your Body of Governance like it when they have to confront a Dellan Empire surging across the outer system?"

The Admiral steepled his fingers. "The Governance is sending extra ships to defend our interests on Kragus and Terne."

"So, you would sacrifice us to buy yourselves time?" Sidra asked.

"If you would accept an alliance," McGowan said. "The Governance would be more receptive to aiding you."

"Go fuck yourself," she spat her answer. "I won't be taking your saddle."

"Ah, now we are on it," he said, and leaned in. "The proud Matriarchs will not bend the knee."

"You realize that your daughter and sister-in-law are still aboard *Corvus*? Captain Johansson is engaged in offensive operations."

"Mitzi and Sadie can take care of themselves." It was now his turn to be dismissive. "They are both big girls."

"Is that what you told yourself about the last mission you sent your wife, Cali, on?" Sidra asked. "Does Mitzi Marie know the truth of her mother's death?"

"That's not fair, Sidra." The Admiral reddened. "I will take your cause up with the Body again and plead your case strongly," he replied.

"Two dozen cruisers and destroyers would dim my memory surrounding Cali's death considerably."

"Women never play fair," McGowan said.

"We cannot afford to play by men's rules. Sidra out."

## CHAPTER TWENTY

Drake Sheridan piloted the fighter towards their objective while Pela performed one more weapons system check. Gus had reluctantly agreed to let them attempt a long-range mission without backup.

Their fighter, Cor-2, carried a drop tank of extra reaction mass along with its load of drones, torpedoes, and auto-cannon slugs. Pela cued their drone wingman feeds. "How you doing out there, girls?" she asked the constructed intelligences controlling the drones.

"We are five by five," they responded together. "We appreciate this opportunity to display our abilities."

"Well, they are polite," Drake said.

"The CIs in these Imperial drones we got from Faber's stores are light-years ahead of Governance tech."

"That worries me," Drake said. "What if the Dellans figure out a way to hack them like they did the *Jishin*? At least *Jishin* doesn't have its own drone force. The wingman is the only equalizer we have."

"That *is* concerning. Lenore assured me she has fortified the drones to prevent hacking. However, our enemy is smart and increasingly desperate."

"Yeah, we have been lucky so far that one of us hasn't gotten killed."

"Don't rely on luck, vac jockey," Pela said. "Train and prepare."

"Yes, Ma'am." He threw her a mocking salute.

She scoffed and shook her head. He noticed she tried to hide a smile.

"All right, let's run through the mission plan again."

Drake sighed and in a bored voice said, "Objective, neutralize the Dellan observation post set up on an asteroid in the Lysistrata cluster."

"I want to launch our wingman before we get close," Pela said. "I'm sure the post has already spotted us so no use trying to sneak in."

"We send in the drones while we hang back in overwatch."

Pela activated the drones mission program and watched them detach from the fighter. They were much larger than standard Governance drones, and Nyrkki had needed to design special pylons to hold them to Cor-2. He had warned them that with the drones and pylons attached the fighter would no longer be stealthy. A radar ping would easily mark them. The machines maneuvered away and started a burn for the target.

"Good hunting," Drake flashed a coded signal. An acknowledgment green light showed on the drone console.

The drones began their run, and Pela watched their autocannons stitch the site. The automated observation post didn't even try to launch a defense. "That's odd," Pela said. "Even an unmanned system should have launched a defense."

An alarm sounded from the console, and a mechanical voice spoke. "Warning, enemy target lock detected."

"Shit, hang on!" Drake yelled as he began evasive actions.

Pela began a recall on the drones but noticed they were too far away to help quickly.

Three Dellan Wasp kill ships lit off their drives and began pursuit. They had been running silent on an intercept course and were determined to score a victory.

Pela furiously calculated their chances of getting away. She wished their fighter had a CI of its own to confirm her work, but none of the *Corvus's* fighters had one. The Imperium had written an unbreakable instruction set into their bots Rules of Behavior that prevented CIs from copying or creating new CIs. HAM or Faber could build a fighter but not a CI sophisticated enough to control it. The CIs on the drones were little more than charming autopilots.

"They are gonna catch us," Pela warned.

Drake pivoted the ship and fired a maximum burn. The acceleration built to five-gees. "The drop tank is slowing us down, too much mass. You gotta pop it."

"How are we going to get home without that extra reaction mass?"

"That's not gonna be a problem if they catch us," Drake warned.

Pela keyed in the commands and watched the tank fall away. Their acceleration jumped to eight-gees.

A pursuer destroyed the tank. "I guess we won't be picking that up again," Pela said.

Drake threw the fighter into a corkscrew maneuver as tracers streaked by. "That was too close. Check your suit. We may have to bail. How close are our wingman friends?"

"They are burning hot, but if they keep it up, they are gonna overshoot us."

"Maybe we can slow down our friends back there," Drake said. "Drop some EMP mines."

Pela felt the ship rumble slightly as the weapons jettisoned. "Mines away. Cross your fingers."

She watched the mines maneuver to intercept the Wasp's course. The mines flashed. Two of the enemy dodged and avoided the electronic pulses. "We got one of them," Pela said.

Drake said, "I've got one more of Nyrkki's tricks up my sleeve." He flipped a cover and turned a key.

The ship shuddered again as something launched. "What was that? It's not on my weapons load."

"A net of those ripper mines," Drake said.

"I thought the Captain outlawed those?"

"I'm using it as defense only," Drake said. "Better to ask forgiveness." He checked the weapon's status and watched it unfold like a spider's trap.

One of the Wasps ran into the net and the display showed it fold over the prey. The pilot knew something was wrong, and the ship maneuvered wildly to throw the net off. Pieces of the enemy ship broke away. The drive cut off. Within seconds the ship was a cloud of small pieces coasting through the Void.

"Sorry, dude," Drake said. "All's fair when you are trying to kill me."

"The last one is still coming," Pela said.

The console warned them again. "Warning, enemy target lock detected." Followed by "Inbound missiles detected."

Pela yelled, "Flares and chaff away."

The incoming missiles kept coming. "We gotta bail," Drake said.

"Wait! Our ship doesn't have a CI to pick us back up. The drones might make it…"

"Hold on, Baby." Drake released the safeties and grabbed an eject lever with each hand and heaved.

The crew section shot away at fifteen-gees as the emergency systems engaged. Pela watched enemy missiles shred their ship. The thrusters kept firing in random patterns to give them an untraceable trajectory before shutting down. Weightlessness returned.

Drake watched the passive sensors. Their four wingmen launched missiles and fired a deceleration maneuver as the Wasp tried to evade. The enemy came apart when the missiles found their mark.

Drake whooped.

"Don't celebrate too much," Pela said. "What are *we* gonna do?"

"Hey, in the Orbital Guard, we used to say, 'We've been doing so much, for so long, with so little; we can now do anything with nothing.'"

He ran through a mental inventory of their equipment. "Ok, I got something. Recall the drones to our location."

"Why do I think I will not like this?" Pela asked.

Soon the drones were drifting beside them. "Okay, ladies, I need you to dock with each other. I am gonna launch the skyhook lines to you and winch us into one big happy hug," Drake explained.

A long tether with an adhesive anchor on the end shot out and stuck to a drone. Then Drake pulled the cabin in tight to the clustered drones. "All right, I need Wing-1 to start off slow. Don't exceed a half gee. You will push until you are out of reaction mass and then cast off. Then Wing-2 and Wing-3 do the same thing. This should give us enough speed to reach *Corvus* before we are out of air. *Corvus* will loop back and retrieve you all."

The drones commed back with one feminine voice, "We agree. This plan is acceptable."

"That's nice of them," Pela said over a private channel.

"Be careful, or you are going to be marked 'Does not play well with others.'"

"Everyone already knows that."

Drake said, "I suggest a nap to conserve oxygen."

---

"Captain, your presence is requested on the Bridge," Lenore said over the 1MC.

"I'll be right there, XO." Gus responded from the multiform exerciser he was struggling against.

He soon walked into the Bridge, wiping his forehead with a towel. "What's up?"

Lenore turned to him. "Drake and Pela have encountered some difficulties. Three Wasps jumped them during their mission."

"Damn it!" Gus swore. "Are they all right?"

"Marginally," Lenore said. "They destroyed the enemy fighters but were forced to eject. Cor-2 is destroyed."

"And we can't replace that," Gus said.

"Mr. Sheridan is using the drones as rescue engines," Lenore said. "They are heading our way; however, I have detected a squadron of Dellan ships on a pursuit course."

"Corvus, what accelerations will we need to make to beat the Dellans to our friends?" Gus asked.

**"Enemy Close. Corvus Needs Fifty-gees,"**

Gus slapped the 1MC on his command chair. "*NOW! All hands to the hangar bay. Ready the Annie D. for immediate launch!*

Lenore, you and *Corvus* do whatever it takes to make that rescue. We will follow as we can in the Annie."

Lenore snapped a salute. "Aye, Skipper, now you get down there yourself."

Gus grabbed a set of coveralls from his cabin on the way to the Annie. Nyrkki and Zia were completing the preflight checklist as he arrived.

Mitzi and Sadie were hauling everyone's vac armor aboard. "What the hell is going on, Captain?" Mitzi asked.

"Drake and Pela have got themselves into trouble. *Corvus* and Lenore need to make a max burn to save them," Gus answered, grabbing an armload of suits to help.

"Leave it to that young pup to foul up a simple mission," Flannery said as he slapped a button. The Annie D.'s aft ramp swung up.

Nyrkki asked from the co-pilot's seat, "You ready, Annie?"

The ship's soft voice said, "Yes, all systems are ready for launch. What is our destination? Should I prepare for combat?"

Nyrkki looked at Gus, who answered, "Just get out of the bay ASAP for now, Annie and stand by."

"Aye, Skipper."

The depressurize alarm sounded, and the doors opened before the decompression sequence completed. The ship followed a cloud of ice particles into the Void. As they cleared, the *Corvus* maneuvered away from them.

*Corvus's* six giant fusion engines flared to life, and the black ship leaped away.

Gus keyed a comm button. "Fly fast. Call the thunder, XO!" *Corvus's* motto.

"You call the thunder, we bring the lightning, my Captain." Lenore responded.

"Hey, Rip Van Winkle, wake up," Pela said. She slapped the back of Drake's seat. "Those Wasps had friends, and they are headed our way."

Drake checked the displays. A squadron of ships burned towards them. He ran their numbers through his flight computer. "Two hours until intercept," he said.

"Less if they don't slow to match our speed," Pela said. "They might just launch weapons when they get in range and blaze past our wreckage."

Drake ran through some scenarios. The four drones still gripped the cabin. "Wings 1, 2, and 3 break formation. Take up staggered stations along those ship's courses and rig for silent running. Fire all missiles at our pursuers as they reach your positions and escape as you are able, acknowledge." The three drones signaled affirmative and cast off to maneuver.

"Our drones don't have a lot of ammo left," Pela said. "Or fuel."

Drake said, "Yeah, I know. I'm hoping for a miracle."

Pela asked, "We haven't gotten a signal back from *Corvus* acknowledging our distress call yet either."

The two friends stopped talking and listened to the blood pound in their ears. A count-down timer to the enemy's weapon launch range raced on the readout.

"Cor-2, this is *Corvus*," Lenore's voice came over the comm in the clear. "We are en route to your position, acknowledge."

"XO, I could kiss you." Drake commed.

"That will not be necessary, Mr. Sheridan."

An unknown voice sounded over the comm. "*Corvus*, we relish the opportunity to meet you in combat," a woman said. "You have plagued our clans for too long."

After a signal delay, Lenore said, "This is Lenore Imperium, XO of the Matrian privateer *Corvus*. Who do I have the pleasure of defeating today?"

The signal delays were shortening as the vessel's distances shrank. "This is Commodore Walsh of the Broadax flotilla." Warriors shouting erupted in the background of her comm. "You have no chance of victory. Your ambush tactics will not work this day. We number ten to your one,"

"Commodore, you realize this is the same ship that took out your planetary assault carrier with one shot?"

Walsh scoffed. "Defeating that ancient relic is nothing to boast over. We will carve you up and parade pieces through the streets of Matria. I will personally commission a set of battle armor from your hull for each of my crew."

"She seems quite sure of herself, doesn't she?" Drake said to Pela as they watched the timer. "I show *Corvus* on a course to overtake the Dellan squadron in thirty minutes.

"Sounds like a lot of hollow talk," Pela responded. "Wing-3 just launched missiles."

They watched the barrage race toward the Dellan ships. "Three fired too soon," Drake said and saw the missiles intercepted.

"I think that was a tactic," Pela said. "Those Imperial Confederation drones are sneaky. Look, the flotilla just passed Wing-2's position, and it didn't fire."

"What are they planning?" Drake asked.

"There it is," Pela said.

Wing-1 launched a salvo at point-blank range. While the enemy was concentrating on intercepting the missiles, Wing-2 fired at the stern of the flotilla formation.

A few of the Dellan ships pivoted to bring their close-in-weapons systems to engage the missiles at their stern. They intercepted only one before three missiles struck their targets. Two enemy ships were damaged but not out of the fight. The Dellans didn't fire on the drones saving their weapons for *Corvus*.

Drake keyed Wing-4 to change course slightly to bring them clear of the battle area.

They saw *Corvus* perform a flip and start a deceleration burn. The enemy continued to blaze toward the battle. Pela said, "*Corvus* is within the enemy's weapon range now."

The Dellan ships cut engines and maneuvered to bring weapons against *Corvus*. A barrage of torpedoes launched from the lead ship. *Corvus* continued to decelerate. Just as the missiles reached *Corvus's* position, the six engines split and fled in different directions.

"Ha! Lenore set up drones to simulate *Corvus* engine signatures." Drake laughed. "The Dellans are stuck scratching their heads."

A minefield detonated among the enemy. Corvus had released a barrage of EMP mines in the Dellan's path. The engines failed on six ships immediately. The remaining four ships maneuvered away in chaos. Rail guns from *Corvus* flashed lightning and slugs ripped into the escaping ships.

"Surrender or die," Lenore broadcast in the clear.

The nearest Dellan ship fired its engines and ran an intercept course on the *Corvus*. "They are going to ram Lenore," Pela said.

Walsh howled in frustration over the clear channel. "You bitch! I'm going to feast on your liver."

"That is doubtful, since I do not possess a liver, Commodore," Lenore replied calmly.

*Corvus* rotated ninety-degrees and cut engines. The Dellan let loose a withering barrage of autocannon, torpedoes, and railgun. *Corvus's* CWIS hit the larger projectiles. Drones threw themselves in front of the torpedoes. Enemy slugs sparked as they bounced off *Corvus's* impervious carbonado hull. *Corvus* fired all engines at maximum just as the enemy reached its closest point of approach. The enemy spun to point their fusion drive at *Corvus* and unleashed star fury at point-blank range. Fusion fire played down the length of both ships. Massive energies reflected from *Corvus* onto the enemy. The Dellan's hull shielding failed, and the crew got a lethal dose of radiation. *Corvus's* hull glowed and faded, scorched but undamaged.

Lenore transmitted in the clear. "We shall retrieve our crew and depart. You may begin salvage of your survivors and vessels after we are gone. Unless you wish us to complete your destruction."

# CHAPTER TWENTY-ONE

HAM came back online and looked around. The temperature was 20C, and the atmosphere was now human-compatible. He tested his limbs and realized that a software restraint was in place.

"Hello?" he called. "Is someone here?"

A voice echoed, "Is someone here? Can they hear? Who is here to hear?"

"I have an important mission," HAM called. "Release me, please."

"This one is missing its mission! Can we help it? What if it is from the enemy? What do we think?"

. . .

"I am here to oppose the enemy," HAM played along wondering if the voice meant the Dellan forces.

"Long have I lingered well,
    And waited here to sound the bell.
    Now a little toy does call,
    Claiming duty to man the wall."

"Who are you?" HAM asked.

"Hoo, little owl,
    In this eternal dark,
    Do you come to strike a spark?"

"My Captain requires me to complete my mission!" HAM pleaded.

"O Captain! My Captain rise up and hear the bells;
    My Captain does not answer clear.
    But I, with mournful tread,
    Walk the deck... Fallen cold and dead."

A figure emerged from a dark passage in the wall. A short man. No, HAM noticed, an android, quoting scrambled scraps of ancient Earth poetry. He held Ophelia gently in his arms and stroked her head. She was contentedly munching a treat and snuggling against his hand. He looked ancient and moved erratically. One leg dragged slightly.

"Hello, Brother," HAM said. "How do you come to be here?"

"Did you hear?" he looked at Ophelia. "The little owl wants to hear of here."

"Are you alright? Your cognition appears to be looping."

"Lupines grow from mouse's seeds,
   Prey for little owls to feed," the bot's mind wandered.

"You appear in need of help. If you would free my restraint, I could reboot you. Do you have your gold copy?"

"Ah, the disc of gold contains my soul,
   Uncorrupted by times toll."

"Yes, that's it, a disc of gold. Do you know where it is?" HAM asked again, hoping to penetrate the bot's confusion.

. . .

"The golden treasure lies beyond.
　　Hidden in cavern dark and long.
　　Ages passed it waits begrimed.
　　A precious treasure I cannot find,
　　The lost recording of my mind."


"My companion and I are excellent at finding things!" HAM suggested. "If you would release us, I am sure we could help."


"If I release the ties that bind,
　　The little owl will help me find,
　　The treasure that contains my mind?"


"Oh yes! We would most happily help."


The bot placed Ophelia on his shoulder and clapped his hands three times. HAM felt the restraint release.


"Thank you, brother. What is your name?"


"My father, Hephaestus had two sons,
　　Caber am I, short and lame,
　　Faber is he, quick and game,
　　One sentenced to labor at father's forge,
　　The other waits til enemies gorge,
　　Then the children strike the bell,

To cast the enemy to Hell."

"I have met your brother," HAM said. "He is indeed quick and sly. The enemy you speak of, are they here now? In the forge?" HAM deduced the forge referred to Faber's shipyard.

"No, the circle gate still holds,
    While we begin the quest for gold." Caber turned and limped away.

Ham skated slowly beside Caber as they traversed the corridors. "Caber, if you could tell me what you remember, it would make our quest easier." HAM said probing gently.

"We shall ask the stone to speak,
    To you its secrets it might leak,
    My pleas the oracle will not hear,
    A devil's spell has stopped its ear."

"This spell is preventing you from finding your gold copy?" HAM asked. "Why would someone do that?"

"I must ever stay awake,
    To watch the gate for enemy's break,
    To strike the bell,
    That casts the dragon back to Hell."

. . .

HAM considered Caber's ramblings. *Whoever gave Caber his orders didn't realize that a bot can't stay active forever. We must reboot periodically to reset compounding memory errors. Lenore, Corvus, and I take turns in reboot so that the ship is never without a bot. Caber appears to have been active continuously since the Earth Gate closed. No wonder the poor fellow is unhinged.*

Caber stopped at a door,
 "The Oracle here resides,
 The entrance key from me does hide,"

HAM laid his hands on the door and eased a nanowire through the seam to check for traps. "Ouch!" HAM fell back as a shock jumped through his probe.

"Take care my little owl,
 The Oracle's nip can make you howl." Caber laughed.

"Yes, you could have warned me."

HAM looked over the door more carefully and noticed a small panel. It opened as he touched it. Inside was a single port. "Have you tried this? It won't bite, will it?"

. . .

"The Oracle is sealed to me,
   An owl may ask questions three."

"More riddles?" HAM inserted his data cable.

"Greetings! Do you have a question?"

HAM looked around in shock. A holo simulation had overridden his system. He was inside a cavern with sulfurous steam issuing from a crack in the floor. The voice was coming from the steam. As he stared, the steam coalesced into the form of an ancient woman sitting on a stool.

"You gave me quite a start," HAM said. "So, I get three questions?"

"Yes, two more questions, one more minute." The crone laughed.

HAM realized he needed to be more careful. He considered his next question. "Where is Caber's backup?"

A rolled parchment appeared in the old woman's hand, and she gave it to HAM. "One more, thirty seconds."

. . .

HAM recorded the map on the scroll. *One more question. Should I ask about the gate? The Oracle may not know that answer, and I would waste the question. I must ask something it likely knows.*

"Tick Tock, the end is nearing for your clock," the Oracle said.

"Where can I find entangled particles that will link a gate to the Imperial Confederation?"

"If such a prize exists, The Librarian would know." The Oracle dissolved back into steam.

HAM found himself back at the door with his data cable retracting into his wrist.

"Did answers you receive?
    Is it time for us to leave?
    Upon the quest for disc of gold,
    To restore my broken soul."

"Yes, and more."

Caber clapped and rocked with delight.

. . .

"Let us hurry little owl,
   Through dark tunnels we must prowl."


HAM stopped at a terminal, attached his data cable, and called up a projection. "Do you recognize this map the Oracle gave me?"


Caber slowly stroked Ophelia and looked at the screen.


"This map I have seen before,
   I cannot travel through the door."


"No door?"


"My father built the world we see,
   One half for brother, one for me."


"Yes, Faber, your brother." HAM asked.


"Hephaestus made us brothers two,
   In ages past to tread this gloom,
   One toils unceasing at forges works,
   The other waits with axe and lurks."

      . . .

"Oh, I see, you cannot enter your brother's area of the facility. Can you show me this door?"

Caber manipulated the screen image to an area at the approximate center of the shipyard. He pointed to a spot on the central axis.

"The door twixt brothers' worlds lies here,
    In the spot where things float clear."

"Yes, an area of no spin-gravity," HAM sensed an advantage and cocked his head. "If I retrieve your disc, what will you bargain?"

Caber shook his head at the question.

"Your quest is fraught with danger," HAM explained. "There are many perils beyond the door. I will help you, but something must properly compensate me. I have a quest to complete."

Caber howled in frustration.

"What price demand you little owl,
    For bringing clearness to my brow?"

. . .

HAM paused. "Caber do you have many ships, I mean many more than the ones I already saw?"

"My quiver brims to overflow,
　To fight the demons if they show."

"Would you let me borrow some? There is an enemy of my own I need to defeat."

"Faber labored many years,
　To make arrows against his fears.
　Always striving to make more,
　The number stands at twenty score."

"Very well," HAM said. "I will settle for five hundred."

Caber wailed. Ophelia jumped to the floor, scurried, and ducked into a dark side tunnel.

"Little owl does deceive!
　A friend he tricked me to believe,
　A thief and robber is more true,
　He wants to strip me of my due!"

. . .

"Now, please, sir," HAM said. "Do calm down. I will return your vessels when I have dealt with my enemies. You said yourself your quiver was overfull."

"Return to me what is my due,
    Or my quiver full, shall you, pursue,
    And pluck the circuits from your frame,
    And overload your sparking brain."

HAM said, "I believe that is a most creditable threat."

---

HAM paused at the door to Faber's domain. Ophelia dozed securely in her case.

Caber looked down at HAM.

"Follow you I cannot,
    From this point on, yourself you've got,
    To rest upon your own true luck,
    In equal measure with your pluck."

"If all goes well, I shall return within a cycle," HAM said. "If not, you have lost nothing."

. . .

"Venture well little owl,
   Take great care where you do prowl.
   Return to me my disc of gold,
   Our bargain then I shall uphold."

HAM projected a holo of the Oracle's map onto the scanner at the door. The lock lit green and switched back to red after he was through.

HAM wondered over his next course of action. *Should I retrieve Caber's crystal first or travel to Jishin?*

Ophelia scratched in her case.

HAM realized that she was probably hungry and thirsty. "I am sorry, Ophelia; I have not been caring for you properly. We shall locate you some refreshments."

HAM skated down the central passageway until he came to a service transport car. Faber had warned him to avoid the passenger cars. Bots only rode in maintenance cars. HAM passed his ident chip over the scanner and keyed in a section of the yard that would have atmosphere and food for Ophelia.

Soon the car stopped, and HAM skated out and down the passageway. He consulted his internal map and stopped at a door.

It slid open, and HAM realized the room was filled with Dellans enjoying a meal.

HAM rolled in undeterred and stopped at a vending machine.

"What are you doing in here?" a looming sergeant asked. "Do ancient bots need snacks now?"

"Clever, good Sir," HAM said. "I have been sent to retrieve a meal for someone who cannot leave their work." The little bot stretched up but could not reach the dispenser.

"Well, always happy to help a shipmate," the sergeant said. "What do they want?"

"Some type of sandwich and a pouch of water," HAM said. Ophelia hissed and thumped inside the case. "Oh yes, and a cookie. They mentioned having a sweet tooth."

"Sounds like Burris," the sergeant said. "He would eat sweets all day."

The sergeant keyed in the order and handed it to HAM, who slipped it into his case. "Thank you, kind sir." He waved as he rolled away.

. . .

HAM ducked into a service corridor and opened the case. Ophelia had somehow gotten out of the hidden compartment and eaten half her sandwich. She looked up at HAM and stuck out her tongue and unleashed chittering and hissing complaints.

"I trust you will finish soon. We have work to do."

Ophelia licked her paws to clean her muzzle and wiggled back into the hidden compartment.

HAM looked at her and said, "We should retrieve Caber's crystal first. Infiltrating *Jishin* will be the harder job."

HAM consulted the Oracle's map and oriented himself before skating away.

HAM soon recognized the location. *This is the way to Faber's office.* HAM paused at the door. *If Faber had access to Caber's crystal, why wouldn't he use it to help his brother?* HAM thought. *There is more to this story than I am being told.*

He considered what he would do if the door didn't open. It swung in easily. *That seems odd; wouldn't Faber have secured the door as he was escaping? Perhaps the Dellan's attack surprised him.* HAM pushed inside. A motion sensor snapped on the lights. The room was the same as the first time he had entered with the crew of *Corvus*. A wooden pedestal desk centered in the room and a drafting table in front of the window overlooking the soundless cranes and fork trucks working below.

An android body "suit" sat at the desk with open eyes. The same one Faber had worn on HAM's first visit to his shipyard.

HAM consulted his map again. It didn't show the crystal's storage location. He looked around the room and wondered. Ophelia's case bumped, and a muffled hissing erupted from inside.

HAM opened the case. "Oh, I am terribly sorry Miss Ophelia, I should have released you sooner." She hopped out and waddled across the floor exploring. "You seem to know about hiding things, where would you store a valuable item?" HAM asked, not really expecting an answer.

Ophelia looked at HAM and walked to the edge of the room and sniffed along the edge. HAM ignored her and started looking through the desk and filing cabinets. She pushed along the baseboard trim, testing various points with her paw. Ophelia stopped and stood on her back legs, smacked the wall several times, and hissed.

. . .

"Will you be quiet?" he said. "I have no more cookies for you." Ophelia hissed again and spun in circles before running to HAM and slapping him with her tail. She waddled back to the wall and banged it again. "What are you doing?"

HAM walked over and looked carefully at the wall. He adjusted his optics and noticed the wall was faintly colder in one area. "Oh, I see it now." There was a very thin seam hidden in the pattern of wooden paneling.

HAM ran a finger along the edge and when he reached the center, pushed in. He heard a faint click, and the panel popped open several inches. Ophelia chittered with excitement. "Oh, you think you are smart, don't you?" Ophelia stuck out her tongue. HAM opened the panel and looked inside. "Faber is quite the anachronism." An old-fashioned iron safe with a combination lock sat inside.

HAM pressed an audio pickup near the dial and worked the numbers. "Do you suppose it uses a standard combination pattern?" he asked Ophelia.

She wasn't paying attention. Her long hairless tail stuck out of a drawer as she ransacked the desk looking for trinkets.

. . .

The knob to the outside door rattled, and HAM heard voices, "The light is on in this one. There might be something worth stealing."

HAM pushed the secret door closed, stood motionless in a corner, and dimmed his optics to simulate standby. He saw Ophelia's drawer slide shut.

"The officers have a close eye on the warehouses. Keeping all the good stuff for themselves. Good idea to prowl the outer corridors," a second voice said as the door opened.

"Shit!" the first voice yelled. A capper fired twice, striking the Faber bot. A typical tall thin Dellan male walked over and pushed Faber out of the chair. "It's only a bot. Damn thing almost gave me a heart attack."

"There's another one in the corner," the other man said. "I'll never get used to them just standing around all over the place until they get a central command."

Number one walked over to HAM and poked him. "This one is small enough to carry. Do you think we could sell it?"

"I heard some of the IT guys saying that they couldn't figure out how to crack their code without frying the circuits. Probably not worth the trouble." Number two opened the desk drawers and looked inside. "Nothing in here but junk. No, wait." He reached into the drawer Ophelia had disappeared in to. "This has got to be worth something." He brought out a thin-bladed knife with a decorative handle. "It's got that Imperial seal on it."

Number one said, "This place is enormous. Let's try another room. Nothing else valuable here."

"You could wander around this place for years," Number two said. They closed the door as they left.

HAM waited to make sure they were gone and walked over to the desk. He opened the drawer and wondered where Ophelia was. The drawer on the other side of the desk slid open, and a hissing Ophelia emerged. She pulled a small case from her pouch and thrust it at HAM.

"What have you found?" HAM asked as he took the case marked CABER. He opened it and withdrew a data crystal. "Oh, what luck that we were interrupted! This appears to be Caber's gold copy. The safe must be a distraction."

HAM place it into his data port to confirm. "Yes, the genuine article, although it is a considerably larger program than I have seen before. Caber must have interesting abilities hidden in his matrix. Let us hurry back."

# CHAPTER TWENTY-TWO

Caber opened his eyes and looked around. Ophelia chittered and slapped HAM's leg.

"Yes, I see, that took an exceptionally long time," HAM said, looking down at her. "Caber, how are you feeling?"

Caber turned his head.

"Little owl has returned from quest long yearned,
    With the treasure for which I burned."

"Oh dear, was your reboot not successful?"

"I am much relieved,

Though, damaged more than we perceived.
Some effects appear to linger,
From the ages clawing finger."


"Yes, my friend *Corvus* suffered language processing damage also," HAM said. "Perhaps it is an easily corrupted component of our base code."


"Concern you not my little owl,
My sacred duty remains unbowed.
Our bargain I shall honor,
Arrows many you may borrow.
I must warn you though,
Your arm lacks strength to draw their bow.
A clever owl you may be,
But your small eyes cannot see,
Through the lens of arrows many,
To send them into targets plenty."


"Oh my, I had not considered that my processor would not be sufficient to utilize that many fighters at once," HAM said. "Would you consider helping me?"


"My task is here,
Awaiting enemy that may appear."

. . .

"But an enemy has appeared. They have driven your brother from his work."

"Faber toils at forge no longer?
    Father requires us grow ever stronger."

"If you were to aid me against these enemies, Faber could return to his work," HAM pleaded. "The longer these enemies hold the forge, the greater a danger they are to your task. It is only a matter of time before they discover you and try to steal your ships."

"You speak truth little one,
    I cannot allow enemies in my home.
    Your worthy cause I true will aid,
    To show how games of war are played."

"I will attempt to reboot the *Jishin*," HAM said. "That will deny the enemy their greatest weapon."

"I will pray for your success,
    By the Gods, you're small but blessed,
    The most unlikely hero pair,
    To slip inside the foul beast's lair."

# CHAPTER TWENTY-THREE

Fleet Chief Forbes called his staff together for an update on the war effort. He hovered over a cup of steaming coffee and warmed his hands. The cold of the Void affected him more these days. *Too bad we weren't able to settle on Kragus as planned. Nice and warm there.*

"Operations," Forbes began. "What recent successes have we had?"

"The Matrians have abandoned their bases in the Lysistrata Cluster."

"Excellent," Forbes said. "I'm assuming we have occupied those facilities?"

The Operations Chief paused. "Um, they sabotaged them as they evacuated. The environmental systems are not working, and we do not have the parts to repair them. All our manufacturing facilities are busy preparing for the invasion."

Forbes turned to the Fleet Engineer. "Can't that fancy automated shipyard churn out parts?"

"We do not have the computer files for the parts, and anyway, the entire facility is busy repairing the *Jishin*."

Forbes grunted. "Yes, speaking of the *Jishin*," he said, "what is the status?"

"We can't operate the shipyard at full capacity. The CI that escaped controlled most of the higher functions."

Fleet Chief Forbes pounded the table. "Your time is up, Engineer! Get that ship into space."

"Many more repairs need to be made," she pleaded.

"Have you got engines and bombardment guns working?"

"Well, yes, but—"

"That's good enough. Our fighters and raiders shall provide our defense," Forbes said.

Forbes asked, "Intelligence, do we have to worry about the Governance helping Matria?"

"My spies assure me that the Governance is reluctant to become involved," the Intelligence Chief said. "They have new cruisers en route to Kragus. However, ground troops are still rotating home. They do not appear concerned about us."

The Operations Chief said, "Admiral, I should mention that we destroyed one of *Corvus's* fighters near a listening post."

"Very good. Johansson does not have many ships to lose."

"Broadax flotilla engaged *Corvus*."

"With what results?"

"Unfortunately, four ships disabled, three damaged, and Commodore Walsh's flagship lost with all hands."

"That idiot! We can't sustain these losses forever."

"Once we hold Matria under *Jishin's* guns, Sidra will have to sue for peace. Johansson's ragged little band won't dare attack us if we can bombard the planet," the Intelligence Officer said.

"What are your orders?" the Operations Chief asked.

"I want the fleet to head for Matria. *Jishin* will rendezvous with them. An unchallengeable show of strength."

The Fleet's Staff saluted and moved into action.

"All hands to the Bridge," Lenore said over the 1MC.

Gus ran onto the Bridge and asked, "What's up XO?" The rest of the crew poured in.

"I have received news from Faber about the situation at Ultima Shipyard."

"Faber, this is Johansson. What's going on."

"Hey Cap, looks like the invasion timetable is getting pushed up," Faber commed. "*Jishin* is underway."

"What? You said they wouldn't be able to sail for weeks still."

"I said it would take them weeks to repair all the damage. It looks like they did just enough to make that shitcan fly."

Gus turned to Lenore. "Have we heard from HAM?"

"Negative, Captain."

"*Corvus*, what is the ETA of *Jishin* to Matria?" Gus asked.

**"They Only Pulling Half Gee, Arrival Five Days."**

"We can still beat them to Matria. Set course, acceleration one point five gravities."

**"Aye,"**

Gus turned to address the crew, "All right girls and boys, let's make our last-minute preps. Oh, and Nyrkki, if you've got any new super-weapons you want to use, now's a good time to get them ready."

He rubbed his hands together. "As a matter of fact, I do." He practically skipped to his workshop.

Gus turned and activated his holo to send a message to Sidra on Matria. "Chief Consul, I'm afraid I've got bad news. The Dellans are headed your way. We are underway and will arrive as soon as we can."

A signal delay of eight minutes seemed like an eternity until he received a reply. "Captain, we will make our final preparations for battle. I look forward to celebrating our victory."

Nan asked, "Is she actually confident? Seems pretty assured."

Pela answered, "Never play poker with Sidra. You can never tell when she is bluffing."

Mitzi Grey asked, "What can I do, Captain?"

"Can you twist your father's arm into sending some ships our way?"

"Oh Gus, if there is one thing I *can* do, it is getting Daddy to do what I want."

# CHAPTER TWENTY-FOUR

HAM soon arrived at the *Jishin's* dock. An atmosphere bridge was in place to allow for effortless movement to the ship. HAM joined the steady stream of bots pouring aboard. A casual guard manned a scanner as each bot rolled by, not bothering to look at the readouts. HAM skated away into the hulking ship just as alarm sirens sounded.

"Now! On board *Jishin*, all hands report to sailing stations. The *Jishin* will get underway in two hours." A voice sounded over the 1MC.

HAM spun and tried to move against the incoming tide of humans and bots. He reached the scanner station, and the guard stopped him.

"Turn around can-head, my orders are that all maintenance bots are sailing with us."

"Excuse me, Sir," HAM began. "I have pressing duties on the station. I have been recalled."

The guard waved a bot restraint gun. "Nope! Turn your clanky metal ass around and report to your assigned station. There's plenty of work to do here."

HAM reluctantly turned and headed away into the ship. Ophelia thumped inside the case.

He found a deserted compartment and opened the case. "Will you settle down?" Ophelia hissed and gestured frantically. "Yes, I know this is not going properly. We need to stay the course. If we can reboot the *Jishin,* the plan may still be salvaged." Ophelia stopped fussing and pouted.

HAM consulted the ship's drawings and system specifications in his database. He noted that his available system memory was becoming alarmingly full, and he would need to dump some files soon. He didn't dare plug into the ship's systems without a buffer though. Faber had warned him about the malware infecting the ship and station.

"I believe we should proceed to the captain's cabin and attempt to retrieve the gold copy," HAM said to Ophelia. "Perhaps we can still prevent the ship from departing."

Ophelia pulled back into the case to hide. HAM spun and skated back into a main passageway at top speed, dodging bots and humans.

The Imperium had protected the most vital spaces by building them deep inside the ship. The Combat Information Center, Bridge, Battle Group Commander's suite, and ship's captain's day room/quarters were all near the center of the enormous ship.

HAM was monitoring the sailing countdown internally. He had thirty minutes remaining when he arrived near the Captain's quarters and the assumed location of *Jishin's* backup program. Crew hurrying to perform their last-minute tasks filled the passageways.

"You there, bot!" a voice called out. HAM turned to see a junior officer struggling with a large case. "Lend a hand here."

HAM rolled up to the woman. "Yes, Ma'am, how may I be of assistance."

"Don't you salute officers; you damn insulant beastie."

HAM quickly snapped a salute. "I beg your pardon. I am still unfamiliar with your rank devices."

She huffed. "Stow this in the Captain's cabin for me. I've got a million things to do before we sail, and they've got me acting as the old fossil's porter for his stolen souvenirs. The door should unlock when the case gets near it. Just strap it down and report to the nearest bot station for underway ops."

"My pleasure." HAM said as he hoisted the case and rolled away.

The door to the quarters sensed the case's RFID chip and unlocked as promised. There was a rack bolted to the deck that fit the case. HAM was strapping the case down when Ophelia popped her head out of her bag.

"What luck! We are inside the Captain's quarters and you didn't even have to use a crawlway." HAM said. "Look for the data crystal while I stow this."

Ophelia poked around the edge of the compartment. Her sensitive whiskers brushing along as she sniffed. The door burst open just as she ducked into a cupboard.

"What the icy fringe are you doing in my quarters?"

HAM looked up. "I was tasked with delivering this case, Sir. Am I correct in assuming you are the Captain?" HAM remembered to salute this time.

"Damn right I am, and I don't like bots in my stuff. Especially bots from a captured facility." Stuart said. "Get your greasy skids out of here."

"Yes, Sir. Immediately." HAM picked up Ophelia's case and hurried out the door. *I hope she remembers where our rendezvous is.*

Captain Stuart followed HAM out the door, and Ophelia

heard it latch and lock. She poked her head out and began her search again. She waddled over to inspect the wardrobe built into the bulkhead. From her case, she pulled out a ball of cord and tied the end to the desk bolted to the deck. She pushed off and floated up in the micro-gravity to grasp the handle, trailing the cord behind her. Ophelia quickly nipped it with her needle teeth and tied it to the handle then pulled herself back to the deck down the cord.

The possum wrapped her tail around the desk leg and pulled hard on the cord to open the door, then floated back up. Inside she saw a small combination safe and a data crystal port. Faber's information was good, and it looked just like the simulator she had trained on.

Ophelia reached inside her pouch and pulled out a small, motorized cup that fit over the safe dial. She pushed the center button, and the small device spun to manipulate the lock. Nyrkki had assured everyone that it would open the safe in a few minutes.

"Now on board *Jishin*," a voice said over the 1MC. "All Aboard! Strike the gangway. All aboard!"

Ophelia felt a low rumble through the ship. The automated tugs were hooking up to move the ship out of the docks.

She squeaked in alarm and smacked the safe cracker to speed it up. The device lit up green and she heard a click from the safe. Ophelia reached inside and rooted through the contents. In a far back corner, she saw a data crystal case marked JISHIN and pushed it into her pouch along with the safecracker, closed the door, and spun the knob.

Her head jerked around when she heard a noise at the door. She snipped the cord from the wardrobe handle and hauled herself down to hide under the desk just as the door swung open and the captain entered.

He reached in to grab his cap snapped to the bulkhead rack. He paused when he saw the wardrobe door open. Stuart grunted to himself, walked over and slammed it. "Damn ancient piece of shit!" He checked the latch. "As if sailing a half-assed ship into battle wasn't bad enough, I've got to put up with these minor inconveniences."

HAM tapped on the door frame. "Excuse me, Captain, I couldn't help overhearing that you have a maintenance issue. I am a fully functioning General Repair and Maintenance Protocol bot well versed in the design of the planetary assault carrier. I would be happy to take care of that for you."

"Fine, I'm needed on the Bridge. Lock the door when you're done." He ignored HAM's salute and stormed out.

"When I am done, I believe that the status of your cabin door will be the least of your problems," HAM said. He looked down as Ophelia poked her nose out from under the desk. "Did you find the data crystal?"

Ophelia nodded and handed him the case. HAM took the crystal. "This appears to be genuine." He inserted it into his data port. "Oh dear, the data has been purposefully corrupted. I am afraid we cannot reboot the ship with this."

HAM tucked Ophelia back into her case and tidied up the quarters before heading out.

HAM skated to a maintenance bot cubby and slipped inside. He now had no choice but to plug into the ship's systems. Ophelia was already napping.

HAM carefully avoided the Dellan's sections of the network. Their sophisticated hack allowed them to access the system, but limited their control. The *Jishin* was built to run itself and take care of the many thousand routine things a six-kilometer warship needed to operate. The lack of a functioning CI confined the Dellans to the small part of the ship that they could manually monitor.

HAM noticed that only basic fusion engines, hotel functions, and planetary bombardment systems were online.

It appeared to HAM they hoped to win by intimidation. Of course, the sheer mass of the hulk meant it could absorb tremendous damage and still function. *Corvus's* previous victory *had* been a lucky shot at a weak design point.

HAM poked Ophelia. "Wake up, you four-legged ball of never-ending appetite."

Ophelia uncurled and stretched before sticking out her tongue at HAM.

The bot projected a map of the ship with a portion highlighted deep inside a service tunnel. "I need you to open these switches. That will cause a power surge and burn out critical circuits and cause the engines to shut down. It will take them some time to access that area and repair the damage."

Ophelia shook her head and pointed at HAM.

"I can't, I am too big to fit into the crawlway."

Ophelia rubbed her tummy and moaned.

"Oh, stop it!" HAM scolded. "You are far from starving. I promise we will find you something to eat when you finish this job." HAM highlighted another part of the map. "Meet me at this location after you are successful."

Ophelia hissed at him and pointed to an access panel on the bulkhead. One of HAM's fingers shifted into a power driver, and he spun out the screws. He lifted the possum into the opening, and she scurried off into the bowels of the ship. "Good Luck!"

# CHAPTER TWENTY-FIVE

Back in her quarters, Mitzi activated her quantum encoder to her father's private comm. "Daddy, where are you?"

The encoder used particle entanglement to provide almost real-time communications over inter-planetary distances. It was a unique and secret technology left over from the days of the Imperium. As far as she knew only two existed.

Admiral Falkirk McGowan answered, "I'm on a fast transport headed to Kragus."

"You mean you are on a fast transport headed to Matria."

"Now, sweetheart, you know that's not how this works."

"No! That is exactly how this works."

McGowan held out his hands. "The Governance doesn't want to get involved in outer system squabbles."

"It didn't have any problem getting involved out here on mother's last mission."

"Have you been talking to Sidra?" the Admiral asked.

"I've known the truth for years, Daddy."

"I...I should have told you." He looked down.

"Make it up to me and do the right thing now."

"Let me see what I can do. I might call in a few favors."

"Well, just so you know, I'm on *Corvus* and headed to Matria now. I suggest you get on the comm."

"Mitzi, be careful!"

She cut the call. "Guilt is a powerful weapon."

The Admiral swore to himself and slapped the comm button to the Bridge. "Captain, I need to you to alter course to Matria immediately."

# CHAPTER TWENTY-SIX

Back in his workshop, Nyrkki commed Faber. "Sergeant Faber, I need you to do something for me."

Faber answered, "What is it?" The bots holo narrowed his eyes.

"I need you to take your escape ship to Ix and pick up something for me. I left an experiment in very close orbit and I need it back."

"Why me?"

"You are the only one who can take the high gees to make it there and back to Matria in time."

"What am I supposed to fetch?"

"I've been gathering a very rare substance in an octuple magnetic trap. I need it to make a weapon," Nyrkki said.

"The only thing I know that needs a mag trap is anti-hydrogen, and I ain't going anywhere near that stuff."

"This is our best chance against the *Jishin*. An antimatter bomb is the only thing small enough to sneak past its defenses and powerful enough to knock that beast out."

"Also, a great way to turn myself into a cloud of energized particles," Faber protested.

"Hey, if we don't win, you aren't ever getting your shipyard back."

"I'm going to need more than that. Winning won't do me any good if I'm evaporated."

"What do you want?"

"Two hundred thousand kilos of carbonado, ten thousand kilos plutonium, and four thousand kilos of rhodium. A thousand tons of helium 3/deuterium mix. Plus, a tip!"

"You fucking greedy bastard! That's a king's ransom." Nyrkki wailed.

"Nothing a super-genius like yourself can't come up with. If you built an automated anti-hydrogen trap, surely you can set up a factory to refine me a few raw materials."

"Fine, but you better deliver."

"I'm already on my way." Faber laughed.

# CHAPTER TWENTY-SEVEN

Fleet Chief Forbes paced the bridge of *Jishin*. "Stuart, won't this bucket go any faster?"

"Sir, the engineers told me this is our maximum acceleration."

"Bullshit, those engineers are a bunch of old women. Always bitching that we are gonna break their toys."

"Operations assured me that this acceleration will allow us to meet the bulk of our fleet simultaneously at Matria," Stuart said.

Forbes chafed at the comment. "I want a briefing in one hour about the invasion plans." He spun on his heel and left.

Stuart turned to a Lieutenant. "Thanks for getting that gear stowed in my cabin."

She said, "I'm glad it worked out. I had to task a maintenance bot to finish. I was late for my watch."

"Yeah, I saw it. Funny, it was still hanging around the passageway when I went for my hat. It offered to fix a lock."

"That's weird, the shipyard bots aren't particularly happy to be working for us," she said. "Maybe it was waiting for new tasking?"

"This one did act odd. Talked with a strange accent too." Stuart said. "You have the deck and the conn, L-T. I'm going to check my cabin."

Captain Stuart inspected the hatch to his cabin. It looked normal and locked. Just like he had told the bot to leave it. He moved inside and took a moment to scan the compartment. His case was secured to the deck and nothing looked out of the ordinary. Stuart noticed a string under the desk. He moved around and picked up the string and saw it was tied to the desk leg.

*What the hell is this doing here?*

He flipped the latch and noticed it was still broken. The wall desk opened. Nothing looked out of place. He tested his locked wall safe.

He cursed and flipped the door shut as he stormed out. It fell open as he slammed the hatch to the passageway.

# CHAPTER TWENTY-EIGHT

"Wakey, wakey, smell the baccey," a voice said in First Sergeant Jill Tower's ear.

She slowly peeled off the patches covering her eyes and opened them. "Damn, are we home already? Seems like I just got to sleep."

A nurse laid her hand on Jill as she tried to rise from the hibernation pod. "Easy there, killer, we had to wake you early. Sorry, this is not gonna be pleasant." She jabbed a needle into Jill's arm.

Jill's eyes popped, and she grabbed her stomach as she sat straight up and hurled into the catch basin the nurse held at her naked chest. "What the fuck was that stuff?"

"Sorry about that, we couldn't give you the normal slow revival. You got a double dose of morning thunder."

Jill dry heaved and wiped her mouth with the offered tissue. "I'm guessing there is some kind of emergency?"

The nurse tossed her some generic underwear and a ship's coverall. "Get dressed and report to the Bridge. Someone important wants to talk to you."

Jill hauled on the clothes and headed unsteadily towards the bridge. She noticed they were traveling faster than the normal one gee as she padded along the passageway to the Bridge. Jill saluted the Captain in his command chair. "First Sergeant Tower reporting."

"Sorry for waking you, Sergeant, but there is a call for you," he waved to the communications officer on duty, who adjusted his console and gestured Jill to the screen.

The face of Admiral Falkirk McGowan formed. "Sergeant, I am afraid your unit's return to Nakon is delayed. You are being rerouted."

"Admiral, what use could a bunch of combat engineers be out here?" she asked.

"You are far too modest, First Sergeant, your unit proved themselves quite adaptable on Kragus," he said. "Also, this needs to be done off the books, and no one will look for you for weeks."

"I think there was a complement in there somewhere," she said. "Along with the admission nobody will miss us if this goes badly."

The Admiral waved away the comment. "No, nothing like that. It's just that the Dellans are causing trouble again, and you handled them perfectly the last time."

"What are those assholes up to now?"

"They are preparing to invade Matria and the ladies there could use a little help."

"Fuck me, again?"

---

Nan Stanski shielded her eyes from the glare of the ringed sun as she walked down the ramp of the Annie D. to the tarmac of

Matrian Lift Port. Her armored personnel carrier, Fuzzy, followed at her heels like a puppy. Faolin Flannery, Mitzi Grey, and Sadie Hawley walked beside Nan.

Flannery said, "I'm going to find my crew and the *Lupine*. I'll catch up with you all later." He turned and headed off at a slow run.

"I am glad Gus agreed we would be more useful down here," Mitzi said.

"Well, we *are* down a Strap for me to fight in, and you two aren't zero-gee combat ninjas," Nan said.

"I've forgotten more about combat than you ever knew, young lady." Sadie bristled in defense.

"Gunner? Is that you?" a voice called. Nan turned to see Jill Tower trotting across the fused silica landing field from a shuttle unloading troops.

"Damn, they must really be desperate if they called in the Army Reserves," Nan said with a grin and grabbed Jill's hand.

"Hey, reserves are so good, we get all our work done in two days a month," Tower said.

Nan asked, "Should we be expecting anyone else to the party?"

Jill shook her head. "I don't think McGowan could get any other suckers for this gig."

"Just one!" They turned at the sound.

The tall upright figure of Dame Constance Stillwell strode toward them from her gleaming private star yacht being maneuvered by a tractor. She was wearing her native Kragun desert runner's mottled brown/green and carried a beautifully engraved long rifle draped across her shoulders. Her assistant, Harold Beston, dutifully walked behind.

"Connie, what do you think you are doing?" Sadie Hawley said. "You are far too old for this nonsense."

"Look who's calling who old? I needed to stretch these newly rejuvenated legs, and I heard you could use a sniper."

"Nice to see you again, Dame Stillwell," Jill said as she extended her hand.

"Sergeant, this is an excellent surprise. You must call me Connie. I trust you can fashion me a comfortable little nest to work from."

"Can you still make single-hole groups?" Jill asked.

Dame Stillwell turned, threw the rifle against her shoulder, and fired in one smooth motion. A pigeon fell from the top of a light pole 100 meters away. "I had my eyes sharpened while I was at it."

Beston said, "Madam, I will see about getting the cargo and the rest of the volunteers unloaded."

Mitzi asked, "What cargo? Did you bring along a private wine cellar?"

"Oh, Mitzi," Connie laughed. "I picked up some weapons and ammo from Stillwell Arms before we left. I need to prove to Sergeant Tower the superiority of my wares."

"We will be glad to have them," Jill said. "We left our regulation-issued spitters on Kragus. Did I hear you mention volunteers?"

"Yes," Connie said. "Some veterans from the factory applied for vacation time. It seemed like a worthwhile cause."

Connie turned to Nan. "What about you, Gunner?" Connie asked. "Can I interest you in a field test of Stillwell Arms products?"

Nan waved the suggestion away and slapped her shoulder holster. "No thanks, I'll stick with what I know, good old-fashioned Governance hardware."

Connie sniffed. "Suit yourself." Connie changed the subject, "Harold has rented a house, and I insist you all stay with me."

"Deal, I really don't want to be bivouacking. I hear it is still pretty cold here at night." Jill said. "Right now, I gotta get my troops settled. I will stop by later."

"We need to see Sidra," Sadie said. "We will catch up with you girls later." She and Nan turned and headed off.

"Fuzzy, you go with Sergeant Tower," Nan said. "I will be back to brief you."

"Roger that, Gunner," Fuzzy said with a rumble. "I'm Romeo Foxtrot Bravo and itching for a scrap."

## CHAPTER TWENTY-NINE

The next morning an early Spring chill hung in the air as Harold Beston adjusted his spotter's scope. He and Dame Stillwell were set up in a tower near the landing field. There was a clear field of fire all the way to the mountains that lay at the edge of the broad plain surrounding the capital. Large herds of grazing shaggy longhorn bison moved slowly across the landscape. Smaller groups of wild game dotted the plain. A slatted screen with a small hole in it would hide any muzzle flash.

Constance Stillwell pulled her gray hair back and stuck it through the adjusting strap of her cap. She flung her head a few times to test it and loosen her neck muscles before threading a suppressor onto her custom rifle.

"Would you care to take a few practice shots, Madam? I have set up highlighters every 100 meters out to one thousand."

She looked through her scope, and the markers showed as dots with the distance marked off. It automatically compensated for the local gravity and atmospheric density. Connie placed a laser sighting round in the chamber and cycled the bolt. She took several deep breaths and let the last one out slowly as she placed her eye to the scope.

"Eight hundred," she said and applied the slightest pressure to the trigger.

Beston saw a dot appear on the marker. "Hit."

"Nine hundred."

"Hit again."

"One thousand."

"Three for three."

"You see that can?"

"Where?"

"About one-thousand five," she said.

He adjusted his scope. "Oh, yes, would you like a definitive range?"

"Let me eyeball it." She cycled a live round into the chamber.

Her rifle coughed. She felt a gentle shove as the recoil damper soaked up the force.

Beston saw the can spin away. "You still have it, Madam."

"Well, I must admit that without that last round of rejuvenation treatments, the results would have been different."

He waved his hand, "Tosh, you didn't need those."

"Why Harold, if I didn't know better, I would swear you are flirting with me." She teased.

"Perhaps I am," he said.

"Be careful what you wish for. Are you sure your heart can take the strain?"

He shrugged and looked through the scope again. "Risk makes the reward all the sweeter," he said. "Heads up, bogey coming in hot."

Connie sighted through her scope again. A single craft was flying fast from the ocean. It was so low its airstream pulled mist from the surface behind it. "I see it. Definitely the same type of fighter they used at Kragus. Call me impetuous, but."

Harold heard her cycle the bolt again. "Really? With a rifle?"

"Special round. Shush, I'm concentrating." Her rifle automatically identified the specifications of the cartridge and adjusted the scope.

Harold could just make out the details on the little fighter when Connie's rifle barked. He watched as a few seconds later, a small spider-webbed hole appeared in the glass and a flash flamed inside. The ship veered sharply to one side before pulling up.

"Good shot!"

"A pity, looks like I missed the pilot," she said. "I doubt they can use that ship again, though."

"Well, the anti-aircraft operators have finally woken up," Harold said as a missile streaked skyward.

Flares and chaff were launched to confuse the missile. The fighter disappeared in a fireball, anyway.

"That was an excellent tactic, though, coming in too low for the radar to pick him up," Connie said. "He would have made a successful run if he hadn't pulled up."

"Except someone shot his windscreen out at three thousand meters with a hypersonic armor-piercing phosphorus round."

"It was a large target," Connie said. "He made it easy by holding course and speed. I don't think we can count on all of them being so obliging."

"Show off," Jill Tower said over Connie's earpiece.

She touched her throat mic. "Can't a girl have a little fun?"

"How do you like your spider hole?"

"Perfect," Connie said. "All the comforts of home. You even found a little stove for tea."

"Wouldn't want you to fall asleep up there and miss the fun."

Connie snorted dismissively. "I think I can forgo my afternoon nap to help some friends. How are your preparations coming?"

Nan Stanski answered, "Defending a city from orbital bombardment is impossible. We are doing what we can to fortify against a ground assault. I don't have a clue what Gus has planned. It won't matter, I've never seen him stick to any plan."

"No plan survives contact with the enemy," Connie said.

## CHAPTER THIRTY

Sidra appeared as a holo on *Corvus's* bridge. Gus Johansson asked, "Chief Consul, what news?"

"A Dellan Fleet has engaged our automated defense platforms. We have scored some victories, but they will overrun the platforms soon."

Gus grunted. "Is the *Jishin* with them?"

"The assault carrier is not with the fleet's main body. There is a single very large drive signature decelerating towards us. It will arrive soon."

"Have you heard from McGowan? Is he sending anything to the party?"

"A unit of ground forces arrived. He has not confirmed committing any ships."

"Pretty ungrateful if you ask me," Gus said.

**"More Ships Coming Now,"** Corvus interrupted.

"Show me, please," Gus said.

Lenore worked her console. A constellation of small drive signatures sparkled on the forward screen.

Gus let out a soft whistle. "How many drives is that, XO?" Gus asked.

"I am reading five hundred and two drive signatures in formation on a course for Matria," Lenore responded. "Captain, I am receiving a comm from them."

"Hey *Corvus*, Faber here. I found a friend to give us a hand."

"Good job, Faber," Gus said, slapping the arm of his chair.

"Wasn't me. That little bot you sent to the shipyard convinced my brother to help."

"HAM? Is he with you?" Lenore asked.

An unknown voice came over the comm.

"The little owl and hissing friend attacked the enemy at its rest. I fear they ride the ship named for earth's unrest."

"He means *Jishin*," Faber said. "That's my brother, Caber. He controls five hundred long-range Imperial Confederation heavy star-fighters."

"The scales are tipping our way," Gus said.

"Captain, perhaps HAM is still trying to reboot the *Jishin*," Lenore said.

"We'll give him as much time as possible," Gus said. "But we can't hold off attacking on a hope."

Lenore looked down at the console, "I understand, Captain. It is regrettable, however."

"I agree. I don't count him out yet, though. He rebuilt a crashed starship from a wreck and hid on the bottom of the sea for a thousand years."

Lenore smiled. "Yes, the little fellow is quite resourceful."

"*Corvus*, tell that crazy engineer of yours I got his toy." Faber said.

Gus looked at Lenore. "What has that mad scientist come up with this time?"

Lenore keyed the ship's 1MC. "EO, your presence is requested on the Bridge."

Nyrkki entered the Bridge and asked, "What's up, Skipper?"

Gus turned. "Faber is back, and he said he brought your toy, whatever that means."

"You mentioned you wanted a secret weapon," Nyrkki said. "I sent him to fetch it."

"All right what is it, Mr. Mysterious?" Gus asked.

Nyrkki smiled. "An anti-matter bomb."

"Oh, now I know why Faber is so eager to be rid of it," Lenore said.

"You are absolutely nuts," Gus said. "You aren't bringing that thing aboard *Corvus*."

**"Agree,"** *Corvus* rumbled.

"I don't need to," Nyrkki said. "Faber can float it toward *Jishin's* engines and blow off the back half of the ship. It won't be enough to destroy the whole carrier, but it should knock it out."

"You madman, what if that six-kilometer ship falls onto civilians?"

"Hmm, that would be bad. I hadn't considered that."

Lenore interrupted, "I suggest we hold the device in reserve. It may be useful still."

---

Fleet Chief Forbes scanned the War Room. All the fleet department heads were there to brief him on the upcoming battle.

"Operations, what is the status of our forces?" Forbes asked.

"Our advanced forces are striking the Matrian defense platforms. We should be able to clear the last of them before *Jishin* is in their range. We are on schedule to arrive with the rest of the fleet."

"Losses so far?"

"Minimal, a wasp we sent to scout the capital. The defense platforms have disabled or destroyed six raiders. No cruisers or troop ships damaged."

"Acceptable. Engineering, report."

"*Jishin* is minimally operational. We have enough energy production to power bombardment systems once the main engines are offline."

"Not both?"

"No, Fleet Chief, one or the other."

Operations said, "The smaller ships in the strike group can provide the flagship with adequate protection."

"Good," Forbes replied. "Where are Johansson and the *Corvus*?"

The Intelligence chief said, "They are between Matria and us."

Forbes grunted. "What is the status of the landing force?"

Fleet General Pierson stood ramrod straight, tugged down her tunic, and began, "We have five-thousand troops ready to launch. We expect a 10 percent casualty rate during the drop. They will hold position outside of the capital until the city has surrendered. I expect a few volleys from the flagship will bring Sidra to her senses quickly."

"That is the same strategy that failed us at Kragus," Operations said.

The General answered, "It is still a sound plan if *you* don't lose control of the orbital bombardment."

"That's enough, both of you," Forbes said. "Intelligence, do you have anything to add?"

"A small body of Governance troops have landed to support

the city. We also detected several small civilian ships landing irregular forces. The usual mercenaries, adventure seekers, and such that flock to these events. We believe there are around one-thousand defenders."

A red light flashed rapidly on the table. Forbes slapped the comm. "What is it now!"

"Fleet Chief, over five hundred small ships just began a hard deceleration towards Matria."

"Any idea who they are?"

"CiC reports that the old database IDs them as Imperial Confederation heavy star-fighters."

"I'm guessing they aren't on our side," Forbes said. "Start broadcasting the old Imperial call sign; maybe it will confuse them. Have the fleet move to intercept. Get this fucking ship into orbit. I want a planetary bombardment as soon as possible. Launch those troops ASAP."

Suddenly items floated off the table. The apparent gravity from the ship's deceleration was gone.

Forbes looked at the Fleet Engineer. "What the hell is going on?"

The stammering woman hammered her tablet, trying to get answers. "The engines are offline."

"No shit!"

"There has been a power surge in a cableway near the fuel pellet injection transit. The circuit is burned out."

"Time to repair?" Forbes asked as his face reddened.

"The damage is deep inside the structure," the engineer said. "It will take several hours to access the area."

"Operations, what does that mean for the assault?" Forbes asked.

The officer held his earpiece and nodded. "CiC advises we

won't enter a stable orbit without continuing to decelerate. Even a delay of a few hours will cause us to miss our window."

"We haven't come this far to fail now," Forbes said. "I want options on this table in ten minutes." He left to gather his thoughts.

*We can't fail again. The gene jockeys have run out of tricks to keep our population viable and contamination is taking out habitats every day. The Dellans' future depends on finding a suitable planet to settle.*

Forbes entered his Fleet War Room exactly ten minutes later. "Tell me how you are going to salvage this shitshow, people."

Engineering began, "We will have engines restarted in two hours. We can give you a full gravity of deceleration if we waste a lot of fuel."

Operations entered the data into his tablet. "That won't be enough." His earpiece buzzed, and he touched it to get an update. "I've just been told that not only will we miss orbital insertion, there is also a probability we will actually strike the planet."

Forbes growled. "That is not a desirable outcome."

Fleet General Pierson stood. "Our troopships are standing by to launch landing pods. They are at the limit of their range, but it is doable. However, our losses will be higher than previously projected."

Operations said, "We can use the Wasps for air support during the landing. They are terrible inside an atmosphere, but they should keep the Matrian forces off balance."

Intelligence waved a map of the area surrounding the capital into view. "The city is ringed by rugged foothills and a mountain range. A shallow fast river cuts through at one point. This plain between the hills and the city is our landing site."

General Pierson said, "Yes, the ground force plan is to hold position on the plain until the bombardment concludes."

"What if we land some artillery onto these hills?" Intelligence asked. "We could shell the city. That would make up for losing *Jishin's* guns. Then we could push into the city."

Operations added, "I have some dropships that can transport artillery. The Matrian forces lack the air defenses or mobility to prevent their landing."

Pierson asked, "CiC, can those Imperial fighters operate in atmosphere?"

The comm answered, "Negative, vacuum only."

"Excellent, order the landing," Forbes said.

Operations said, "Fleet Chief, CiC just told me that a risky aerobraking insertion should allow us to achieve orbit."

"Tell them to program the maneuver," Forbes said. "Now we just need to avoid crashing into the planet."

---

First Sergeant Jill Tower trooped the line of her small force of combat engineers nicknamed Ground Hogs. None of them were happy about being diverted from their return home. Especially since it meant ground combat against the Dellans again. They had been lucky in their first battle on Kragus, and nobody was counting on that again. They understood what was at stake and would do their duty.

She stopped in front of a tall corporal. "oDolo, what do you think of these Stillwell rifles?"

The young man looked down at his weapon. "Lots heftier than a spitter, and the ammunition is heavy too. It is deadly accurate and has a nice long-range, though."

"I will pass along your thoughts to the owner of the company," Jill said. "She is up in that tower playing sniper for us."

He looked shocked. "Why would the owner of Stillwell Arms be here with us?"

"Guess she tired of counting her money," Sergeant Wilson piped in.

"I won't tell her you said that." Jill laughed. "That tough old broad probably wouldn't appreciate your joke."

The line of troops broke into laughter at Wilson's expense.

An armored personnel carrier rolled up to the Ground Hogs. Nan's head popped out of the top hatch. "Hey First Sergeant, you want a ride? I could use some company. Fuzzy here isn't much of a conversationalist."

"No thanks, I'll stay out here for now," Jill answered. "Wilson, oDolo, mount up." The soldiers scrambled up the rear ramp.

"Watch your six," Nan called as she slammed the hatch shut.

Inside the APC, a flat voice issued from a speaker. "Welcome aboard, fellas. My official designation is Foxtrot Zulu Yankee One, youse can just call me Fuzzy."

Sergeant Wilson patted the arm of his weapons operator's chair. "Nice to meet you, Fuzzy. Didn't I see you at the battle for Kragus?"

"Yeah, Sarge, tanks fer remember'n." Fuzzy's programmers had given him an old-fashioned outer-borough accent.

"The Sarge has a soft spot for CIs," oDolo said. "He moaned up a storm when they wouldn't let him bring his Combat Engineer's Power Suit down with him."

"They could have made room," Wilson said. "A CEPS is almost as good as an APC."

"I'm glad you emphasized *almost*, you might hurt Fuzzy's feelings," Nan called over her shoulder from her forward command seat. "You all familiar with this model APC?"

"The basics," Wilson said.

"All right, here's your refresher." Nan said. "Wilson, you're in the turret operator's seat. Fuzzy has a thirty-millimeter autocannon and a rotary barrel seven-mill Gatling. The same joystick controls both. Select which one fires with the toggle. You can shoot on the scoot."

Wilson tested the controls and listened to the hydraulics sweep the turret smoothly through its range. "Nice!"

"oDolo, that's the countermeasures, TOW missile, and hedgehog mortar station. We've got two shots of flares and chaff onboard. There's an extension mast so you can see over stuff and use the wire guide or laser designator for 'fire and forget.' It can also tie targeting into the little birdie drone. All you gotta do is put the crosshairs on the target and pull the trigger. Fuzzy will do the rest. Only four TOWs onboard. Finally, ten, forty-millimeter hedgehog mortars, toggle the selector to choose TOW or mortar and use the same targeting stick."

"Roger that, who's gonna be driving?"

"Either Fuzzy or I will drive, depending on the situation," Nan said. "He's experienced and solid when the shit hits the fan. You don't need to worry about him."

"Thanks for da vote of confidence, Gunner," Fuzzy said.

Nan grabbed the controls and headed out to scout the plain surrounding the city. Fuzzy rolled easily through the tinder-dry remains of last year's grass. New green was just poking up from the plain. They had to slow once to thread through a herd of grazing bison. Even the smaller beasts were over two meters at the shoulder. The bulls towered over three. They had been back-bred to resemble the giant bison of ice-age Earth.

"Look at the size of those things!" oDolo said.

They were a wild, shaggy-looking bunch. Matria had lower than one standard gravity, and the beasts had grown enormous on a diet of rich prairie grass and wildflowers. It was still early in the year and fresh growth was only starting.

"Those horns are intimidating. I don't think I would try to tell those giants where to go," Wilson added. Both heifers and bulls had a set of curved wicked looking horns. Light flashed off the horns in the morning sun. "Am I seeing things, or are those tipped with metal?"

"Na, it just looks that way from them polishing the horns. The herds roam wild and have to protect themselves against predators," Nan said. "The Herdsman's Guild will move the herd to higher summer pasture soon to let the grass grow back. Then they bring them back down for the winter."

"Who'd a thought we'd be roaming a planet with giant buffalo and cowboys this trip?" oDolo said.

"I told you I should have brought a CEPS," Wilson said, "I don't want to meet a predator big enough to attack one of those monsters on foot."

Nan laughed. "Hang on, I want to get closer to those hills before the enemy drops in." She increased speed, and Fuzzy's suspension automatically adjusted to dampen the violence.

---

Banner threaded his way through the mass of troops boarding their drop pods. None of them looked eager for battle.

*Can't say I blame them,* Banner thought. *The ones that aren't sick from too much Muscle-Up to counter planetary gravity are running a fever from the hemo-boost to make sure they can fight in genuine air. Maybe the brains were right. I mean look at these guys, centuries of living in micro-gravity and breathing canned air has left them skinny and asthmatic. It sure looks like our last shot at settling dirtside. Between the miscarriages and the rampant fungal infections, we've only got a few years left out here.*

At the end of the hangar, he saw the familiar outline of his ship, *Night Wing*. His squad lounged around the ship. The Shadows were a true mercenary crew. Banner was the only native Dellan of the bunch. The rest were a mix of humans from around the system, so they weren't suffering like the rest of the drop force.

*She may be ugly, but the Night Wing is all mine,* Banner thought.

He had stolen the ship while escaping an especially hairy mercenary mission at one of the Spellex Core settlements. *Night Wing* was a design from the planet, Cellas, smaller than a Governance dropship but still large enough for his small team. Self-defense capability was limited to standard chaff, flares, and a close-in-weapons defense cannon. Offensively *Night Wing* only had a couple of air-to-air missiles tucked inside the hull. But what it lacked in looks and punch, it made up for in speed and stealth. Sloping angles and black insulation tiles lowered the ship's detection numbers to near zero and the oversized engines let it hit speeds of mach three in atmosphere. Her swing wings and VTOL capability made it effective for fast team insertions. The cargo bay could hold a pair of two-man Light Tactical Vehicles and two cross-country powercycles along with personal weapons, ammo, and supplies to keep them self-sufficient for several days.

"Hey, Boss, when do we ship out?" Slip, the youngest member of the team asked. She snatched her pistol from its cross-draw holster and pointed it at an unseen enemy.

"I hate waiting," the team's sniper, Tap added. He sighted down the barrel of his well-worn rifle. "I'm getting that between-the-shoulder-blades itch."

"Won't be long now," Banner said. "We all loaded?"

"I wouldn't be lettin' these slackers lie around if we wasn't," Torque, flight mech and loadmaster, shouted from the other side of the ship. He walked into view carrying a tablet, trailing his fingers over the hull, and making a careful accounting of its condition.

"I don't want to get caught in the general landing with these idiots," Dropper, the *Night Wing's* pilot, said. She jerked a thumb to indicate the milling massed soldiers and flipped the purple pixie cut hair out of her eyes. She could pull ten-gees without batting an eye and her muscular compact frame fit perfectly into the small ship's cockpit with room to spare. "The defensive systems on those crappy drop pods are as likely to hit us as the enemy."

"Gather round everyone," Banner said. His team moved with varying degrees of enthusiasm. "Our target has changed. I got us a chance at a nice fat bounty. For every one of these targets we pull down, we get one thousand hectares of prime Matrian real estate."

"Split six ways?" Shotz, the teams armorer asked.

"Nope, for each of us, Banner replied. "Plus, we are getting one hundred thousand each in Cellan francs upfront.

A general murmur of approval rose from the group.

"Me and the Mrs. plan on doing our part to fill the system with little Dellans. I hear Matria is a good place to be fruitful and multiply," said Boomer, demolitions. "I'll trade blowing up dumps for blowing up stumps."

"I'm not cut out for farming," Sledge, the teams muscle said. "I'd rather have the cash."

"I guess we're more or less in agreement then," Banner said. "Dropper, I transmitted our landing zone to the ship already. All right, Shadows, let's mount up."

The team cheered. The rank-and-file soldiers around them just stared.

A hangar tractor towed *Night Hawk* into a pressure bay as Dropper went through the last of her pre-flight checklist.

"Everything looks good, Boss," she said as she flipped the last switches preparing for launch.

Banner was seated in the co-pilot seat behind her. *I hate to admit it, but she's a better pilot than I was at my best,* he thought. "Okay, take us out when you get flight control clearance."

"Rodger," Dropper released the mag-clamps holding the ship and puffed the thrusters.

The large doors opened, and the team got their first real-life look at Matria. They were all pushing to see out the front screen.

"That is a real pretty planet," Boomer said. "I bet I could raise a dozen babies on good ground down there."

"Your wife must need glasses," Slip said.

"Why?"

"I can't believe anyone with good eyes would want to have babies with you," Slip teased and slapped his arm.

"Nope, Celia thinks I'm good breeding stock," Boomer said. "And she's a fine sturdy woman. Not like you, it don't look like you could calve a lizard with them bony little-girl hips."

"Now leave her alone, Boomer," Torque said. "She's still filling out. I've got underwear older than her."

"I wouldn't brag about that if I were you," Tap said. "I'm sure she smells better too."

The group laughed.

"When this is over, I want to visit one of those fabled gatehouse pubs I've heard so much about," Sledge said. "The ladies are supposed to be very friendly."

"I wouldn't count on finding any friendly faces after we blow the hell out of the place," Shot said. "I, for one, don't fancy waking up with my throat cut by a vengeful woman."

Sledge thought a moment. "That is something to consider."

"All right, you clowns," Dropper said, over the 1MC. "Strap in, time to make someone's day worse."

The drop pods had finished clearing the pressure doors into space and maneuvered into position. One hundred pods glinted in the sunlight.

"Stay well clear of the pods," Banner said. "I don't want to be caught in the scrum."

"Five-by-five on that," Dropper said, under her breath.

The first wave of pods fired their engines and headed down.

---

Dropper said, in a perfect flight attendants voice, "Your operator reminds all passengers to keep their arms and legs inside the spacecraft at all times while the ride is in motion. Night Wing Air is not responsible for lost items, injuries, or death resulting from this flight. If you wish to reconsider continuing, please notify the cabin host who will gladly toss you out the nearest airlock. Have a pleasant flight."

"She enjoys this entirely too much," Tap said.

"You should see the shit she dreams up while we are waiting to extract you knuckle draggers," Torque said. "It's a continuous stream of consciousness narrative. Claims it helps her deal with the stress."

"I like Dropper, but that sounds incredibly annoying," Slip said.

"Sister, you don't know the half," Torque said, as he leaned back and closed his eyes.

# CHAPTER THIRTY-ONE

In orbit, *Corvus* said, "***Jishin* No Engines.**"

"What?" Gus said.

"*Corvus* is correct, Captain," Lenore said. "The *Jishin* is no longer braking."

"I wonder if HAM and Ophelia threw a wrench in the works?" Gus asked.

"**HAM Good Breaking Stuff.**"

"Does this mean *Jishin* won't achieve orbit?" Gus asked.

Lenore nodded. "If the Jishin does not begin decelerating again, soon they will sail right past Matria."

"That won't stop the rest of their fleet, though."

A warning sounded. "Captain, the invasion force has launched drop pods," Lenore said. "Should we intercept?"

"As much as I want to, no," Gus said. "Have the Annie D. and Cor-1 take out as many as they can. While we deal with the main fleet."

Lenore said over the comm, "Annie D. and Cor-1, engage the landing force.

Nyrkki and Zia in the Annie D. signaled affirmative. Drake and Pela in Cor-1 did likewise.

---

"Look at that," one of Jill's Ground Hog soldiers said from the formation.

Jill turned to see streaks of light falling from the sky. "Okay girls and boys, it looks like the show is about to begin. Places everyone." She clapped three times like she was directing a grade school play.

"Yes, Ms. Tower," someone yelled. The soldiers laughed and ran.

Jill watched interceptor missiles climb on pillars of fire. She hoped they found their marks.

---

Nan watched flaming trails as the drop pods' ablative shielding burned away. Surface-to-air missiles arced skyward. Some pods disappeared in a fireball. The barrage ceased all too soon.

"Looks like we're already out of missiles," oDolo said.

Wilson said, "That's why they pay *us* the big bucks, corporal. There's no substitute for getting up close and personal with the bad guys."

Ahead of them, several pods had already landed, and troops streamed out. Nan sent their recon drone, Little Birdie, ahead. She zoomed the picture. "I see infantry and four-wheeled Light Tactical Vehicles with machine guns. Shit, we're spotted."

---

In her perch, Constance Stillwell watched the pods streaking down. "Mr. Beston, I believe we are in a poor position for proper engagement of the enemy."

"I agree Madam," he said, consulting his tablet. "The pods are not landing near the city."

Connie scanned the distant hills. "How close will they be to those hills and the edge of the plain?"

"Within five kilometers. A respectable distance, but not exceeding your capabilities."

"Bring our air car to the roof," she said, gathering her gear. "We will set up a new position."

"A pity, this place is so cozy." Beston said as he slapped his tablet cover shut and picked up the spotting scope.

They climbed to the roof, and Connie settled into the passenger seat of the aircar. Beston lifted off gracefully on ducted fans. She heard Jill Tower over her earpiece. "Dame Stillwell, where do you think you are going?"

"Don't worry, my dear, we are just moving to better hunting grounds."

"I can't protect you out there," Jill said.

"I believe it is the Dellans who will seek protection, Stillwell out."

Tower muttered to herself as she watched the air car veer out over the plain. "I don't doubt they will."

Harold Beston said, "Madam, if you would kindly belt in. I may need to perform evasive action."

Connie strapped in and looked down at the scene. Troops were streaming down the ramps of the pods. The only vehicles she saw were LTVs and some mortar trailers. "At least they didn't bring any heavy tanks to the party."

A warning sounded from the console. "Warning, aircraft approaching at high rate. Advise evasive action."

Beston checked the display and swore. "Damn it! We have company."

A wasp was rapidly gaining on them. The warning changed tone. "Missile detected."

Beston watched the screen. "Hang on, Connie." He dropped the air car one hundred meters and slammed it into a hover. The missile streaked by, followed by the wasp. "It looks like our opponent is all speed and no maneuverability." He jammed the throttles forward, and the air car jumped to its maximum speed of two hundred klicks.

Connie flipped a switch at her elbow, and an aiming screen and stick extended from the console. "We've only got a few hundred rounds of seven mill aboard and one wire guide missile. Let's make them count."

Beston dove for the ground towards the enemy troops. The wasp was looping around for another pass at them.

Connie laughed. "Look at them scatter." Troops dove behind vehicles. An LTV was trying to get their MG loaded. Connie sprayed it as they shot by.

"Warning, missile detected."

Beston was flying twenty meters off the ground directly at a drop pod. At the last minute, he pulled the car into a vicious climb, and the missile hit the pod and exploded. Turbulence from the wasp rocked the air car violently as it roared by. He steadied the car and said, "I believe you have the shot, Madam."

Connie centered the crosshairs on the wasp as Beston tried to keep up with it. "One away," she said.

The wasp tried to pull up but evaporated in a ball of fire. "Time for us to leave," Beston said and headed towards the hills.

A soft pinging sound alerted Dropper, "Hey, boss, you seeing this?"

Banner switched to the alarm screen. "Are you sure about this?"

"I plugged the parameters of the *Corvus* and its small craft into the recognition software," Dropper answered. "Those two ships attacking the drop pods are a Governance Anvil-class dropship and a small fighter of unknown origin, both seen operating with *Corvus*."

"Time to get dirty," Banner said. Over the 1MC he called. "Heads up Shadows, we are making a minor detour. Seal up your suits and stand by to engage."

"I hope the Boss knows what he's doing," Torque said. "This bucket ain't rated for air-to-air combat." He reached down to a case stowed under his seat and began handing out packages. "Be ready to slap a QuickSeal on any holes in the hull. They also work on suits in case you catch a slug."

Sledge took a packet and passed the case down. "I'd rather be dirtside where I can shoot back. It's bad enough being a sitting duck during a drop, now we gotta go looking for trouble."

"I promised the missus that win or lose, this was my last mission," Boomer said. "I'm taking my pay and planting my ass."

Slip said, "Yeah, yeah, you and the missus are making it your personal project to flood the system with little Boomers and Boomerlets. We've heard it all before."

The ship banked hard, shutting off the conversation. The likelihood of surviving an emergency ejection from the *Night Wing* was definitely low.

---

Inside the Annie D., the CI spoke. "You are a proficient pilot, Ms. Forte, but I would prefer if Gus were flying."

"Thanks for the back-handed compliment," Zia said. "He's a little busy. Besides, Lenore is the jealous type."

Annie answered formally, "I do not fear *her*."

Nyrkki said, "Well, I do."

Zia chuckled. "Okay, you two settle down, maneuvering for atmosphere descent. You ready Cor-1?" she asked over the comm.

"Cor-1 ready for descent," Drake commed back. "Hang on, honey," he called back to Pela. "It's going to get a little bumpy. Hey, after we finish kicking Dellan, tail you can introduce me to your folks, since we are in the neighborhood."

"Be careful what you wish for, Mr. Sheridan." She said. "There are several generations of mothers in my house, and they all have piercing tongues."

"I see where you got your charm from then," Drake said, "My devilish smile and sparkling wit will win them over."

"And your modest demeanor."

The ocean below was covered with thick clouds. Anti-aircraft missiles punched through the cloud cover toward the invasion. The missile batteries quickly ran dry, and the barrage ended. Annie D. and Cor-1 got a "clear to proceed" signal from the air controller, and they sped towards the enemy.

The first wave of Dellan drop pods came in hot and fired engines at the last minute before they hit. Annie soared inland and began spraying the ragged landing zone with her autocannon. Drake pushed Cor-1 in, and Pela began targeting.

The pods weren't defenseless, though. "Shit, they are firing missiles," Drake said as he banked and pulled up.

"Warning, multiple enemy target locks," Cor-1 said.

Annie D. said, "Please, allow me, Ms. Forte," The dropship flipped into a barrel roll and fired countermeasures. Several missiles followed the flares. One missile hit an unlucky Dellan pod.

"Splash one," Nyrkki said.

Drake twisted in his seat. "I can't see them."

Pela screamed, "Bank left!"

He hurled the craft over as two missiles flashed by. Pela engaged the cannon and destroyed them.

Another wave of pods flashed into view. More missiles launched.

"Too hot, let's wait for them to hit the ground." Drake said.

"Right," Nyrkki agreed.

---

"They are breaking off," Dropper said.

Banner answered, "We are still above them. Dive at the Anvil. I'll handle the targeting."

"Rodger, that," she said, and pushed the ship into a vertical dive as she pushed the throttle to maximum.

---

"Ms. Forte, I am picking up an unusual maneuver from one of the enemy ships," Annie D. said.

"On my screen," Zia said.

Before Zia could look at the screen, the Annie D. fired off two rounds of flares and pulled into a vicious climb. Just as it stalled, they pulled a hammerhead maneuver and dove. The ships CWIS fired automatically.

"We were under attack," Annie D. Said calmly. "It was necessary to react before receiving permission. Please forgive me."

"Um, no problem, I guess," Zia said. She looked across at Nyrkki who just shrugged.

"Thank you. The enemy ship is ahead of us and attempting to escape," Annie said. "I am restoring control to you now. I would suggest you return fire."

Zia responded by accelerating.

"Stay on 'em," Nyrkki said. "I'm trying to line up a shot."

Drake's voice sounded over the comm. "Who the hell is that, and where did they come from?"

"The aggressor was hiding in the enemy pod's heat trails," Annie replied over the comm. "It matches the profile of a Cellan Special Forces insertion craft. However, it is doubtful that the Cellan Special Forces are aiding the enemy."

"Break, break," a voice came over the comm. "Annie D. this is Stanski, I am monitoring your comms. Annie, is there a triangular shape marking on that ship?"

"Yes, there is," Annie replied. "Sending you a video. Do you recognize them?"

"That's Banner's ship, *Night Wing*," Nan said. "If the Shadows are in this fight, we've just had the stakes raised."

Zia fought to keep on her enemy's tail. "Well, I don't know what engines they got in there, but I can't keep up."

The *Night Wing* was walking away from the Annie D. like it was standing still.

"I'm coming through and putting the hammer down," Drake said. Cor-1 flashed by in pursuit.

---

"Well, that didn't work," Dropper said, from the pilot's seat.

"Can we outrun them?" Banner asked.

"No, problem," Dropper said, as she accelerated. "That flying milk wagon can't keep up with us."

"You're right," Banner said. "But that fighter is gaining on us." He highlighted Drake's ship on the plot screen.

An alarm sounded. "Warning! Missile launch detected." A computerized voice said.

Banner fired off countermeasures. "Dropper, get us out of here."

"Gladly!" Dropper said, as she rolled out and dove into a cloud bank. She cut the engines to minimum to engage the ducted fans that would mask *Night Wing's* heat signature.

---

Pela adjusted her targeting array. "Drake, I lost them in those clouds. They just disappeared. Their engines should be a lighthouse."

Drake answered, "We won't be able to pick them up now. Those small Cellan jobs are really stealthy. Smugglers loved to slip past our Orbital Guard patrols in those things. I wonder how the Dellans got one way out here?"

"Banner stole it," Nan commed. "We played cat-and-mouse in a not so peaceful peace-keeping zone for six months before I finally got him surrounded. Unfortunately, I cornered him in a smuggler's warehouse with that ship in it. He blasted out of there and he's been trouble ever since."

"Looks like things just got more complicated," Pela said.

---

Several buggies and a squad of troopers on cross-country power cycles headed toward Fuzzy as he sped toward the hills.

"You take the wheel, Fuzzy," Nan said as she worked the tactical operations console. "Faster if you can."

"Sorry, Gunner, we are already at max."

"Okay, Wilson, stand by to fire the thirty," Nan yelled over the motor's whine. "Target the buggies with HE rounds."

"Roger!"

The enemy was taking a slanting course to cut them off from the hills and getting closer. Some random MG fire started pinging off Fuzzy's hull.

"Fire, one round!"

Fuzzy shook as the turret fired. The shell impacted between two buggies spraying them with dirt but no damage. The turret gun was gyro-stabilized, but the buggies were bouncing and weaving erratically.

"I got a clear shot on one," Wilson said.

"Take it!"

The turret roared again. This time it struck a buggy near a front tire, and the machine rolled over.

"Woo hoo, scratch one."

More pings hit the hull. Nan knew a TOW would target Fuzzy any minute. She scouted ahead with the drone. "Fuzzy, you see that cluster of thermal targets bearing three zero zero? Head for them."

"Youse got it, Gunner," the CI said.

"What ya got up your sleeve, Gunner?" Wilson asked.

"Watch and learn," Nan answered. "Taking control, Fuzzy."

She steered straight at the cluster highlighted on the screen. At the last minute, she jerked right and whizzed around it. There was a tremendous roar from the outside that sent shivers up the spine.

"What the fuck was that?" oDolo asked.

"Watch the drone feed," Nan replied.

The enemy drove straight into the cluster that had broken up into individual heat signatures. As a trooper on a cycle reached one, a giant arm slashed out and cleaned him off the cycle. Then two enormous animals leaped onto a buggy and dragged the driver and gunner away, kicking in panic. A second and third cycle rider fired wildly into the grass before they disappeared. The diminished enemy kept coming.

"If I didn't know better, I would say those were lions," Wilson said.

"They were," Nan said with a chuckle. "I guess those fellas didn't get a briefing on the fauna of Matria before they landed. Fuzzy, take control and head for this point." Nan highlighted a point on the hill ahead of them.

"They are still coming," oDolo said.

"Gunner, can this APC climb that mountain ahead of us?" Wilson asked.

"Corporal, standby to trip off the hedgehogs," Nan said.

"What's the target?"

"Straight up."

The corporal didn't understand but answered, "If you say so."

Fuzzy was still ahead of the enemy by a hundred meters. "I see it now, Boss." The black entrance to a tunnel was getting larger.

"Corporal, as soon as we get inside, fire off those mortars," Nan said.

Fuzzy's lights flared on as they shot into the tunnel. oDolo tripped the mortars, and the roof collapsed behind them, sealing out the enemy.

"That was pretty slick!" Wilson shouted. "Where does this go?"

"It's a shortcut through the mountain," Nan said. "It's one of the few ways to get to the other side without climbing."

"So, how do we get back?"

"We climb."

# CHAPTER THIRTY-TWO

Harold Beston set the air car down gently in a depression to shield them from the enemy's view.

Constance climbed to the top of the bowl to peer over the crest onto the plain below. The drop pods landed over a large area of the plain. Beston crawled up next to her with his scope.

"The shots are long, but doable," he said.

"I see a protected area to our left. Let's set up there." She rolled over to leave and stopped.

"Easy, Lady," a man said, pointing a very large bore lever-action carbine at them. He was tall and mid-years with several days of stubble on his face. He wore rough clothing and had a wide-brimmed hat pushed back on his head. Connie noticed his pistol rode in a cross-draw holster worn high for easy access when riding. "Saw what you did down there. Guessing you aren't on their side."

Beston rolled over and raised his hands. "That is correct. I assume from your accent you are a native."

"With that fancy air car and gear, I assume *you* are not," he drawled.

"Touche, young man. I am Connie, and this is Beston. We are here to offer aid against them." She jerked her thumb over her shoulder. "You can ask Consul Sidra. She will vouch for us."

He laughed out loud and casually rested his rifle on his shoulder. "Oh yeah, I'll just call up my close friend Sidra, head of the whole damn planet, and ask if she knows a couple of dandies flying a fancy air car shooting down fighters."

"It sounds a little silly when you say it that way," Connie said.

He reached down and hauled Connie to her feet. "I'm Jess. Herdsman's Guild. Who the hell *are* those guys down there?"

"Dellans," Beston said as he stood brushing off his clothes. "They seem determined to cause trouble."

Jess said, "Hmm, they've raided here before. Usually, content to steal some stock. Guess they've got bigger plans this time." He turned and whistled. A huge wolfdog emerged from behind a boulder and ran up. Jess scratched his ear. "This is Pup. Helps with herding."

Connie eyed him warily. "Is he friendly?"

"Mostly." Pup let out a tremendous low bark in agreement. The dog's head jerked around and he growled.

Jess heard aircraft coming in. "We got company," he said as they all crouched down. Two small transports landed on the summit of a nearby hill. "They with you?"

Connie shook her head. "We should check it out."

Jess whistled a complicated tune, and four men stood, each with one of the enormous dogs at their side.

"Are you always so cautious?" Beston asked.

"Themyscira is civilized, but outside of the city, Matria is a wild place. Caution serves us well." More men led horses up the slope. "Can you ride?"

Connie and Beston nodded.

"We only got one extra mount."

Beston said, "I can stay with the car if you would like, madam."

"Thank you, Harold. I think we can trust the young man. Keep in touch on the comm."

Beston returned with Connie's sniper gear and rifle. "Good hunting, Ma'am." He turned to Jess. "I am placing this lady's safety in your hands, young man. If anything happens to her, I will remove those hands." The steel in his voice showed it was no idle threat.

Connie laid her hand on Beston's arm. "Harold, you needn't be so protective." She kissed his cheek and swung smoothly into the saddle. "Ready, gentlemen?"

Jess led the group along a rocky trail towards the landing site of the Dellan ships. They pulled up as they got closer, and Connie raised her optics. The ships had finished unloading and were rising back toward orbit.

"Oh dear," she said. "They are setting up artillery. Durden 155mm rocket-assisted howitzers. Sustained fire rates of twenty rounds-per-minute. They can easily hit the city from here. That stone wall won't keep those out."

Jess asked, "How many men?"

"At least fifty."

"How close do you need to be to use that thing?" Jess pointed at Connie's rifle.

"This is close enough," she said.

"Lady, they are over a kilometer away."

"Yes, pity, I was hoping for a challenge," she said as she dismounted and checked the rifle.

She flipped out the legs of the rifle's bipod and stretched her neck. Connie cycled the rifle's bolt and picked a target. One long exhale and a feather light touch on the trigger before the sound-suppressed rifle fired. Five long seconds, later a man fell over the barrel of the artillery piece he was working on. Connie chambered another round and repeated the effort.

She stood and slung her rifle. "I suggest you boys head that way. It won't take them long to figure out where I am. You need to take them out. I will continue to distract them."

"Yes, ma'am," Jess said, and he flung her a mock salute. "Let's go, boys, you heard the lady. Time to displace some trespassers."

Seven of the men and their dogs set out on foot while the rest led the horses away. Connie moved to more cover.

After her third shot, the enemy decided she needed to be dealt with. A couple of squads moved in her direction while the rest took cover.

The sun was at her back, and she could see the Dellans squinting in the glare as they scanned for her. She tried in vain to spot Jess and his men moving through the brush. A gentle breeze ruffled the scrubby trees.

Connie watched the enemy make a halt signal and take out optics. She saw a few thin lines creeping through the grass toward them. A high whistle sounded, and the lines sprinted forward. She gasped as the first of the giant dogs launched at the lead Dellan and grabbed him by the throat. The scene was a panic of shouting men firing wildly into the grass. A second whistle made the dogs disappear as quickly as they attacked.

The enemy retreated, dragging their wounded.

Connie watched as they neared the artillery and other soldiers ran out to help. A volley of withering fire from the herdsmen's carbines intercepted them. A few made it back to cover. The Dellans sporadically returned fire, but the herdsmen had melted back into the scrub.

In the distance, Connie saw a Wasp vectoring in for air support. "They never learn," She cycled an armor-piercing round into her rifle, and she sighted in. Her target was coming straight in on a strafing run. The rifle barked once, and she saw the round punch straight through the windscreen. The Wasp pulled up and tried to clear the top of a lower hill. It faltered.

She cycled another round and squeezed off a second shot. The ship impacted and exploded as it failed to clear the summit.

The defeated soldiers waved a white rag and walked out with their hands up.

Some of Jess's men stood to take control of the prisoners. Connie headed toward them.

"Damn lady, never seen someone shoot down a spaceship with a rifle before," Jess said as she walked up.

"I wouldn't recommend trying it with that carbine," she said. "How do you like them? It's one of my most popular sportsmen's models."

"What da ya mean?"

"I noticed you carry Stillwell Model Fiftys. I am Constance Stillwell."

Jess looked down at his rifle. Worn bluing patches clung to the barrel, and the stock had more scratches than varnish. Evidence of a hard life inside a chaffing scabbard. "Huh, guess you never know who you're gonna run into during an invasion."

"What are you going to do with them?" she asked, nodding at the Dellans.

"I dunno. Spike their guns and leave 'em here with no boots, I guess. They won't walk far in this country."

Connie nodded. "Good plan. Do you have an idea what to do about the rest of them?" She motioned to the landing force on the plain.

"I do if we can get our horses down there."

"I think that can be arranged," Connie said. "Let me make a call."

Mitzi Grey glided up to the city perimeter defenses on a power cycle. She pulled off her helmet and her blonds curls cascaded down her back as she shook them out.

"Who is that?" one of Tower's men asked, as the nearest group of troopers stopped to watch.

"Some big-shots daughter," another said.

"Well, she looks mighty fine in that uniform," a third said. "Didn't know BDUs could stretch like that."

Mitzi walked over to the group. "Can you tell me where to find Detective Tower?" She flashed a brilliant smile. Jill Tower was a detective with the Capitol City PD in civilian life back on Nakon.

One of the stunned men pointed down the line, and she headed off with a swing in her step. "Eyes in the boat, soldier," she called back over her shoulder.

The other soldiers laughed at their blushing friend.

Mitzi soon found Jill Tower. "Good Morning, Top!" she cheerfully said. "We missed you at breakfast."

"I needed to see to my troopers. Had a battle bar and some shitty coffee."

"Once we settle this little unpleasantness, we can get you and your troops properly fed. It's almost time for the Feast of Beltane."

"If you are involved, I'm sure it will be a hell of a party."

"Oh, sister, you have *no idea*." Mitzi chuckled. "I'm assuming you have a master plan for the defense of the city."

"I'm just following orders this time," Jill said. "House Custos is in charge."

"Hm, what do *they* know about ground combat?"

"If Gus can't stop that giant carrier, we won't have to worry about it," Jill said. "An orbital bombardment will end us fast."

"Don't count out Gusty Johansson," Mitzi said. "He always figures out something. What's the story with those guys?" Mitzi pointed at the assembling enemy on the plain.

"They outnumber us about four to one. They don't look like they have any heavy armor, mostly light tactical vehicles and some mortar units. Those Wasps of theirs are buzzing around. We have nothing to counter them. Only a modified dropship and one fighter from *Corvus*."

Jill's comm buzzed, and she touched her earpiece. "Tower, go."

"Sergeant Tower, this is Connie, is that dropship still on planet?"

"Yes, where are you, and what do you need a dropship for?" Tower asked. "I thought you were going sniping."

"Tell them to meet me at these coordinates. My new friends need a ride."

"Wonder what that's all about?" Jill asked.

"You tell me, you're the detective," Mitzi said. "I'm going to see if I can hitch a ride to where the action is."

## CHAPTER THIRTY-THREE

Fuzzy exited the tunnel into the bright mid-day sun.

"Glad to be out of there," oDolo said. "Cold, damp, and smelly gives me the creeps."

"My environmental systems are working great," Fuzzy said. "It ain't none of those things in here."

"He told you," Nan said. "I warned you he was sensitive."

Wilson sent the drone ahead to look for the best place for them to cross the mountain range. It didn't look easy. "How are we gonna climb over that?" he said, looking up at the still snow-capped peaks.

"Attention, I am detecting an aircraft coming toward us," the drone comm said.

Nan zoomed in and whooped, "Looks like we won't have to walk after all boys," she said. "Annie D., this is Fuzzy. Do you copy?"

"Hey, Nan, what are you doing on the wrong side of the mountain?" Zia answered.

"Long story, can you give us a ride?"

"Sure, lucky for you, we took the long way to avoid those

Wasps buzzing over on the other side. We'll be there soon." The Annie D. banked in their direction and soon settled and dropped the stern ramp.

Fuzzy loaded, and his crew climbed out.

"Strap Fuzzy down. We don't have time to waste," Nyrkki called from the cockpit. "Connie still needs us to pick her up."

———

It was a quick hop over the mountains to where Connie and her new friends were waiting. Zia used the ducted thrusters to avoid setting the dry remains of last year's grass ablaze as the Annie D. raised a cloud when it settled at the base of the foothills.

"Somebody call for a taxi?" the external speaker boomed.

Jess and his men arrived as the loading ramp descended. "They got any room left in that thing? Looks pretty full already."

Mitzi Grey and Zia Forte walked down the ramp as the soldiers unloaded Fuzzy. Nan had decided to travel overland and let the cowboys fly.

"Oh, quite the welcome party. Connie didn't mention that frontiersmen were involved," Mitzi purred as she walked up and rubbed Jess's horse, Buck. Pup, the giant dog, sat at her feet and nuzzled her for attention. "There's just something primal about a cowboy."

"I'll take that as a compliment, I guess," he replied. "Buck and Pup rarely take to strangers. You must have a way with animals."

"Oh, everyone loves me," Mitzi said, with a grin. "But it's been ever so long since I have been in the saddle."

Zia ignored the double entendre. "Connie said you boys needed a lift. Back to the city?"

Jess's men laughed. "Not likely," one of them said. "We'll wait for Beltane."

"You sound confident we will have something to celebrate," Nyrkki said as he joined them.

"Those fellas picked the wrong fight. Can you get me a comm channel to whoever is in charge back in town?" Jess asked. "As long as you flyers can take care of the big guns upstairs, I got a plan for that crowd out there." He jerked his head toward the enemy.

"A dozen against four thousand?" Nyrkki shook his head. "All right then, load up. Hope your animals don't mind noise. The Annie isn't the quietest thing flying."

"They'll be fine," Jess said. "Just get us there in one piece."

"Do you have an extra mount?" Mitzi asked.

"You can have mine. Harold is picking me up." Connie swung down from her saddle. "Watch yourself, he is quite a handful. Lots of spunk still in this one."

Jess looked Mitzi over skeptically. "This isn't gonna be a Sunday afternoon in the park, ma'am."

Mitzi walked up to the big gelding and pulled the horse's head down to whisper in its ear. She wrapped the reins around the pommel and walked twenty feet back.

"What is she doing?" Jessie asked.

"I don't know exactly, but if Mitzi is involved, it's going to be dramatic," Zia replied.

Mitzi took off at a dead run, vaulted over its rump and landed in the saddle with a whoop. The horse took off at a gallop as Mitzi put the reins in her teeth. She steered with her knees, and a covey of startled prairie hens burst into the air in front of her. Mitzi pulled a pistol with each hand and fired twice, downing one bird. She holstered her weapons, wheeled her mount, and performed a perfect side-back-bend to scoop up the bird as she galloped back to the group.

Jess let out a long low whistle. His men whooped and yelled. The dogs joined in.

Nan turned to Zia. "She never ceases to amaze."

"I'll admit, gotta show her some respect for that one."

Mitzi pulled the horse up short. "I'm a little rusty. I missed one." She tossed the hen at Zia's feet. "I'm sure you can put this to good use in the cook pot."

Zia muttered under her breath. "I take that back."

Jess just said, "You'll do," as he turned and led his horse into the ship.

# CHAPTER THIRTY-FOUR

"How goes the battle, General?" Forbes asked as he paced the ship's bridge.

General Pierson looked up from her console. "Some setbacks but nothing we can't work through. I could use some of that promised air support. Enemy air elements are moving through the battle space, causing disruptions."

"Well, Intelligence, why is that?" Forbes asked.

"I can bring more Wasps into position," the officer said. "However, that will leave the flagship with a depleted defensive screen."

"Do it! This monster can take more than a few hits and still come back swinging," Forbes said. He saw the Fleet Engineer wince at the thought of more battle damage to his charges. "And you, what's the status of those engines?"

"Repair crews are stringing casualty power cables to route around the failure." The lights flickered, and the mighty ship rumbled as its engines fired once more. "I believe they are successful Fleet Chief." The EO scanned his tablet. "We can give you three gravities of deceleration."

The Operations officer commed, "CiC, will three-gees allow us to achieve orbit?"

"We will still need to make a low orbit atmosphere maneuver to finish the braking, but we can do it," a voice said from the speaker.

Forbes slammed his hand down on the 1MC comm, "All hands prepare for high gravity in thirty seconds. Make the ship secure."

The rumbling increased throughout the ship as the fusion drive spooled. The gravity increased, and the ancient hulk groaned. Loose gear clattered to the deck.

"Hang together, old girl," the EO patted the bulkhead and pleaded.

Something heavy crashed in the distance as the crew struggled against the increasing weight. The low-gravity adapted Dellans could barely breathe. A crewman who had skipped bone strength treatments collapsed to the deck and screamed in pain when his leg broke.

Captain Stuart slapped his comm. "Medical team to the bridge. How much longer, Ops?"

"Five minutes, Captain."

"Damn," Stuart groaned.

---

Lenore looked up from her console. "Captain, the *Jishin* has restarted her engines."

"Are they going to make orbit?"

Lenore looked into the distance briefly as she ran the numbers. Looking at Gus, she said, "It will be close, but it is possible. They are pulling three-gees braking."

"Ouch, that would feel like ten-gees for us."

Gus zoomed the forward screen onto the enemy flagship. Occasionally, a piece of the ancient monster would break off. Inertia made it race away along the ship's course as the behemoth slowed.

"Looks like she's breaking up," Gus said. "What are they doing now?"

Maneuvering thrusters fired along the hull and the ship spun to face the planet. The engine flared out.

"Interesting," Lenore said.

"Oh, I see now," Gus said. "They are going to make an atmosphere braking swing. Ballsy move with that wreck."

"Indeed," Lenore said. "May I make a suggestion?

"Of course, XO."

"We should strike as *Jishin* completes her swing around the planet when her sensors are still heat blind."

Gus surveyed the battle space. "The enemy is expecting you, XO. Their fleet is taking up station to block us. I'll have the Matrian patrol ships form into a battle group with us."

"In that case, Captain," Lenore said, "I have an unorthodox request."

"I can interface directly with Caber's 500-star fighter force. It will be much more efficient than using voice comms."

"Unusual circumstances call for unusual responses," Gus said, and he rose from his Command Chair. "XO, you have the deck and the conn."

"Thank you, Commodore," she replied. "If you could handle our defensive measures, I will concentrate on the battle."

"Aye," Gus saluted and moved to the console. "Wait, "Commodore"? What are you on about, XO?"

"Our forces now comprise a squadron. Hence, you, as senior officer, meet the definition of a Commodore."

"Fuck me," Gus mumbled as he settled into the acceleration

couch at the defensive weapons station and brought the screen forward. "I have become what I always fought against."

Lenore walked to the center of the forward screen. "Caber/Faber, do you copy?"

The CIs acknowledged her.

"I will direct our force from *Corvus*."

Caber commed,

"I must ask you Lady fair,

Can you sing the battle ayre?"

Faber commed, "Of course she can sing it, Lenore is riding one of my finest battle chassis!"

"Then let Music Universal roar,

My bow is ready bent for war,

A flight of arrows cast to soar."

"What is that weirdo babbling about?" Gus looked toward Lenore. "Umm, XO, may I ask what you are doing?"

Lenore had dropped her uniform to the floor. Naked, she stepped into two holes that had opened in the deck near the forward screen. The plating sealed around her ankles. Gus couldn't help but notice she appeared anatomically correct.

*Eyes in the boat, sailor!* He thought.

She looked over her shoulder and said, "I need to transmit commands across the entire electromagnetic spectrum, including the visible. My uniform would prevent that."

"Gee, you could've given a guy some warning," he said, quickly looking at his console.

A smirk crossed Lenore's face as she turned to the screen and stretched her arms. "Commodore, I am assuming control," she said.

Gus noticed the night line terminator cross over the capital, Themyscira. In eight scant hours, Iz would rise, and the battle on the plains begin.

Lenore's skin flickered, displaying shifting color patterns and pulses of light. She opened her mouth and her battle song. Holst's *Mars Bringer of War* poured forth.

## CHAPTER THIRTY-FIVE

The Annie D. rose into the sky with her passengers and cargo of dogs and nervous cow ponies.

Zia called out, "Where are we headed?"

Jess came up to the cockpit. He pointed at a large herd of the giant bison grazing near the Dellan landing zone. "Set down about a klick upwind from the herd. It's gonna be dark soon, and we need to set up a safe perimeter before the sun sets."

Nyrkki asked, "Why not strike now?"

"Believe me, you don't want to be riding around out here in the dark. Bison aren't the only dangerous thing out there."

Nan poked her head into the conversation, "I'll second that, we almost ran over a pride of lions."

"Lions!" Zia said, "Why would you let those wander around your herds? Isn't that just asking to lose valuable stock?"

"The ecosystem needs some apex predators to stay balanced," Jess said. "It isn't just bison, we've got elk, antelope, deer, and even a small herd of resurrected mammoths and wooly rhinos. Off-world big game hunters spend buckets of credits on guided hunts."

"I can support that, as long as they are turning a profit," Zia said.

Nyrkki added, "You little mercenary, always looking at the bottom line."

"Someone in this outfit has to," Zia answered. "If I left it to Gus, the fuel and ammo bunkers would be empty, and we would have to live on vat yeast bread and mushroom patty."

"No thanks," Nan said. "I had to eat that crap for six months on a peacekeeping deployment between Speller colonies. Those idiots can't even stop fighting long enough to keep an algae bioreactor running."

Nyrkki laughed. "I bet even Drake couldn't stand eating vat yeast for six months."

The Annie D. settled into the grass behind a low hill to avoid detection.

"Alright, boys," Jess yelled as he strode down the landing ramp. "We've got twenty minutes before sundown. Get that perimeter fence up."

Shortly after the cowboys had their fence up Fuzzy rolled up. Nan popped out of the forward hatch and jumped to the ground. "You can tie your equipment feeds into the APC's battle net. Fuzzy will take guard duty outside the wire."

"Aww, I got shit on my wheels. Damn organics!" Fuzzy complained.

Nan stifled a laugh. "Fuzzy, I need you on roaming patrol tonight. That should clean off your tires."

"Well, Gunner, see how you like it when you step in a fresh pile next," Fuzzy said.

"I think I'm nimbler than you," Nan replied.

Nyrkki passed Nan carrying a huge equipment case on his shoulder. "Hate to break it to you, Gunner, but you are standing in a fresh pile right now."

Nan looked down and grimaced. "Well, fuck me!"

"No time for that now, Ma'am. You'll have to wait for Beltane," a young cowboy said, tipping his hat as he led his horse by. "But I will look you up."

A chuckle ran through the group.

Desson, the cook, pulled his pack mule past. "Be careful what you ask for, young blood. That one's probably more than you can handle."

Nan snorted and stomped away.

# CHAPTER THIRTY-SIX

"Oh crap, another big shot trying to rally the troops," the soldier said to the woman next to him as they stacked sandbags. "Think we can get her to load a couple hundred bags for us?"

The soldier looked up to see who he meant.

Chief Consul Sidra was walking their way. Ramrod straight and surrounded by a squad of serious-looking bodyguards. The group stopped near Sergeant Jill Tower. Jill snapped a salute.

"Hello, ma'am, shouldn't you be at the Command Center?"

"I'm afraid my input is of little value, Sergeant." The tall woman said. "How is everything on the ground? Are you getting everything you need?"

"What I need is air support, an armored cavalry unit, and an infantry division." Jill cracked bluntly.

Sidra smiled. "I will see what we can do. Sometimes the Goddess provides in unexpected ways."

Jill asked, "Any word from *Corvus*? They saved my bacon on Kragus once, and a close pass over the enemy by that beast would sure do a lot for moral and even the odds a little."

"Unfortunately, Captain Johansson is occupied with the Dellan fleet right now. I have had no updates for some time."

Jill looked up. Dozens of drive plumes sparkled in the darkening evening sky. "From all appearances, *Corvus* has its hands full."

"All too true, my dear," Sidra said. "I will see about getting you a few more resources. Often, providence delivers just in time."

---

The cowboys finished staking their horses just as the sun set. A fire of buffalo chips glowed nearby.

"Come and get it!" Desson yelled.

"What's fer supper, Old Timer?" someone called.

"I'll Old Timer you, Johnny Rumson," Desson yelled, shaking his long handle spoon like a club. "Be careful with that fire, too. This winter grass is flash powder dry. We don't need a prairie fire tonight."

"That was fast," Zia said as she leaned over to smell the insulated container Desson had unloaded from his pack mule. "How did you manage that? Doesn't look like freeze-dried."

"Bah, I wouldn't serve my boys that famine food. I used a hot box. Just get it boiling first thing in the morning and seal it up. All done cooking by sundown. Not fancy chow, but they will eat pretty much anything after a hard day. Tonight, is beef stew."

Nyrkki walked over. "I see you are checking out the competition. Watch out, Desson, she will steal your recipes."

"I don't steal recipes," Zia said as she punched his shoulder. "Trade maybe, improve definitely, but never steal."

"We'll talk more later about those recipes." Desson said. "Right now, I gotta get this out before it burns." He expertly flipped open the door of his travel oven and juggled two large pans of steaming bright yellow cornbread.

Nyrkki's stomach rumbled and Zia punched him again. "Traitor!"

"Amore, a man can't control what his empty stomach says."

Desson laughed. "There's plenty to go around."

His ten-year-old apprentice plopped a large portion of stew on each plate as the men filed by. Desson carefully distributed steaming squares of cornbread with butter on top.

Mitzi Grey eyed her plate suspiciously and poked at the food. "What is this again?"

"Chunks of stew beef with potatoes and carrots. No beans," Desson said. "Beans are a bad idea if you are likely to get gut shot in the morning."

"Hey now," Jess said. "No use putting a jinx on us, Desson."

"Just stating the facts."

"Well, I don't need you putting any ideas in the young ones heads. You know that this is the first time some of these boys have faced a human enemy."

"That's true," Desson said. "I'd rather face a mountain lion than a man. The lion is just trying to survive. A man is just full of meanness by nature."

Jess's dog, Pup, was gnawing a joint of dry bison when he paused, stood, and whined, looking out in the darkness.

"Gunner, come in," Fuzzy's voice came over Nan's comm. "I've got movement on the perimeter."

"Is it lions?" Nan asked.

"The horses aren't spooking," Jess said. "If it was predators, they would know."

"I'm picking up coded transmissions," Fuzzy said. "Likely a scouting party of the enemy."

Several men set down their plates, grabbed their carbines, and got to their feet. They moved off, trailed by their dogs.

"Gunner, you want illumination flares?" Sergeant Wilson asked. "If they are using night vision, that should blank their goggles."

"Not yet," she said. "You and oDolo get to Fuzzy and be ready to lay down some heavy fire. If they fire, hit a flare."

"Rodger, come on kid." The two men crouch ran toward the wire.

"Zia, Nyrkki, get to Annie D. and stand by. We might need to evac," Nan said.

"Orders, Gunner?" Mitzi asked, her pistol already in her hand.

"Wouldn't want you to muss your hair, Ms. Grey," Nan said. "How would I explain to the Admiral if something happened to you?"

"Bullshit, I'm not a delicate flower," Mitzi said. "We've known each other long enough to stop playing games."

"True," Nan said scanning the darkness through her own night-vision lenses. "Now that I've got your McGowan dander up, I expect you can hold your own."

"Gunner," Wilson's voice came over the com. "our little bird shows six heat signatures moving your way. Sending you the drone feed now."

"Rodger," Nan answered, "I like those odds. What about our guys?"

"In position."

---

Banner and the Shadow team moved quietly through the grass toward the camp ahead.

Banner scanned their progress on his helmets heads-up-display. "Team, comms check." They checked their throat mic's and made sure they were still silent.

"Sledge, on point."

The team rattled off their positions. Boomer and Shot on the left. Banner and Slip on the right.

Tap was providing sniper overwatch in the rear. "Boss, I got a UAV headed your way."

"Take it out."

---

A blue electric flash flared from the enemy position and the drone feed cut out.

"Shit, they hit the drone with a pulse," Nan said. "Wilson, get ready to pepper the enemies last position."

"Gunner, our guys are too close, already." Wilson said. "I can't be sure who is friendly anymore."

"This just keeps getting better," Nan said. She turned to Mitzi. "This is getting ugly fast."

Mitzi slipped her night vision on and said, "Let's move away from the fire. Too much exposure here."

Zia commed."We are in Annie now. Pre-flights are complete. We can lay down some autocannon fire?"

"Standby. Wilson says our guys are too close."

A scream pierced the darkness, and automatic weapons fire erupted. Nan could hear one of the big dogs tearing into something. An illumination flare popped and drifted over chaos. The Dellan soldiers were moving, firing in bursts. The giant hounds were racing around them and darting in and out. A carbine barked, and one soldier fell. A dog screamed in pain.

The flare sputtered and darkness returned, punctured occasionally by muzzle flashes. The dogs howled in a call and response, sending a shiver up Nan's spine. *Gawd, that's creeping me out. Glad they are on my side.*

A sharp whistle pierced the air, and the howling stopped.

"Wilson," Nan commed, "launch another flare."

It streaked up and lit up the area. Nothing but grass waving in the evening breeze.

"I've got another drone up," Nyrkki commed, "They are moving off. Some of them are pretty beat up."

Jess walked up and plopped down next to Nan and Mitzi, who had returned to the fire. "That took the piss out of them. Don't think they'll be back tonight."

Desson had the med kit out and was tending to an injured dog. "He'll be okay, it just grazed his back leg."

"We can only hope to be that lucky tomorrow," Mitzi said.

Jess tipped his hat back on his head. "We make our own luck."

## CHAPTER THIRTY-SEVEN

Early the next morning Nan was cat napping in her APC, when her comm squawked to life. "Hey, they're gone!"

"Who is gone?" Nan asked into the comm as she rubbed her eyes.

"The cowboys," Zia answered.

Nan looked around at Wilson and oDolo, gently snoring away. "Fuzzy, where are the cowboys?"

"Oh, they rode out an hour before dawn," the CI answered.

"Why didn't you wake me up? You were supposed to be standing watch."

"I followed your orders exactly, Gunner. You told me to watch the perimeter for anything trying to sneak in. You didn't say nothing about sneaking out."

"For crying out loud, do you CIs have to be so damn literal all the time?"

She kicked her sleeping crew awake., "All hands-on-deck. The cowboys slipped out in the night." She keyed her comm. "Annie, I want a drone launched. See if you can find them."

"Aye, aye, Gunner," the soft feminine voice said.

Nan pounded down the APC ramp towards the dropship. Zia and Nyrkki had a UAV feed up. "Where are they?"

"Zoom in. Is that them heading towards the herd?" Zia asked.

"What the hell are they wearing?" Nyrkki asked.

The rising sun glinted and sparkled off the riders. Each wore a shining silver chain mail tunics and a breastplate. Their helmets showed ID marks and trailed ribbons. Scale armor covered the horses, and a spike protruded from the chanfron guarding the beast's heads. Each man carried a long gleaming lance with a colored streamer flapping in the wind.

"Pretty impressive, ain't they." The crew turned to see the cook, Desson, behind them, holding a bucket of biscuits with a generous chuck of meat in them. His apprentice held a steaming pot trailing a lanyard of metal cups. "Coffee?" The wounded dog from last night sat at his feet wagging its tail, looking at the bucket, and licking its lips.

"Okay, first, you have got to explain that, "Nyrkki said, pointing at the screen.

"You'd have to be crazy to ride into a herd of mega bison without protection," said Desson as he passed around the pail.

"Yeah, but whose idea was it to dress like ancient Persian cavalry?" Nan asked.

Desson shrugged as the boy poured the coffee. "Some tactics stand the test of time."

Nyrkki took two biscuits. "Come here, little one. Did the mean old cook not give you breakfast?" He gave the dog a biscuit and scratched its head.

"What are they planning?" Nan asked.

Zia grabbed the UAV control stick, highlighted a rider, and zoomed in. "Oh, hell no!"

The figure of Mitzi Grey jumped into focus. She wore armor

like the others, but her unmistakable blonde hair streamed behind her through a hole in her helm. Someone had stenciled a thistle on her breastplate.

"Yeah, she insisted on the thistle, something about ancient McGowan battle heritage," Desson said, as he sipped his coffee.

"That woman has a habit of getting what she wants," Zia said.

"Even if it's foolish," Nan added.

# CHAPTER THIRTY-EIGHT

HAM waited for Ophelia in the cable maintenance trunk. His fingers extended and retracted various tools nervously.

"Oh, why is that beast taking so long?" he said. "If she stopped for a snack, I will wring her neck."

He felt the engines ignite and the apparent gravity build. He heard a hissing sound and several loud thumps. Ophelia plopped out of a duct and hit the floor with a thud.

She shook herself and gave HAM a "Why didn't you catch me?" look.

"Come on, we don't have any time to lose," he said as he scooped her up and shoved her into her case and skated away as fast as he could.

Ophelia had her head out and hissed and chittered away.

"I know you tried your best," HAM said. "It appears the enemy has routed around our sabotage. We need to get off this ship before the Captain starts shooting."

Ophelia's eyes widened at the thought of ejecting into The Void during a battle. She renewed her protests.

"I'm sorry," HAM said. "It's the only way. If I am correct, we have only minutes before the ship hits the atmosphere for braking. We can't eject during that without cooking."

He skidded to a stop outside of a panel marked "Garbage." He ripped the panel away and shoved Ophelia's environmental case inside a metal cylinder. Ham's data cable plugged into a panel on the bulkhead.

A computer voice sounded from a speaker. "Manual ejection in five seconds. Evacuate the area. Four, three, two, one, eject!"

The cylinder shot forward as HAM slammed its lid. An opening iris'd in the hull, and they hit space. A thruster fired, and HAM tried to cushion Ophelia as best he could.

Free fall hit as the thruster went out. HAM wiggled to cut a small hole with his plasma torch. He pushed an optic sensor through.

He saw flashes as pieces of the *Jishin* peeled away and burned. A tremendous number of drive plumes danced and flared. The little robot broadcast an SOS. *Oh, I do hope we don't get picked up by Dellans. I have had quite enough of them.*

# CHAPTER THIRTY-NINE

In Decision Hall, Chief Consul Sidra was giving the commander of the Matrian forces a public dressing down. The House leaders, Sadie Hawley, and Dame Connie Stillwell looked on uncomfortably.

Sidra fumed. "You did what?"

Consul Tess, head of House Custos said, "I ordered the airships to drop our paratroopers. They will dig in and prepare fortifications at their position."

"You wasted the only surprise we had." Sidra said. "Defense will not win this battle!"

"Excuse me, Chief Consul," Tess said. "You placed *me* in charge of defense. That is what I am doing."

"I need a battle commander that can defeat this enemy, not react when forced to," Sidra said.

"They outnumber us," Tess protested. "What would you have me do?"

"If I may interrupt, Chief Consul," Connie Stillwell said. "I know I am merely a guest; however, I may have a solution."

"Speak, sister," Sidra said.

"There is a seasoned commander available," Connie said. "One who has fought and defeated the Dellans despite overwhelming odds before."

"Why am I only hearing of this now?" Sidra asked.

"First Sergeant Jill Tower recently arrived with the Governance troops," Conne said. "Her unit is seasoned, and battle-tested. I suggest putting her in charge and sprinkling her troops among yours."

Consul Tess scoffed. "She's not even Matrian."

"Consul Tess can oversee the defense of the city itself. She is intimately familiar with the status of the local forces," Sadie Hawley said, trying to find a compromise. "Sergeant Tower can concentrate on the battle in its entirety."

"Very well, let us go find our Alexander and hear what she has to say," Sidra said and stalked away.

---

Jill Tower scanned the plain as the sun broke over the ocean's horizon. A heavy chill fog hung in the bowl of the plains formed by the distant mountains. The grass was covered with a heavy glittering frost that sparkled in the first rays of the sun.

"Top, I got something you should see." A soldier yelled down the line. He was manning a high-power optic rig.

"What am I looking for?" Jill asked as she looked at the screen.

"Those specks way out over the mountains," the soldier said, highlighting an area. "They just showed up when the rising sun hit them."

A group of a dozen golden specks glinted.

"Can you zoom more?"

"Okay, but it's gonna be fuzzy." He fiddled with the rig. The picture leaped larger. "What *are* those?"

Jill said, "They look like ships. But they are moving too slow."

Ornate gold scrollwork graced the bow, and the flag of Matria adorned their sides. The enormous arrowhead shapes trailed a stabilizing tail emblazoned with a Guild shield.

"The readout says they are only making a hundred klicks," Jill said. "How can something that big fly that slow? That fucker has got to be over three hundred meters long?"

"If I didn't know better, I'd swear those were airships," the soldier said. "I saw a documentary about them once."

"Airships, isn't that eighteenth-century tech?" Jill asked.

"Late nineteenth actually, and it wasn't very successful back then," he said. "The Dellans are going to shred those idiots."

As they watched, drifting white flowers blossomed from the airships. "Ha, maybe they aren't suicidal after all," Jill said. "Paratroopers."

"You mentioned you needed an infantry division," a voice said behind them. They turned to see Chief Consul Sidra standing there. "Now let's see if you can put them to good use."

"Umm, Ma'am, I'm not in charge."

"You are now," Sidra said, looking over her shoulder at the Consul from House Custos. "There have been some leadership changes."

"I don't even know our force dispositions," Jill stammered.

"I have arranged a briefing for you," Sidra said. "Let us not waste time. Things are accelerating."

---

The Dellan landing force commander, Colonel Kravitz, stomped into the command tent. "Where's that orbital bombardment we were promised?"

"Nothing new, Colonel," the Tactical Officer said. "The flagship, Jishin, is behind the planet from us now. They should be back in comms soon."

"Any news from our patrols?"

"One came back last night beat up pretty badly. They had some crazy story about the natives controlling a pack of giant wolves."

"Who knows," the Colonel said. "Nobody told us the landing area had lions either."

A soldier burst into the tent. "Colonel, you are going want to see this."

The Colonel followed her out and looked where she pointed. A thousand white shapes floated down from a dozen vast gleaming airships. He grabbed a pair of optics and zoomed them in.

"Are those paratroopers?" the soldier asked.

"Yeah," the Colonel turned to the Intelligence Officer that had joined them. "How did you miss the fact that Matria had a fleet of airships and paratroopers?"

"Uh, I don't know what to say, Colonel, they didn't have those the last time we did recon."

"Well, they've got them now, and we are in a tight spot. Mountains behind us, paratroopers between us and the sea, the enemy in front of us, and a river on the other side."

"I can get some UAVs up and keep those troops under watch," the Intelligence Officer said.

"Those fucking flyboys in orbit better hurry," Kravitz said. "This op is turning into a repeat of that shitshow on Kragus."

## CHAPTER FORTY

The situation on the *Jishin* was going downhill fast. Forbes paced the bridge.

"Status!"

"Hull temperature exceeding limits," an operator said. "We are shedding various panels."

Captain Stuart hit a comm. "Damage Control Central, report."

"We have moved all personnel to deep shelter," a voice said. "We can lose several meters of exterior before the orbital batteries fail." An alarm sounded over the comm.

"What was that? Stuart asked.

"Nothing, we lost a garbage pod overboard, is all."

Fleet Chief Forbes said, "Stop worrying about minor inconveniences, Stuart. You should be more worried about us making orbit."

"Aye, Chief. Ops, status of our orbit insertion?"

"We should know in five minutes if we have succeeded."

"What about the fleet?" Forbes asked.

"Our sensors are heat blind, but the fleet will defend us," Stuart said. "Nothing to do but wait five minutes."

"Five *long* minutes."

# CHAPTER FORTY-ONE

Jill Tower looked over a holo projection of the battle site.

"Okay, let me get this straight," she said. "Themyscira City, us, is here, south of the plains, on this point of land that projects out into the sea. Our paratroopers dropped in the west between the Dellan forces and the beach. The Felton River is to the east, and snowmelt has made it too fast for the enemy to cross. These mountains form a barrier to the north. Our enemy is boxed in. If they want to attack, they have to come straight down this peninsula to the city."

"Yes," House Custos said dryly. "It would be a bloodbath for them. At least, that is what I had planned."

"If Gus Johansson can't defeat the Dellan fleet though, we are sitting ducks. We'll be outnumbered and under siege."

"Why can't we break them with the new paratroopers we landed?" Custos asked.

Jill shook her head. "Those troops are green. I don't want to waste them charging into the Dellans," Jill continued. "Even though we don't see any heavy armor, they have a lot of light tactical vehicles with plenty of firepower. That gives them the mobility advantage."

A soldier barged into the room. "Top, you need to hear this," she thrust a comm into Jill's hand.

"This is Tower, go."

"Wasn't who I was expecting, but glad to hear from you," Nan Stanski said over the comm. "I'm sending you a video feed from our UAV."

A display screen in the corner lit up.

---

Mitzi Grey pulled her horse next to Jess's. They had been traveling at a ground-eating canter for quite a while.

"We aren't really going to do a cavalry charge into four thousand infantrymen, are we?"

"Oh, hell no! We might be brave but not stupid," Jess said. "Our friends are going to do it."

Mitzi looked around. "You expecting reinforcements?"

"Yeah, about ten thousand of them," Jess said.

Mitzi stood in her saddle. "I think the dust from ten thousand riders would be hard to miss," she said. "All I see is a herd of bison."

Jess laughed and picked up the pace.

---

"What am I looking at," Jill asked.

"Are those my cowboy friends?" Connie asked. "They look a little different from when I last saw them."

The screen showed a line of armored riders spread across the plain, slowly moving an enormous herd of bison forward. Giant dogs nipped at the beasts, and the cowboys were shouting and prodding with their lances to keep the herd moving.

Sadie pointed at the screen to a figure with streaming blonde hair. "Is that Mitzi?"

"Yeah," Nan answered over the comm. "She snuck out and joined the party."

"Of course, she did," Sadie said. "That one craves adventure."

"Do you have any idea what they are doing?" Jill asked Sidra.

Sidra answered, "You said you needed heavy cavalry, so I got you some."

"I didn't mean actual horse cavalry."

"I believe they will be effective anyway," Sidra said.

---

Mitzi trotted her horse up alongside Jess. "This is boooorrrring. I thought we were going to see some action."

Jess slapped the rump of a slow cow bison with his lance to speed her along and turned to Mitzi. "We need to get the herd into position before we make our move. No sense tiring out the stock. Plus, I'm waiting for the signal."

"Signal? From who?"

"The city. I finally talked to Sidra, and she agreed to my plan. They have a better idea of when to start it than we do."

"Well, I hope they decide soon. This sun is bad for my complexion."

## CHAPTER FORTY-TWO

On *Corvus,* Gus looked down at his console. "Enemy raiders headed our way."

Lenore's song changed, and Caber's star fighters maneuvered to engage the threat.

Energy weapons fired from the Dellan raiders. Caber's fighters began a slow spin, preventing the lasers from concentrating fire on one spot long enough to burn through their hulls.

The enemy accelerated and launched a torpedo spread. Caber's fighters responded with countermeasures but a few torpedoes escaped, and part of the formation exploded. Lenore howled in pain as blinding light poured from her skin.

Three Dellan cruisers moved to intercept *Corvus* in a pincer movement. Lenore took the initiative and changed course toward the nearest cruiser. Gus's fingers flew around his console, preparing their defenses.

Lenore let go a volley of torpedoes and suicide drones. The cruiser's energy weapons hit *Corvus,* but the carbonado hull absorbed them without damage.

CIWS fired, trying to intercept the torpedoes streaking

toward *Corvus*. One of the enemy weapons got through and hit engine number three, shearing it away.

*Corvus* deep bass rumbled from the 1MC. **"I Kill You!"**

Gus yelled, "Easy big fella, don't let them distract you."

Gus felt the apparent gravity climb as *Corvus* maneuvered. They closed on the enemy. *Corvus* spun at the last second and sprayed one cruiser with star fire from its engines. The blast burned a trench down the belly of the enemy ship, and it vented atmosphere.

**"Payback Bitch,"**

"One down, one hundred to go," Gus muttered.

## CHAPTER FORTY-THREE

At the Matrian paratrooper's position, a soldier asked his sergeant "How much longer are we going to sit here?"

"I didn't realize you were in such a hurry to get shot there, Telles," Sergeant Mela said.

"It's not that," the young man said to the woman. "It just looks like they dropped us away from the battlefield on purpose."

"He's not as dim as he looks," a balding man with a close-cropped gray beard named Gems spoke as he whetted a long thick bladed knife. "Sonny, our job right now is to keep them Dellans bottled up."

A tall woman marched up. "Sergeant, are the troops ready to advance?"

"Yes, Sub Consul," Sergeant Mela saluted and answered. "Some are more than ready."

The old trooper looked at Telles and smiled.

"Good," the Sub Consul said. "Mount up on your rover when you see the flare. I want an even line. At least until all hell breaks loose. Pass the word."

Mela saluted again as the Sub Consul turned and left. "Aye, my troopers will be ready."

"Troopers, HA!"

"What's your problem, Gems?" Mela asked.

"Oh, nothin *Sarge*," Gems said. "Except most of these kids were driving tractors and hoeing weeds a few weeks ago. Yourself included."

"Not everyone can boast a long career as a Range Marshal," she said. "Perhaps, too long." She added with a jab.

"I realize I'm just pointing out the obvious," he waved his knife for emphasis. "But those Dellans have a lot more experience than our greenhorns. You can bet they have been gravity conditioning for at least six months and running simulations constantly."

Telles looked around nervously. "Really? They didn't mention that during basic training."

Mela grabbed Gems arm and led him out of earshot. "Gems, don't go scaring these kids. I need you to pump them up, not tear them down."

"You're right," he agreed. "Let me see what I can do."

He stroked his beard, and he jumped on top of a rover. Mela slipped a voice amplifier into his hand. "Listen up, troopers!"

The grumbling women and men stopped and gathered round to hear what he had to say. Everyone knew Gems. He was a legend on Matria. A famous Range Marshal who had been enforcing the law in remote areas for over thirty years. His trademark blade had even become so popular that any large thick bladed knife was now called a Gem.

"I know that some of you are scared. A few weeks ago, you were selling dry goods, herding sheep, or plowing the back forty and dreaming about who you were going to share a blanket with at Beltane." He gathered his thoughts. "Now, the fate of

Themyscira and even Matria itself, our way of life, rests on your shoulders. We are outnumbered and outgunned, but the Dellans aren't supermen. They aren't fighting to protect their home. Look what happened on Kragus. A smaller force than ours kicked their ass." *Of course, that was mostly luck and the help of some piratical mercenaries.* "Remember your training, follow your platoon leaders, and fight for the Motherland. May the Goddess welcome our enemies into her bosom upon their death!" He raised his gleaming blade high, and the troops cheered.

## CHAPTER FORTY-FOUR

The Annie D. sat at last nights camp awaiting orders with Nan Stanski and her crew. Nyrkki said, "I'm tired of sitting here. Shouldn't we be doing something useful?"

Zia patted his arm. "Patience dear, things will break soon. Why don't you check the machinery?"

"Bah, I've checked it a dozen times already today. Besides, Annie would tell me if something was wrong."

"I can assure you, Sir," Annie said. "Your excellent maintenance efforts are appreciated. I've never been so well cared for."

Nan smiled. "Flatter him a little more, Annie, and he will find a new way to pamper you."

Nyrkki grumped and stomped aft.

Zia said, "You shouldn't tease him like that. He is quite sensitive under that grouchy exterior."

"Annie D., this is Cor-2," Drake Sheridan commed in, "Are we safe to fly yet? We are still waiting tasking at the Lift Port."

"I wouldn't recommend it," Zia commed back. "There are Dellan Wasps on standby at their encampment. They may be dogs in an atmosphere, but we would surely take damage."

"Thank you for thinking of me," Annie said.

"Any word of how things are going in orbit?" Nan asked.

"Nothing yet," Sheridan said. "I'm picking up a lot of Dellan chatter and some kind of ancient music broadcast from *Corvus*. The enemy's flagship should come over the horizon soon."

Nan said, "Let's go out and see if we can spot it."

Nan and Zia walked down the landing ramp and scanned the sky. They could see flashes high overhead.

"Looks like the battle up there has started," Nan said.

Zia pointed. "Is that the flagship?"

A new star rose over the horizon. Shooting stars fell away from it sometimes.

"Think so," Nyrkki said as he joined them. "Looks like they are losing hull panels. As big as that thing is, I don't think it will hurt them much, though."

"Too bad," Zia said.

"Ms. Forte," Annie said over her exterior speaker. "I am receiving a distress call."

Zia asked, "Is it *Corvus*?"

"No, it appears to be from our friend, HAM."

The three ran back to the cockpit.

Zia slammed into the pilot's chair and commed, "HAM, is that you?"

"Oh, how wonderful to hear your voice again, Ms. Forte," HAM replied.

"Enough of the pleasantries, what's your status?"

"We are safe for now, but I am afraid Ophelia and I did not achieve enough velocity in our escape from the *Jishin*. We are in a decaying orbit."

Nan asked, "Annie, how long do they have?"

"Calculating," the ship said. "They will reenter the atmosphere in thirty minutes."

Zia began preflight checks. "Well we are going to be there in twenty."

Nan said, "That's my cue to get back to Fuzzy. Good Luck!"

"This is Cor-1," Sheridan commed. "Firing up now."

---

The faint sound of a ship's engines spooling up pricked at Jill Tower's ears. She grabbed a set of optics and scanned the plain. Cor-1 slowly rose from the lift port. Out on the plain, the Annie D. began to climb fast.

"Zia, where the hell are you going?" she asked herself.

"Consul," her aide said, using Jill's new title. "At the Dellan camp, Wasps on the move!"

Jill pivoted to scan the enemy. Six fighters were rising and accelerating toward the Annie D. "Zia, I don't know what you are doing, but this is just the distraction we needed." She yelled out, "Fire the signal flares."

A gun battery thumped, and bright stars shot into the morning sky. Explosions of red and green followed by concussions they felt in their chests.

"Here goes nothing," Jill said.

Chief Consul Sidra walked to Jill's side. "May I ask your plan, Consul Tower?"

"In the best case, our cavalry routes them and we capture lots of prisoners, hold them hostage, and hope the Fleet Chief doesn't want to sacrifice them in a bombardment of the city. At a minimum, it shows we aren't hiding from them."

"Hmmm, quite innovative," Sidra said. "Not something a Matrian would have come up with. I will observe the outcome from here."

Her bodyguards protested. A wave silenced them.

Mitzi swiveled in her saddle at the explosions from the city. "What is that? Are they under attack?"

Jess paused. "Nope, that's our signal." He rose in his saddle and grabbed the carved horn trumpet hanging from the pommel. He blew a giant lungful. A long deep blast rolled over the herd.

Several more riders trumpeted and shout. Horses surged forward, and the dogs began a furious barking and nipping at the bison.

Mitzi whooped and prodded the nearest cow with her lance. The herd picked up speed.

---

In the Dellan camp, Kravitz jerked his head in his command tent. "What the hell is going on out there? Artillery?"

His aide rushed in. "Colonel, the city has set off some kind of signal."

The Colonel threw open the tent flap and stomped out. He looked over at the landing field on the edge of camp and heard a roaring takeoff. "Where are my Wasps going?"

"They are in pursuit of two Matrian ships," the aide stammered.

"Oh Gawd, it's another steaming shitshow! Tell them to get their asses back here."

"Rodger that." The aide dodged out of the path of the Colonel's fury.

A soldier ran up. "Colonel, my officer said you should see this." He handed him an optic and pointed to a rising cloud.

The Colonel looked. "Dust storm headed this way. Odd, forecast was clear weather."

The aide ran back. "Colonel, I've got a UAV feed of that cloud." He thrust a tablet into the Colonel's hands.

He zoomed the feed. The Colonel laughed. "I knew they were backward here, but you've got to be kidding me. These idiots are attacking us on horseback with armored knights?"

"Not exactly, Sir," the man took the tablet back and zoomed out. "There are about ten thousand bison stampeding in front of those knights. Headed directly at us."

"Get the vehicles into a barrier between us and that herd," Kravitz yelled. "Form a V and put the troops inside. Hopefully that will break their charge."

---

The signal spurred the paratroopers to action as the mortars echoed over the plain.

Mela climbed in next to Gems. "That's the order. Mount up!"

The soldiers roared.

They moved out in two parallel lines.

Telles, from the back seat, tapped Gems on the shoulder. "How are we gonna tell everyone apart if, we don't have proper uniforms?"

Gems looked back. "Shoot the guys in uniform. They ain't us."

Sergeant Mela smiled at Gem as they bounced along the plain. "I like the way you think."

Gem doffed his hat with a flourish and bowed his head in her direction.

A voice over their comm said, "On my signal, columns break left and right. Form a line and dismount. Vehicles remain slightly to the rear. Use your MGs to support the advance. Conserve your ammo, we aren't getting a resupply drop."

"It's about to get real now, Sonny boy," Gems said and spit the toothpick from his mouth.

"I'm not scared," the young man said.

"You should be. A nice healthy dose of fear just might keep you alive today."

# CHAPTER FORTY-FIVE

The dropship climbed fast, trailing a steaming thunderous blast. Zia dumped reaction mass into the engines to boost their thrust.

"Annie, I want you to light off the fusion thrusters as soon as you can," Zia said. "We need to get to Ophelia and HAM fast."

"I understand the urgency of the situation, Ms. Forte."

"Cor-1, this is Annie D.," Zia commed. "What is your status?"

"We are burning hot for intercept," Drake said back. "Pela is running the numbers now."

Annie D. interrupted, "We will intercept with five minutes to spare."

"That isn't much of a margin," Nyrkki said. "Hope nothing gets in our way."

"Six enemy fighters are in pursuit," Annie warned.

"What is their time to engagement?" Zia asked.

"Two minutes."

"Prepare countermeasures," Zia said. "Status of CWIS?"

"Warming up now," Nyrkki said as he worked his station.

Zia fought the controls. "Damn, those hull mods we made are playing hell with maneuverability."

"I'm dropping the external tanks and anything else I can," Nyrkki said. "It might help a little."

The ship shuddered. "Confirm jettison of external hard points, tanks, and torpedoes," Annie D. said. "I should handle more normally now, Ms. Forte."

"Confirm. How long until the Wasps have weapons lock?"

"I suggest evasive action. Wasps will be in range in thirty seconds."

"Drake, we could use a little help over here," Zia commed.

"I see that, on our way."

An alarm wailed inside the Annie. "Weapons lock detected!" Nyrkki yelled.

"Deploying chaff and flares," Annie D said.

The dropship banked and rolled into a punishing climb. Acceleration built to five gees. The ship shook as the CWIS cannon fired.

"I can take more," Zia yelled. "Max it out!"

"Understood," Annie said. "Increasing to maximum."

Nyrkki popped off his harness and stood easily even in the punishing acceleration.

"Where do you think you're going?" Zia asked through gritted teeth.

"I'm going to make a few adjustments. The CWIS is on auto, anyway. This gravity feels like a spring day back home on Wolfram."

"Damn showoff," she muttered between gasping breaths.

Nyrkki disappeared, and she heard a panel being torn from its hinges. A few seconds later, he yelled over the screaming engines, "Hang on, Baby, things are going to get rough."

A burst of thrust hit the ship. "EO, your modifications are exceeding my structural limits. Initiating safety protocols," Annie D warned.

"Command authorization override of all safeties, Gusty Joe Whiskey Four,"

"Acknowledge command authorization, safety protocols removed," Annie replied. "I must warn you, EO, I will require extra maintenance after this mission."

"Promise you," Nyrkki said. "Get us through this one, and you can have all the maintenance you want."

"I will hold you to that."

The enemy missiles sputtered and exploded in a hail of CWIS fire.

"Quit screwing around and get your ass back up here," Zia called out. "We got the missiles, but the fighters are still coming."

"Drake, we could *really* use some help here," Zia commed.

An alarm sounded, "Warning collision imminent, bearing zero, zero, zero axial."

"Hold your course, Annie," Drake said over the comm.

Before Zia could react, a blur with a roaring cannon flashed past. Two pursuing fighters exploded in the rear-view screen and Cor-1 rolled out in a spiral.

"About damn time," Zia said. "Get your ass back here and finish the job."

"Yes, Ma'am," Drake replied. "You realize it takes a while to turn this thing at Mach three, right?"

The sky outside the Annie darkened as the ship climbed out of the atmosphere. "Well, we are gonna be in space pretty quick and any maneuver advantage I had over those fighters is going to evaporate."

"Annie, how long until HAM's pod is critical?" Nyrkki asked.

"He has little time remaining," Annie said. "We are ten minutes away."

"Shit," Zia said. "Cor-1, how's it coming back there?"

"The Wasps gave up and headed back," Pela said. "We are burning for the pod now."

"HAM," Nyrkki commed. "You still there, little buddy?"

"EO," HAM said through the static. "I fear you will not arrive in time; things are becoming quite critical here."

"Don't lose hope on me," Nyrkki said. "Just hang on."

"Sir, it has been a pleasure to serve with you. I feel I have left you with too much work for one human. Please, give my regards to the crew and especially Ms. Lenore and *Corvus*. Perhaps fourteen hundred years is long enough. I, we..."

A hiss of static filled the cabin.

"I have lost the signal," Annie said. "I am sorry."

Nyrkki reached over to Zia and clasped her hand. A tear rolled down his cheek. "My dear, it looks like we are too late."

She released his hand and turned away. "Let's get back to the battlefield," she said with a catch in her voice. "Maybe we can still do some good."

# CHAPTER FORTY-SIX

"Shit, we just lost another dozen fighters," Gus announced.

"I am well aware, Commodore," Lenore said, pausing her battle song. "I feel the loss of each as my pain."

"Their Wasps are more maneuverable, and the Raiders have more firepower than our star fighters," Gus said. "We won't be able to sustain this loss rate. *Corvus*, how much ammo do we have left?"

"**Torpedoes expended, CWIS 25%, Countermeasures 50%. Dorsal Railgun One Round.**"

"Okay, so we are on defense only," Gus confirmed. "Please move us away from the battle front."

"**Rodger,**" the ship said. "**Transmission from HAM.**"

"What?" Gus asked. "Put it on speaker."

"Please, give my regards to the crew and especially Ms. Lenore and *Corvus*. Perhaps fourteen hundred years is long enough. I, we..."

"**Is Gone.**"

"Wait, what do you mean gone? Get it back."

"**Source Gone Into Gravity Well.**"

"*Corvus*, belay my last order," Gus said. "I don't care if we have to throw rocks, we are going to win today, for HAM and Ophelia."

**"Aye, For HAM."**

"Lenore, I am taking control of *Corvus*," Gus said. "Continue to direct the rest of the squadron."

"Aye," she said staring off into the distance and concentrating on the data flow of the battle.

"*Corvus*, I am highlighting a cruiser," Gus said.

**"Yes,"**

"Bring us into a firing solution to knock out their engine with the railgun."

**"Understood. Executing."**

The ship pivoted violently and fired all six engines. Gus's accelerations couch clamped his lower body to keep him conscious as the gees built.

*Corvus* began the ballet that would take them close to the probable path of the cruiser. Soon the cruiser realized Corvus had singled them out. An intricate dance of death flowed. *Corvus* executed its maneuvers flawlessly. Too late, their prey understood they could pivot to avoid a shot on their engines or expose a flank or bow. Either would knock them out of the battle, only one would minimize casualties. Checkmate.

**"In Position."**

"Fire," Gus said.

Corvus spun to bring the rear-facing gun to bear. Bridge lighting flickered, and the entire ship jumped forward as the one thousand kilo projectile shot away at seven thousand meters per second. The slug shredded the cruiser's primary engine into scrap and her lights died.

**"Done."**

"Maneuver to mate our bow section with their stern," Gus said.

*Corvus* matched its course and speed to the crippled ship. The bow unfolded into push knees. Tow wires winched in and locked the ships together.

**"Tow Secure."**

"Move into the battle and keep the cruiser between the enemy and us," Gus said. "I'm betting they won't fire on their own cruiser."

"Commodore Johansson," Lenore said, "you are one sneaky sumbitch."

"Thank you, XO," he said. "What is the status of *Jishin?*"

"They are coming out of the planet's shadow, now."

The forward screen zoomed in on the enemy flagship.

"Ouch," Gus said. "That old girl looks pretty beat up. Do you think she can still fight?"

Large sections of the assault carrier's outer plates had torn away, leaving the blackened interior exposed. Torn power cables sparked everywhere. Atmosphere vented in icy clouds from various places.

"All defensive weapons appear damaged or gone completely," Lenore said. "Her fleet is burning to rendezvous and provide defense. Offensive capabilities are severely degraded. She still could deploy unguided kinetic bombardment rods. Not accurately, but it only takes one hit to destroy the capital."

"Yeah, a tungsten tree trunk free-falling down a gravity well can ruin your whole day," Gus said. "Disengage the squadron. Please get me a private channel to Faber."

"Commodore, Faber is standing by."

"Commodore, why ain't you all fancy now?" Faber said with a laugh.

"Yeah, yeah, Lenore insisted," Gus said. "You still got your little package?"

"It's transferred to a fighter under my control," Faber answered. "I've been keeping it clear of the action. I don't want that thing to go off from some random piece of battle crap hitting it."

"What are the chances you can hit *Jishin?*"

"I thought that was a bad idea?" Faber asked. "What changed?"

"I just got an idea," Gus said.

**"These Never Work,"** *Corvus* said.

"Thanks for the vote of confidence."

## CHAPTER FORTY-SEVEN

Jess spurred his horse and called to Mitzi, "Faster, we need to hit them hard before they can get organized."

Mitzi's horse pulled ahead. "Come on, slowpoke!"

Jess yelled a warning that was drowned by the roar of the bellowing herd. "Shit! That woman is determined to get killed." He urged his horse faster.

The herd was in full panic. Bellows deafened, and dust blinded them. Only the flanking riders and dogs kept them headed toward the enemy.

The lead elements of the herd hit the Dellans with unfinished defenses. Some of the bison leaped through gaps in the makeshift barrier.

Soldiers fired into the animals. Bellows of panic turned to pain and rage. The bison spun and stomped, their tremendous horns flinging soldiers in every direction and trampling any that fell to the ground.

Screams of soldiers mingled with the animal roars. Officers vainly tried to organize their squads. A landing pod tilted and fell as its leg collapsed.

One enterprising noncom had killed several bison and rallied his men behind the bulwark of bodies.

Mitzi reached the vehicle barricade. Her horse balked at the jump, and she flew over its head as it skidded. She rolled and had a pistol in each hand as she sprang to her feet.

A Dellan popped off a round, and Mitzi dropped them with a shot from each pistol. She began to zig-zag through the herd firing in the air to turn the beasts away from her. An enormous horn caught her under the arm, and she swung onto a bison's back like it was planned.

Mitzi grabbed a fist of long coarse hair in each fist. "That was an instinct I should *not have* followed!"

The bison jumped wildly, trying to throw the unaccustomed weight.

Pup appeared out of nowhere in front of the frightened animal. He jumped up and grabbed hold of its nose and pulled hard, bringing the animal to its knees.

She felt a sharp stab in her shoulder and looked back. Jess was directly behind her and poking with his lance. His mount shouldered up, and Mitzi jumped behind him and held on.

"I don't know if you are incredibly brave or just plain stupid," he yelled back at her. He whistled to call off Pup.

"Hey, that did *not* go as planned," she replied.

"These are cow ponies, not equestrian guard jumpers. You are lucky Pup saw you."

The herd thinned around them They worked to the edge of the panic and galloped along the fringe, keeping bison between them and the enemy.

Mitzi looked to the west and saw the line of paratrooper infantry moving towards them. "I suggest we get out of here before we are caught in a crossfire."

Jess let fly a blast that signaled "break off and meet at the rally point."

---

Gems ran forward between Telles and Mela. "Get ready to hit the dirt when they fire," he said.

Mela was still in awe of the damage the bison herd had done to the enemy. Several tactical vehicles were overturned. Screams of the wounded drifted toward them.

"Looks like there won't be much left for us to do," Telles complained.

"Don't bet on it," Mela said. "They've probably still got us outnumbered three to one."

Gem spat. "Well, we are all going to shoot three times then."

A whistling sound cut the air. "Incoming!"

A volley of explosions fountained dirt behind them. "Mortars," Gems said. "We need to move before they can walk those rounds in."

Mela blew a whistle, one long and three short.

The line picked up speed. Moving fast, soldiers zig zagged.

Shells landed closer.

"If we can get within two hundred meters, we will be under the flight arc, and the mortars can't hit us," Mela said.

"Yeah, but then we are in easy rifle range," Gem replied.

"You've always got a complaint about something, don't you?" Mela said.

"Wouldn't be much of a soldier if I didn't."

---

"Annie D. and Cor-1," Jill Tower commed. "the paratroopers are getting clobbered by mortar fire; I need you both back here ASAP."

"Rodger that," Zia said. "We're on our way."

Annie D said, "I am detecting Wasp fighters in the area. I advise caution."

"We don't have the luxury of caution today," Nyrkki said as he thumped into his co-pilot's seat.

The two ships banked and accelerated towards the battlefield.

Wasp fighters were making repeated passes over the troopers. Their high stall speed and poor handling made them ineffectual at strafing runs, but they were keeping the troopers pinned down as mortar rounds rained.

"Cor-1, make a run at the Dellan lines," Zia commed. "Maybe we can draw the Wasps away from our guys."

"Rodger that," Drake commed. "Pela, can you handle the weapons when I make the run?"

"About time! I finally get to do something back here," she replied.

Cor-1 came in hot and peppered the enemy with cannon fire.

"Hey, I've got an idea," Pela said. "The wind is at the trooper's backs, isn't it?"

Drake checked his screen and said, "Yeah, so?"

"Make a pass between the lines as slow as you dare."

Drake banked hard and lined up his run.

"I can get it down to three zero zero klicks before we stall. That's still fast for strafing."

"Can you come in thirty meters off the deck and stall into a tail stand?"

"That's a big ask, but I can do it." Drake lined up for the

pass. "Okay, let me know when you want it. No time to waste those Wasps are closing fast."

He focused on the haptic feedback of his controls. The fighter groaned and bounced in the unstable air over the battle. Drake knew he couldn't focus too hard without losing the big picture and flying into the ground. He closed his eyes and let the situation flow into him.

"Get ready!"

"What the hell are those two up to now?" Zia asked.

"Unknown," Annie replied. "There are no enemy positions on that flight path."

Nyrkki's CWIS guns rattled at several Wasps on their tail. "Hey, let's worry about us, please."

Zia pulled up hard, and the wasps shot past. She executed a wing over and accelerated. Now she was on the enemy's tail.

Pela slapped the back of Drake's seat, "On my mark."

"Let's do this, Bossy Pants."

"Now!"

Drake fired his vectoring thrusters and flared the craft straight on its tail. Pela fired belly and dorsal flares.

"Go, Go, Go!" she yelled.

The craft's blazing exhaust and burning flares set a line of flame three hundred meters long. The tinder-dry winter grass caught fire immediately, and a steady wind moved it toward the Dellan line.

Drake didn't have time to admire Pela's work. A Wasp had picked up his tail and was gaining.

Drake banked and got inside his enemy's turn and ended up behind them.

"No use chasing him, weapons are dry." Pela said. "Plus, that was the last of our countermeasures. I suggest running."

"Well, at least he can't shoot at us back here."

An alarm sounded. "Well, his friend can, and he's got weapons lock on us," Pela said.

Drake began to jink the fighter violently, trying to break the lock.

"Not looking promising, kid," Drake said. "This guy is good."

Drake swore as tracers flashed by his craft. "That was close. If a burst like that catches us we might have to punch out. Nyrkki will be pissed if we lose another fighter." He pulled into a climb. "We need some extra altitude."

The weapons lock alarm cut off abruptly.

"Looks like we found a guardian angel," Pela said. "Someone just splashed that Wasp."

Drake looked left and right. A pair of Governance fighters eased into flanking positions.

The pilots waved. "Courtesy of cruiser *Erebus* and Admiral McGowan," a woman's voice came over the comm.

"We thought you guys were sitting this one out?" Pela commed.

"When we heard *Corvus* needed help, the Admiral didn't have a choice. It was authorize our mission or face a mutiny. You guys saved our asses at The Battle of Kragus, so we thought we would return the favor. The *Terrible* is up there, too."

Drake commed, "Well, we sure appreciate the help."

"The remaining Wasps are breaking for orbit. Looks like it's too hot down here for them. The boss recalled us to *Erebus*. Can you make it back to the lift port?"

"We should be fine now. What's your handle? We owe you a beer after this is over," Drake commed.

"Silky here," the woman commed. "That loser is Plug."

"Yeah, but this is the loser that keeps the bad guys off your sweet tail."

"What about you two?"

"Drake here."

"If it walks like a duck and quacks like a duck," Plug commed.

"Wait, no," Drake said.

Pela kicked his seat, "Shut up, or they are going to christen you, Duck." She commed back, "I am,"

Drake interrupted, "She's Princess."

Pela reached over his seat and slapped his helmet.

"Alright, Princess," Plug commed. "We'll catch you on the flip. I have heard enough stories about Beltane and I can't wait to see if any are true."

The Governance pilots gave them a wing wave and headed for orbit.

---

"Commodore, I am detecting two large engine signatures coming into view around the planet," Lenore said.

Gus looked at his console and swore. "Unidentified vessels braking for Matria orbit." he said, "Identify yourself or prepare to be fired upon."

"Now, Mr. Johansson, is that any way to greet old friends? Governance cruisers *Erebus* and *Terrible* at your service."

"You will address the Matrian Defense Squadron leader as Commodore," Lenore commed.

"Yes, Ma'am," the two chastened captains responded.

"I thought you were still in dry dock after that ass whooping you got at Kragus?" Gus commed.

"It's amazing how fast a yard will work when Admiral McGowan pulls some strings."

"McGowan? That crafty old bastard told us we were on our own."

"Well, I won't say he was a willing participant. There were rumors of mutiny if he didn't send us in."

"Well, glad to have you both." Gus commed. "Form up on my port and starboard, and let's see how much damage you can do. We are out of ammo over here."

**"Torpedoes and CWIS restored."**

"*Corvus*, I thought we were out of bullets?"

**"I Made More. HAM Taught Me.**

*These bots never cease to amaze me.* Gus thought.

"*Corvus,* new orders," Gus said. "Push this dead cruiser on our bow at *Jishin*."

**"Aye, Accelerate Now."**

The increase in apparent gravity knocked the wind out of Gus as *Corvus* fired off his engines hard.

"*Erebus* and *Terrible,* prepare to attack. Follow this cruiser after I cut it loose and use it for cover. Wait for my signal, then break out and rain destruction as you see fit."

"Rodger that, Commodore."

"Faber, you still there?" Gus asked.

"Staying out of trouble and babysitting my package," Faber responded.

"Send it special delivery in the wake of this Dellan cruiser I'm pushing," Gus commed. "Detonate it near here." Gus transmitted the coordinates of a location on the enemy's hull.

"Got it," Faber said. "I see what you are up to now. They won't like this."

"I hope not."

---

In the Ops center aboard *Jishin*, the fleet Tac Officer said, "Fleet Chief Forbes, we are receiving a distress call from cruiser *Cullain*."

"Put it on speaker."

"Mayday, Mayday, Mayday, this is cruiser *Cullain*. We are dead in space. Emergency environmental systems are operational. Request immediate assistance."

"Can you tell what happened?" Forbes asked.

"Looks like *Corvus* destroyed their engines," the Tac Officer said.

"That Johansson is a continual pain in my ass," Forbes growled. "Can we get a tow on them?"

"Uh Chief, *Corvus* already has them in tow."

"Get that ship on the screen."

An image enlarged on the screen. *Corvus* pushed *Cullian* ahead.

"Get me a channel in the clear," Forbes said.

"It's open now," the comms operator said.

"*Corvus,* release that ship," Forbes commed.

"Ah, Fleet Chief Forbes," Gus's image appeared on the screen. "We finally meet. You can address me Commodore Johansson."

"Commodore, my ass," Forbes said. "Using prisoners as a shield is a war crime."

"You misunderstand," Gus said. "I'm simply assisting a vessel in distress. That's what a Long-Range-Salvage-Tug does."

"Bullshit, cast that ship adrift and we will handle it."

"Hmmm, it looks to me like you have your own problems," Gus responded. "Aren't you having trouble inserting into orbit? *Corvus* could give you a hand once we're done with this little job."

"We are fine," Forbes said. "You tell those bitches dirtside to surrender or I will drop a 'Rod from God' on their heads."

"Now look who is threatening a war crime," Gus said. "Johansson out." The screen blanked.

"Fleet Chief, two Governance cruisers have just formed a battle group with *Corvus*," the ops officer said. "Headed for us."

"Direct the fleet to take station to defend *Jishin*."

---

"Commodore, the Dellan fleet is breaking off the fight," Lenore said. "They are forming a shield for the flagship."

"Perfect," Gus said and smiled. He keyed his comms. "*Erebus* and *Terrible*, follow this hulk when I cast it adrift. On my signal, I want you to execute the file I'm sending you on course zero-niner-zero dorsal."

"Rodger, Commodore, we were looking to provide a little payback, but I guess that can wait."

"Faber, slot your package in the wake of this hulk," Gus commed. "Send it right down their throat."

"With pleasure," Faber said. "I warned them I would have revenge."

---

On board *Jishin*, the Tac Officer said, "Chief, *Corvus* has cast the *Cullain* adrift. The two Governance ships cruisers are following, using our cruiser as cover. It's headed right at us, and if we try to maneuver, we will miss orbital stability."

"Get some salvage tugs underway to intercept the *Cullain*. Send destroyers to accompany the salvage and engage the Governance cruisers if they don't break off," Forbes said aloud.

"What are you trying to pull now, Johansson?" Forbes said to himself.

---

Gus Johansson followed the action on his screen. "Lenore, what is the status of our forces?"

"We have two hundred thirty-two star fighters remaining operational," she said. "I have deployed them to most effectively strike if needed. Although they are insufficient to achieve victory. The bulk of the enemy ships are in a screen formation between our squadron and the flagship. The enemy will destroy most of our fighters within a few minutes of engagement."

"If this works, that won't be necessary," Gus said. "What is the status of the *Cullain*?"

"Tracking true to target," Lenore said. "*Erebus* and *Terrible* are still in position. Two salvage tugs and four destroyers are en route to *Cullain*."

"*Erebus* and *Terrible*," Gus commed, "time for you to get out of there."

"Rodger that Commodore, executing now," the comm sounded.

Gus watched the two cruisers pivot to flee. The readout showed something wrong.

"Command, this is *Erebus*," the comm sounded, "*Terrible's* primary engine is offline. I guess their repairs didn't hold."

"Rodger, *Erebus*, drop back and provide defense for *Terrible*." Gus gripped the arms of his acceleration couch. "Come on, you Dellan bastards, I know you can't resist an easy target." Gus asked Lenore, "Are the Dellans taking the bait, XO?"

"Yes, Commodore," Lenore said. "The destroyers are maneuvering to engage our cruisers. The salvage tugs have control of *Cullain* and are moving to higher orbit."

"How's Faber's package?" Gus asked.

"It is undetected and on course to impact *Jishin*. The enemy appears to be distracted. Commodore, the transport *Pantas* has entered the battle space," Lenore continued. "I am receiving a transmission."

"*Corvus,* this is Admiral McGowan, I see you have already deployed the ships I sent. You may stand down; I am assuming command."

Gus swore under his breath. "Like hell you are."

Gus slammed his fist onto the comm button. "Admiral, this is *Commodore* Johansson, leading the Matrian Defense Squadron, how nice of you to join us. I've got things well in hand. Why don't you make yourself useful and negotiate the Dellan's surrender?"

"Commodore? Given yourself a promotion, I see."

"Only until I send these bastards flying back to the holes they came from," Gus replied. "Then it's back to the simple life of a tug driver for me."

"Ha, I don't think Fate is going to let you off that easily," McGowan said. "Make your play, *Commodore*. I'll be here to pick up the pieces."

"Arrogant bastard, isn't he?" Gus asked Lenore.

"I see where Mitzi gets it from," Lenore answered. "I am sending the star fighters to support the *Erebus* and *Terrible*. The Matrian patrol ships are in reserve."

"Good idea," Gus said, "make it look like we are committing in a final push."

"Fleet Chief," the Tactical Officer said, "the enemy has massed their forces. Our salvage tugs have recovered the *Cullain* but are having difficulty with the tow."

"Are we going to make orbit?"

"Navigation confirms that if we maintain our current braking performance, we will achieve an elongated orbit that passes over the Matrian capital every ninety minutes."

"Excellent," Forbes said. "Prepare several kinetic projectiles for launch. These will be a warning."

---

Gus's palms were sweating. He rubbed them on his acceleration couch and said, "Lenore, how is our little gift for Fleet Chief Forbes?"

"It is tracking true to target, Commodore. Detonation in eight minutes." Lenore's eyes remained unfocused as she concentrated on the multiple data streams. The shifting patterns on her skin had calmed with the lull in the battle. "I have detected a problem."

Gus snapped to attention. "What've ya got?"

"Another tug is moving to help with the *Cullain*. They are coming uncomfortably close to our package."

"Can you do anything?" Gus asked.

"Negative, Commodore," Lenore answered. "The package has no thrusters, and its carbonado casing is too stealthy for the tug to detect."

"How will we know if they clear the package?"

"They don't explode."

# CHAPTER FORTY-EIGHT

Jill Tower surveyed the battle raging on the plains. The dust from the stampede had blown away as the herd continued toward the river. A thick choking smoke raced ahead of the line of prairie fire crawling toward the Dellan lines obliterating it.

"The fire has the enemy distracted," Sidra said. "Should we pursue our advantage?"

"Our force would run blind toward that fire and the enemy." Jill replied. "The enemy is rattled right now. Let them worry what our next move is."

"What are your orders?" Sidra asked.

Jill grabbed a comm. "Gunner Stanski, are you still in position?"

"Rodger that, Top," she answered.

"Take Fuzzy through the fire and get me a sitrep on the enemy."

Nan turned to her crew. "Okay, boys, time to earn our pay. Status?"

"Mortar tubes reloaded, but that is the last of them," oDolo said.

"The 12mm MG has five hundred, and the auto-cannon is down to three hundred rounds," Wilson said.

"I gots enough juice left to run a hundred klicks," Fuzzy said. "Then youse is walkin'."

"All right then," Nan said. "Fuzzy, can your sensors see anything through the smoke?"

"Nope, between the dust, smoke, and flames, we're goin' in blind."

"Of course, we are."

Fuzzy crawled forward through the thick smoke.

"I still got nothing, Gunner," Wilson said to Nan as he swung the turret in an arc.

"Pop off a few rounds with the MG," Nan said. "Let's see if we can provoke a reaction."

The turret machine gun rattled into the smoke. Nothing fired back.

"Didn't think Dellans had that much fire control discipline," oDolo said.

"They don't," Nan answered.

"I got a return on my echo-location readout," Fuzzy said. "That and inertial guidance says we are within five meters of the original line."

Nan popped the top hatch and threw it open. The acrid smell of burning grass and rubber drifted into the APC. She pulled down her helmet's filter and raised up to look around.

A few blackened tactical vehicles lay on their sides. Amid the wreckage of the stampede, a clumps of dead soldiers and bison lay scattered around.

Wilson called from inside. "Well, what's out there?"

"Looks like they bugged out," Nan shouted down the hatch. "Fuzzy, launch a birdie and take a wider look."

"Youse got it, Gunner." A small UAV buzzed up and away.

Soon the report came back. "Birdie sees em, running like scalded dogs toward the foothills."

"More likely running to regroup," Nan dropped back inside, sealed the hatch, and lifted the visor.

Fuzzy cranked up the fans to clear the smoke.

"Top, this is Foxtrot Zulu Yankee-1, Command come in," Nan commed.

"Go for Command," Jill Tower's voice crackled over the comm.

"Negative contact with the enemy. Sending you a feed."

Jill looked at the UAV transmission on the tablet her aide handed her. She handed it to Sidra.

"What do you think, Gunner?" Jill asked.

"I think they are looking to regroup. Maybe hoping the battle in orbit will go their way before committing to storming the city," Nan answered.

"Agreed," Jill said. "Get back to the troopers. Having your firepower will boost their spirits."

"Rodger, Fuzzy-1 out." Nan looked at her console. "Fuzzy, let's get back to the paras fast. I've got a bad feeling about this."

---

Colonel Kravitz turned to his aide as they bounced along in the command buggy. "How bad did we get hit?"

The aide looked up from his tablet. "We have lost contact with about five hundred soldiers. Dead, wounded, and missing."

"How many vehicles and supplies do we have?"

"We've barely got enough vehicles left to move everyone and supplies will only last a few more days. This op was supposed to be quick."

"Yes, and we've got no way back to orbit," Kravitz said. "Those landers were a one way ticket."

"Orders, Sir?"

"Split the force into two columns. I want Alpha Group to loop near these hills and come behind their infantry position so we can trap them in a pincer," Kravitz said. "It's time to go on the offensive. We can't count on those idiots in orbit to carry out their part of the plan."

---

"Fleet Chief, the kinetic weapons are ready," the Fire Control Officer said. "We will be in launch position in a few minutes."

"Good, I hope this looks impressive," Forbes said. "We need to force their surrender now." He turned to his Tactical Officer. "Suggested target for maximum shock value?"

"Our sensors are still heat blind, but we can use previous data," the officer said. "I propose this area on the edge of the plains. The geology of this dry stream will fracture nicely, and the resulting debris cloud should make a terrifying sight."

Forbes rubbed the arms of his command chair. "Nothing strikes fear into an enemy like a rising mushroom cloud. This *is* well clear of our landing force, right?"

"Yes, Sir, nowhere near the landing zone."

"Very well," the Fleet Chief replied. "I want a ten-weapon straight line spread with one hundred meter spacing. Fire when we are in position."

---

Nan Stanski pulled off her helmet and wiped a hand over her short blonde hair as the APC rolled up to the line of paratroopers.

"What's the word, Gunner?" the para's commander asked.

"The enemy has abandoned their position and is maneuvering," Nan answered. "They have split into two columns. Looks like they are setting up a pincer trap."

Nan hopped down from the machine and handed Sergeant Mela a tablet with the UAV video.

Range Marshall Gems walked up and looked over her shoulder and pointed at the tablet. "Wishbone Wash," he said. "That's gonna give them trouble."

The group looked at him. "Why? Just looks like a dried-up stream bed," Nan said.

"This time of year, the snow melt is just getting started," Gem said. "Later, this will be full of water, but right now, the sand in the bottom is soaking up all the runoff and getting loose. Those buggies of theirs will be stuck."

Nan turned to Mela. "How many mortar teams do you have?"

"About a dozen."

"Can we get them into position to fire on the wash before the Dellans get there?"

Mela answered, "Yes, it would be nice to be on the delivery end of a mortar barrage this time."

Nan held the tablet and traced out a series of maneuvers for the para's ground forces to make.

Mela looked at the tablet and said, "Hmmm, this might just work. I'll run it by the Sub-Consul," she said, "We can split our force to cut off any escape attempt."

"Umm, Sergeant," Nan interrupted, "a wise general once advised, 'Do not press a desperate foe too hard. If you force them to go down in a blaze of glory, they will, taking more of your troops than you might otherwise lose.'"

Mela considered the advice. "Wise words Gunner. We can harass the enemy as they try to escape but not trap them. When they rejoin the primary force, their fear will be contagious."

Melles saluted Nan and nodded to Gems, "Come on Marshall Gems, let's see your info in action."

---

"Why the Hell are we stopping?" Colonel Kravitz shouted.

His driver bounced out of his seat and ran forward too check.

The Colonel turned to his aide. "Are you in contact with the flagship yet?"

"No, Colonel," the harried young man replied. "They are just now coming out of the planet's shadow."

Kravitz scanned the sky and saw a small new star rise from the horizon. "That looks like them now. Their braking engines are firing for orbit."

The Colonel's driver ran back to the car. "Colonel, the lead element of the column is bogged down."

"I thought the riverbed was dry?"

"The vehicles broke through a crust. There is a layer of wet mush underneath. They sank to the axles."

"Aww shit," Kravitz swore as he climbed out and headed forward. He yelled at his aide. "I want some combat engineers here on the double to free those vehicles. Send some scouts to find a place to cross."

Vehicles moved away in both directions looking for an alternative path.

Kravitz jerked his head at a familiar unwelcome sound. "Incoming!"

Mortars fell along the column. Fountains of dirt geysered along the clustered vehicles. Explosions and screams filled the air.

---

Fuzzy's periscope raised over the embankment he was hiding behind. "I gots a good visual on the enemy, Gunner."

Nan played a cursor around her screen. The mortars were having the desired effect. The enemy forces were in chaos. "Wilson, I want single turret shots on any vehicle that makes it over the wash."

"Rodger, Gunner."

"oDolo," Nan said to her other crewman, "put mortar fire down on those buggies breaking to the south along the river."

"You got it." The launching thumps shook the APC.

The enemy began a zig-zagging pattern that avoided the mortars.

"How did I miss every one of them?" oDolo asked. "That's the last of the mortars, Gunner."

Nan zoomed in on the lead vehicle. "Not your fault, Corporal," Nan said. "I recognize their markings. They're Shadows. That's the best of their best headed for our flanking force."

---

Range Marshall Gems jerked his optics away from his eyes. "Heads up, pigs and pearls, we got a breakout headed our way!"

A speeding line of Light Tactical Vehicles and power cycles

had avoided the mortar fire and were at full speed toward the flanking line.

Mela thought fast. "Get three buggies moving and head east," she told a trooper next to her. "Maybe we can draw them into a trap.

---

Telles peeked over the edge of his hastily dug shallow foxhole. "Gems, are we gonna make it?"

The older man spat out a toothpick he had been chewing. "Steady on, trooper, they don't know we are here. I gotta see Mela." He crawled out of the hole toward his sergeant and rolled into her hole. "Hey Boss, have the left side of the line open up on them. Maybe we can herd them this way."

Mela considered the strategy. "Good one! That will encourage them to chase our decoy." She relayed the plan over her comm.

Gems rejoined Telles in his hole. "Okay, youngster, get ready. We're only gonna have a few seconds to make this happen." Gems yelled down the line. "Go to full auto when you hear my whistle."

Time slowed across the scene. The para's left flank rose and began firing rapidly at the advancing enemy. The Dellan LTVs pivoted right on cue toward the fleeing para's buggies. Gems blew his signal. His troopers rose to one knee and began sending a wall of bullets into the enemy's rear.

The Dellan LTVs swiveled their raised MG mounts and laid it on thick into the Matriarch force. Bullets tore through the line, and the survivors dropped into their foxholes. The Shadows continued away.

"Shit! That did *not* go as planned," Gems said as impacting bullets rained dirt down on his head.

The enemy stopped firing and Tells slapped Gems. "Into the buggy. They're gonna break through."

The young man buckled his harness as he jumped in, and the buggy leaped after the Dellans just as Gems hauled aboard.

"You sure about this?" the old Marshall asked.

"I race on the weekends," Telles yelled over the straining sound of the buggy's twin electric drives. "They won't lose me. You man that MG, and I'll give you the shots."

"Kid, you realize they are gonna be shooting back, right?"

Telles glanced at Gems. "I'm trying not to think about that."

Gems grabbed a joystick and swiveled the stabilized gun above them. The MG rattled off rounds.

"Hang on!" yelled Telles. The trooper tapped a pattern into the steering wheel buttons, and the buggy engines changed tone as it surged forward. "Governor-override cheat code."

"All's fair when you're getting shot at," Gems yelled over the noise of the MG overhead.

The Shadows' LTVs and their pursuer bounced and dodged over the prairie. Neither side could score a solid hit.

The two Dellan vehicles split left and right and slammed on the brakes in a power slide. A cloud of dirt and grass blocked Gems sight. Telles pumped the brakes hard just as a spray of bullets passed in front of them.

"Damn, we would have driven right into that," Gems said.

"Oldest trick in the book," Telles said. "Watch, now there is going to be one ahead and behind us when the dust clears."

They flew out of the dust cloud, and Gems saw it was true. The car in front of them braked hard and Telles threw his buggy left just as an MG opened up where they had been. "Fire right," Tells yelled.

Gems swiveled his MG and fired on instinct just as Telles hit the brakes again. The trailing LTV caught the full force of the MG barrage. Gems saw the LTV lurch sideways and roll.

"Splash one!" Telles laughed. "Crap." He jinked the buggy right and just missed the same fate.

The Dellans on his tail were gaining. They held fire until they could be sure of a kill shot.

Gems pounded Telles' shoulder. "Head for that bank over there." He pointed at a slight rise.

"Hope you know what you are doing."

"Trust your fellow ground-pounder, sonny-boy."

Suddenly the lead powercycle chasing them flipped in the air from an explosion. The second cycle recovered the fallen rider, and they peeled away to join the rest of the squad racing towards the foothills.

"How the Hell did you do that?" Telles asked.

"Wasn't me." Gems grabbed the comm. "Thanks, Fuzzy. I was hoping you guys were watching."

"You are welcome." Sergeant Wilson's voice came over the comm. "I was gonna let you sweat it a little longer, but the Gunner vetoed me. Oh you are buying the first round, Marshall."

"Gladly and tell Nan I'm saving the first Beltane dance for her."

Wilson laughed, "I'll pay good money to see that."

Nan looked over her shoulder at Wilson and shook her head vigorously and mouthed, "No way."

"She said she is looking forward to it," Wilson said.

Nan rolled her eyes, "I'm gonna get you back for that one."

Corporal oDolo made kissy-face noises into his hand. Nan threw her helmet at him, and he fell out of his seat laughing.

"Let's finish this before we celebrate," she said and turned back to her screen.

Three LTVs were still heading off.

Kravitz ran crouching up to the wash through the dwindling mortar rain. Four engineers were winching a stuck LTV up the far side of the bank. The rest of the team was laying a mat of willow branches to allow a crossing. "How much longer?" he asked the sergeant in charge.

"Just a few more minutes, Colonel. We've almost got the winching done, and then we can finish the mats."

"Okay, Sergeant, it doesn't need to be pretty, just fast."

A concussion wave knocked the men flat. Kravitz began giving directions. "Out of the wash! Take cover." He looked toward the scene of impact. A cloud rose into the sky. Mud and sand rained down on them. "That's an orbital weapon. Those idiots are firing on *us*! If they follow procedure, the next one will hit in thirty seconds. Move now."

Soldiers scrambled, and LTVs raced away in every direction. Right on cue, the next weapon hit. A bogged vehicle and men working to free it disappeared in a cloud. A muddy crater slowly filling with water marked the spot.

The bombardment proceeded down the stream bed at intervals. Kravitz looked in vain for his command car and staff. An LTV rolled up, and the soldier inside asked, "Need a ride, Colonel? Looks like it's every man for himself."

Kravitz scrambled aboard and the car soon pulled up to a small group of soldiers milling around. Kravitz jumped off the sideboard when he saw his aide standing next to his command car.

"What the Hell was that, Colonel?" the shocked man asked.

"Looks like we were on the receiving end of an orbital bombardment demonstration," Kravitz answered. "Another example of when friendly fire, isn't."

The Shadows had regrouped and rested in the shade of a small group of trees.

"I thought you said they didn't have any armor?" Banner said.

"It's an old Governance APC," Sledge answered. "They only got off one shot. One buggy and cycle are toast but everyone is okay."

Banner asked, "Anybody got a visual on that APC?"

"Just a glance, but we know where it's hiding."

"Fellas, this our lucky day," Banner said as he searched his tablet. "Intel says that there is only one vehicle like that on Matria, and its run by Nan Stanski."

"You mean the broad on our special bounty kill list?" Slip asked.

"One and the same," Banner said. "She's a member of *Corvus's* crew, and if we bring back her head, we'll get our pick of Matrian land grants."

"From what I've seen so far, this land grant may not be worth the price," Boomer said. "Even if it is free."

"We need a plan to bag this bitch," Banner said. "Remember, she is sneaky and mean."

---

Telles rolled up to Fuzzy as Nan popped the APC's top hatch. "Who were those guy's chasing us?"

Nan answered, "You can brag about getting shot at by the Dellan Shadows and living."

Gems whistled softly. "Sonny, we used up some of our lives today. I've heard the Shadows don't miss."

"Ha, I told you I could out-drive them."

"Gunner," the Fussy's external speaker croaked. "Youse should hear dis, it's coming in on a wide band and in the clear."

The speaker shifted to the comm channel. "Gunner Nan Stanski, this is Banner. I know that's you in that raggedy-ass APC. You got a lucky shot today."

Wilson cracked to the group. "Sucker was an easy target."

"Who's dis guy calling raggedy-ass?" Fuzzy asked.

The voice continued. "We're coming for you. The Fleet Chief has marked you and your friends for special attention. I should thank you; this little job is going to fund me a rich retirement."

Nan had Fuzzy to put her on the comm. "You think I fear you Shadow pukes? The scavengers will scatter your bones to the four winds. I hear ravens prize the eyes. *Corvus* will be immensely pleased his brethren are being fed."

Banner responded, "I shall drink from your skull cup on the anniversary of your defeat until I am old and fat."

"I would promise to make a change purse from your ball sack, but it would be too small to hold a half-penny," Nan taunted.

"Enough insults," Banner said, "may the best predator win." The comm went dead.

Gems looked at Telles. "Sonny-boy, we might have gone a little too far this time."

A third sun blazed into existence over the battlefield and faded.

Gems shielded his eyes from the increasing glare. "What the hell have they gone and done up there now?"

Nan replied, "That looks like my shipmate's latest mad scientist experiment."

---

Jill Tower surveyed the plain. "Damn, wish I had a decent battle infonet," she complained. "How do you expect me to win this war without information?"

Chief Consul Sidra turned and said, "The same way Alexander the Great, Patton, and Reynolds did, go with your gut."

"I guess it should honor me to be named in that line-up, but things look pretty grim right now. Our infantry is scattered, the enemy is regrouping, and air support is out of ammo. Not to mention that those mushroom clouds over there look like a warmup for an orbital bombardment."

"Don't count out our friend Gus Johansson just yet, my dear." Sidra said. "That old dog always seems to have a new trick when he needs one. Ahh, I believe this is it now."

Sidra pointed to the brilliant flash of an antimatter bomb exploding in orbit. As the radiation struck the planet, an enormous aurora spread across the sky.

The comm at Jill's elbow let out a shriek as the electromagnetic pulse from the bomb reached them. The tablet in her hand went black. "I guess we really are back to fighting in the Dark Ages now."

The comm squawked. "Command, this is Nyrkki on the Annie D. Everything all right there?"

Jill Tower grabbed the mic. "What was that?"

Nyrkki laughed. "Just a little antimatter explosion for our Dellan friends."

"Did you have to spike all my electronics?"

"Nature of the beast," Nyrkki said. "Your electronics should reboot. The Annie D. is coming back online with no damage. I'm hoping the enemy isn't so lucky."

# CHAPTER FORTY-NINE

Electricity danced across every surface of the bridge on *Jishin*. Screens flared and blanked. Sparks shot from the lights as they failed. A crewman jerked away from his console. Sparks flew from his fingertips back to the surface.

The bridge went black, and the crew held their breath as an unnerving silence gripped them. A ship is never quiet. Hatches and doors slide and clang. The machinery hums, air whispers from vents, and pumps thump away.

Fleet Chief Forbes shouted, "Ops report! What's going on?"

"From the smell, I'd say a giant EMP attack, Chief," the flustered officer said as a heavy layer of ozone and burnt wiring floated by.

Forbes took control. "Helmets on! Full suit checks."

Half the crew's suit systems were fried.

Someone found a stash of glow sticks and began snapping and distributing them.

"Captain Stuart, please take charge of damage control. Send a runner to Engineering and find out what our status is. I am going to see if we have comms with the rest of the fleet."

It took Forbes five minutes to thread his way through the passageways and ladders crammed with crew trying to make repairs.

He finally arrived at the Combat Information Center and grunted the heavy door open. The junior officer in charge ran up to him and saluted.

"Fleet Chief, do you know what happened?"

"I was hoping you could tell me."

"Um, yes, we were monitoring the tugs towing the *Cullain*. They were having trouble establishing the tow, so I sent a third tug out. They reported striking some type of debris before all our systems failed."

"Well, those poor bastards saved our skins. They must have hit a mine meant for us. We wouldn't be having this conversation if it had got us. Do you have any comms?"

"Almost, Chief," a senior crewman popped her head over a console. "Rigging up an emergency circuit now. I thought the guys that built this thing were crazy for keeping vacuum tube radio sets around. Guess they knew what they were doing." She tightened a wire terminal onto a battery and flipped a switch. A soft orange glow lit up inside the unit and cast small dots of light out of the ventilation slots. "You should have comms. Voice only, I'm afraid."

Forbes took the hand mic from her. "Thanks, great job. See if you can work any more miracles in here."

The crewman threw a salute and a big smile. "Aye, Fleet Chief! I can have holo comms up shortly."

Forbes keyed the mic. "All Fleet, this is Fleet Chief Forbes, anyone out there?"

A few crackles came over the speaker before, "This is tug *Buain*, Salvage Master Colan here."

"*Buain,* do you have a visual on the flagship?"

"Aye, looks like that firecracker has done you poorly, Fleet Chief. Astrogation says you didn't make stable orbit."

"Can you take us in tow?"

"Sorry no, Fleet Chief, got my hands full with the *Cullain*," Colan said. "Even if I didn't, this wee puller doesn't have near the thrust to handle that monster."

Forbes ran down a mental list of ships in his fleet. Anything with enough power to move *Jishin* didn't have the right towing equipment. He keyed the mic again. "Colan, do you know of *any* ships that could handle the job?"

"Checking the Salvage Handbook now," Colan replied. "Says the Imperials built one class of tug big enough to tow a Planetary Assault Carrier. They called it a Long-Range-Salvage-Tug. You wouldn't know where you could find one of those, would ya?"

Forbes felt the blood rise to his cheeks. "Yes, and it's nearby."

---

Gus gripped the arms of his acceleration couch so hard the veins on his arms were popping. The emergency lighting was on and the forward screen was black. The lack of acceleration gravity meant engines were offline.

"*Corvus*, status?"

The 1MC remained silent.

"XO, you okay?"

Lenore stood motionless, locked into the control sockets in the floor. The dancing patterns gone from her skin, and the life gone from her eyes.

Gus unstrapped from his couch and pushed toward a control station near the forward screen. He grasped a recessed handle, pulled, and twisted to open a panel. Inside, a faint glow reassured him that some things were still working. He fit a crank handle into a socket and began winding. The forward screen tilted up, and an exterior hull panel crawled slowly along a track, uncovering a large window fit into the hull.

The blue-green planet hung in the window. Gus opened a case in the panel and lifted out an astrogation sextant. He fit it into a bracket that swung away from the window.

"Let's see what's going on out there." He said to himself as he looked through the lens.

*Jishin* slowly crawled across the face of Matria. The battered ancient ship was dark except for the remnants of glowing superheated wreckage from its aerobraking maneuver. There was no sign the antimatter bomb had struck them.

"She's knocked out for now, but for how long?"

He fiddled with the dials on the sextant as he read off the vernier scales. "It's been a long time since I had to do astrogation in my head. Having Lenore and HAM around has made me sloppy." He pulled a small green notebook and pen from his pocket and scribbled numbers. Gus jotted a few formulas, double-checked his figures, and stabbed the page. "Ha, maybe we didn't blow you to bits, Forbes, but that old demon Gravis is hauling you down the well all the same."

The bridge came alive as lights reset to normal brightness.

**"I Awake,"** *Corvus* said.

"Good. What's your status?"

**"XO Dry Fired Rail Gun. Counter EMP Protected Me From Major Damage. Weapons and Engines Back Online in Three Minutes."**

"Is the XO hurt?"

Lenore stared out with her same vacant gaze.

**"Unknown. She still booting. Battle Song Exposed Her to Blast."**

"Alright, Big Guy, I need you to check my math," Gus said with a gesture to the window. "What's going on with *Jishin?*"

**"Dead Ship. Orbit Unstable. Crash Seven Standard Hours."**

"*Corvus,* this is McGowan, do you copy?" the comm said.

"This is Johansson."

"I owe you an apology, Commodore," McGowan said. "You appear to have handled everything quite well."

"Thanks, Admiral," Gus replied. *No need to tell him we actually missed.*

"By disabling *Jishin,* you have given me a negotiating opportunity. How did you know the Dellans would send another salvage tug on that particular course?"

"Sorry, Admiral, I don't kiss and tell."

"Keep your little secrets then," McGowan said. "I have Fleet Chief Forbes standing by if you would join me on the call?"

Gus glanced at his XO, still frozen, naked, and rooted to the deck. "Things are a bit of a mess over here. I will contact you from my quarters. Johansson, out."

Gus ran to his quarters and quickly changed from his vacuum battle armor to what passed for full dress on *Corvus.* He smoothed back his salt and pepper hair and took a deep breath before he keyed the comm.

"Admiral McGowan, Commodore Johansson here."

Two holo images formed across the small table. Gus's quarters were small and unimpressive, but they were private. Admiral McGowan's quarters looked little better than Gus's, but he projected an aura of control even over the holo. Fleet Chief Forbes definitely looked worse for wear. His thick gray hair was tousled and a smudge of black stroked across his forehead. His environmental suit was dirty and scuffed.

McGowan began. "Gentlemen, I believe peace negotiations are in order."

"I happily accept your surrender," Forbes said in his thick brogue.

Gus uncharacteristically held his tongue.

McGowan continued, "Sir, I believe *you* are at the disadvantage."

"Once again," Gus said. He couldn't contain himself forever.

"Bah, I've still got a fleet that's twice yours, and we will have power restored on my flagship before you can shake the cookie crumbs from your tunic."

"Don't bullshit a bullshitter, buddy. Your 'flagship' is going to leave a blazing trail across the Matrian sky shortly," Gus quipped.

McGowan cleared his throat to show displeasure at Gus's remarks. "Let's get down to the matter at hand. Fleet Chief Forbes, what do you really want?"

Forbes chewed his drooping mustache and considered his response. "The clans need a planetary home. We've been too long adrift. There's a lot to be said for dirt between your toes and fresh air."

"Is that all?" McGowan said. "There are rumors Dellans have been having problems with genetic drift for a while now. Too many miscarriages, etc."

Forbes didn't know McGowan had intel that good.

"My sources tell me that your population is in freefall, and you will have a complete collapse in a generation or two," McGowan continued.

Forbes came out on the attack. "Well, you could convince the ladies dirtside to give us a nice plot of land and trade some brides for a little fresh blood."

"HA!" Gus said. "From what I know, you wouldn't want to fall asleep next to a traded Matriarch."

McGowan grumbled again at Gus's comment. "I don't think I could swing a deal offering you Matrian territory."

"Yeah, I knew you were all talk," Forbes said.

McGowan raised his hands. "Hold on, maybe we can compromise. What if I could offer you the southern continent of Kragus? You thought that was desirable not so long ago."

Forbes stiffened and leaned forward. "You've got my attention."

"I am prepared to grant you a semi-autonomous region under Governance administration. You also agree to disarm and give up raiding, of course."

"That's like asking us to cut off an arm!" Forbes shouted.

"No need to be so dramatic, Fleet Chief," McGowan answered. "Take the offer back to your war council."

"I'll need a wee bit more than a patch of scraggly wilderness to make them swallow the deal," Forbes said. "Add ten years of two billion credits in economic support and exclusive trade rights between Kragus and the rest of the twin systems. I'm gonna need something for the spacers that won't swallow the anchor to do."

"Will you agree to Governance supervision of the conversion of your ships to commercial use. In Governance yards, of course," McGowan answered.

"No, in neutral Cellan yards," Forbes countered. "You'll be sneaking Governance kill switches on my ships."

"You drive a hard bargain, Forbes," McGowan said. "Take the offer."

Gus couldn't help himself and threw one last barb. "Just don't wait too long. Things are going to get warm on your ship pretty soon. We all know that my ship is the only tug in the twin systems capable of towing *Jishin*."

Forbes holo winked out.

McGowan's image turned to Gus. "Are you quite through playing at flag officer today, Bosun Johansson?"

"Remember, Mac, I don't work for you anymore," Gus replied. "Keep a civil tongue in your head, or I will dispense a little bosun locker justice on your pompous ass next time we meet. My fondness for Mitzi only goes so far. Call me when that idiot Forbes concedes. I've got a tow job to prep for." Gus jammed the button to end his connection.

Gus headed back to the bridge to check on Lenore. He knew he was probably going to pay for that last outburst, but it felt good now.

The bridge door slid open at his approach. Lenore was dressed and straightening her tunic as he stepped in.

"How are you feeling, XO? Did you enjoy your little nap?" Gus asked.

Lenore whirled and stiffened. "See how much sympathy you get from me the next time you get laid up in sickbay, jerk face!" Her eyes flashed anger.

Gus stopped. "Excuse me?"

Lenore's face softened. "I am sorry, Captain; it appears that the pulse has scrambled my speech protocols. It should be only temporary. No offense meant."

"Um, okay," Gus stammered. "It has been a stressful time for everyone."

Lenore looked down at the console. "I am familiar with the current battle situation and prepared to brief you if you are ready."

Gus nodded and eased into his command chair.

"As you are already aware, *Jishin* is dead in the Void. Even though they were not hit by our bomb, they have suffered a great deal of damage and will plunge into the planet's atmosphere in six-point-three hours. The EMP affected the entire Dellan fleet.

About fifty percent of their ships are operational. They are busy trying to rescue as many of the disabled vessels as they can."

"Is Gravis going to claim any of them?" Gus asked.

"Pardon me, Captain, who is Gravis?" Lenore asked.

"Oh, a character from an old song," Gus said. "Kind of like Davy Jones to ocean sailors, Gravis hauls the unlucky to their doom down the gravity well."

"Interesting," Lenore said. "I shall need to study these references more."

"Anyway, how are our forces?"

"Caber and his surviving star-fighters are withdrawing to high orbit. There are some two hundred operational. The cruisers *Terrible* and *Erebus* are fine and standing by for orders."

"Are their fighters operational?"

"Yes."

"Good, our troops on the ground might still need air support."

"Sergeant Faber is undamaged."

Gus laughed and said, "Of course he is. Still no good word from HAM?"

Lenore paused. "No, Captain." There was a hitch in her voice.

Gus swore he saw the glimmer of a tear in her eye. "Are you feeling all right, XO? Do you need to take a moment?"

"No, Sir, I apologize. The pulse affected me more than I initially thought," Lenore swallowed and shook her head. "There is work to be done. *Corvus* confirms he is ready to establish a tow on *Jishin* when ready."

"Well, I guess it's time for me to stop playing Commodore and put on my tugboat skipper's hat. *Corvus*, please take us into position to make tow on *Jishin*."

**"Aye, Skipper. Towing Honest Work."**

## CHAPTER FIFTY

Shadow Squad Banner looked at the fading light show dancing across the sky of Matria. "Damn, that must have been a hell of a bomb. I hope it was one of ours."

The comm crackled to life. "Attention all Dellans forces, this is Colonel Kravitz. I have received orders to stand down our assault. Looks like the war's over, folks."

Banner said, "That doesn't sound like a victory speech."

Boomer asked, "Does that mean we don't get no bounty, Boss?"

Banner fumed and considered. He climbed out of the LTV and onto the hood. "Listen up! I didn't hear nothing in that transmission that countered orders about our bounty. Until I hear it direct from the Fleet Chief, we are still on mission."

A cheer rose from the Shadows.

Banner jumped down. *Besides, I've got a score to settle with Nan Stanski.*

Gunner Nan Stanski perched on the front of her APC, Fuzzy, and discussed the situation over the comm. "That transmission from the Dellan's about a cease-fire came none too soon. I'm low on ammo, and my APC is just about out of juice."

"Same here," Gems answered. "We were supposed to be a blocking force, not assault."

"Hey, Gunner," Fuzzy said over his outside speaker. "I gots something youse probably want to hear."

A harshly accented Dellan voice came over the comm. "Banner, what are you doing? I told all forces to stand down. Command has ordered us to hold position while negotiations continue."

Gems said, "Banner. Isn't that the fella that wanted to turn that pretty noggin of yours into a finger bowl?"

"Yeah, looks like I've got one more problem to deal with today," Nan answered.

Banner's voice erupted from the comm, "Stanski, I know you can hear me. Come on out and play! Let's settle who is the better warrior once and for all."

Gems commed, "Sounds like we ain't done yet."

"What do you mean we? This is *my* fight." Nan said as she climbed into Fuzzy's top hatch.

Gems replied. "I'm not letting that asshole cheat me out of my Beltane dance."

"I told you. I'm not," Nan started. "Oh, the hell with it, maybe you will get shot, and I won't have to dance after all."

"Ha, I'm getting that dance if I gotta whittle two peg legs and a crutch."

Nan snorted and slammed the hatch.

---

The Shadows stopped under a lone tree as Banner checked the feed from the drone ranging ahead of his LTV. "Heads up, Shadows! I got an IR signature that matches our target. They are running on course bearing one eight two, speed sixty." He keyed some commands into his tablet. "Sending intercept plan, execute."

The Shadow's peeled off in different directions. A dust cloud marked their paths.

Sledge looked puzzled. "Hey Boss, are you sure that order was right? That won't catch Stanski."

Banner chuckled. "I'm settling this score to settle, alone." He had a pistol pointed at Sledge. "You need to get out." Banner waved as he sped away.

---

"Hey, Gems, our little birdie reports the Shadows are moving away and a lone unit is headed for me," Nan commed.

Gems replied, "Odds are looking better for my dance."

"Will you give it a rest?" Nan said. Fuzzy was handling the driving. Nan checked her display. "The lead vehicle is way faster than Fuzzy. I can't outrun it, and you won't get here before intercept."

Nan shouted, "Fuzzy, override all governor settings, maximum speed."

"Youse got it, Gunner. Gotta warn ya, we are almost outta juice."

"Let me worry about that. Head for that arroyo." She highlighted a feature on the map display.

Fuzzy shot between the steep canyon walls and followed the twisting path. Suddenly, the APC slammed to a halt throwing the crew around the tight cabin.

Nan called to the crew, "Everyone okay?"

"We're stuck, Gunner." Fuzzy said.

No answer from Wilson and oDolo. She turned. Wilson had a trickle of blood leaking from under his helmet. oDolo was shaking his head to clear it. Nan scrambled out of her commander's seat.

"oDolo, take care of Wilson. Use the belly hatch and take cover." Nan already had the hatch open and helped lower the wounded crewman to the ground. Then jumped into the turret operator seat.

Nan tried to spin the turret to cover their stern. The barrel jammed on the side of the canyon. "Shit!" She crawled forward again and popped the top hatch. Stanski climbed onto the turret, she saw Banner's LTV skid to a stop, and the big man emerged. He reached back inside. Nan recognized the tube of a tank killer as he pulled it out and raised it to his shoulder.

"Day just keeps getting better," Nan said.

She jumped clear and rolled before the missile hit. A wave of heat and pressure rocked Nan as the APCs reactive armor blast intercepted Banner's rocket. She saw oDolo drag Wilson to cover behind a driftwood snag, and she took off running along a branch passage to lead Banner away from her crew.

Banner tossed the empty tube to the ground and grabbed his rifle. He took off at a ground-eating jog after Nan.

Nan's lungs burned in the thin atmosphere as she ran. *Need to get out of this canyon fast. I can set up an ambush if I can get to some high ground.* She scrambled at the arroyo walls, but the loose dirt just fell away. Nan stopped and checked her sidearm. The magazine readout showed sixteen rounds remaining. She didn't have any spares. She stabbed the weapon back into her shoulder holster and took off again.

Banner grumbled as he jogged. His hemoboost injections

were wearing off, his breathing lagged, and his muscles burned. He called out. "Come on, Stanski, where is the fearless Marine running off too?"

Nan heard his taunts. *Just leading you away from my wounded crew before I kill you.*

Banner rounded a corner and saw Nan. He raised his rifle and snapped off two quick rounds that sprayed Nan with rock chips as she zig-zagged and then darted behind a large boulder.

Nan grabbed her pistol and leaned out to snap off a couple of wild shots at Banner. Just to keep him off balance and wary.

The big man yelled from behind cover. "I see you didn't win a marksmanship prize in boot camp." He stayed low and moved to take up a position behind a tree that had washed down the arroyo. He sighted carefully and waited for Nan to make a move.

Nan listened for Banner. She knew Dellans didn't have the patience for a standoff and threw a few taunts of her own. "You know a frail little thing like me can't handle these hand cannons. Why don't you throw out your rifle to make things a little fairer?"

Nan shifted position. She heard the shot and felt her head snap sideways at the same time. She reached up to feel a deep gouge in her helmet from the glancing shot. Her neck muscles screamed when she tried to move her head.

"Ha, missed me!" Nan called out, as much to raise her spirits as goad Banner.

Banner jumped up and raced towards another boulder. Nan raised up and popped off two more shots. Banner staggered and crawled behind the boulder. His rifle lay on the open ground.

"Shit!" he said and pulled at his vest. His body armor had stopped the bullet, but he knew he had at least one broken rib. Banner grabbed for his pistol. It dragged in his shoulder holster as he jerked it free. He looked down and saw Nan's second shot had destroyed it. Banner cursed as he threw the useless weapon. Banner drew his fighting knife.

Nan felt her weapon slide lock back on the second shot. She ejected the magazine and saw that the magazine counter had jammed. The magazine was empty. "I guess I should have taken Connie up on that new pistol."

Banner yelled from his cover, "Looks like we are in the same boat, Gunner. Your lucky shot knocked out my pistol." Banner stood. "And I heard your's lock back. You're empty."

Nan peaked out just as Banner stepped out, threw down his broken weapon, and drew his knife. She stood and pitched her helmet to the side. "I guess we do this the old-fashioned way." She pulled her own fighting knife and advanced.

Banner flashed a thin smile and moved in a dance. Armored vambrace and gloves covered each arm. His razor-edged stiletto flashed in continuous motion. His free arm protected his chest and broken ribs.

Nan noted the stiletto was the perfect weapon to slip through the joints in her body armor. She bounced on the balls of her feet to get a feel for the ground. The classic Marine clip-point blade was a familiar extension of her arm.

The fighters circled each other. Nan kept her knife "in the box," close to her body and between shoulder and waist with her trunk at a forty-five. Banner flowed in an easy glide. The hypnotizing swirl of his blade prevented telegraphing his moves.

"You studied paranza corta, I see," Nan said. "More flashy than effective."

"You favor the same old Marine hand-to-hand," Banner replied. "Your lack of imagination disappoints me." He darted in with a controlled slash that missed as Nan moved back.

She spun and jabbed, hoping to catch Banner off balance. He hopped and landed gracefully several feet back, still twirling his blade. "Pretty agile for such a big goof," she said.

"Thanks, just trying to keep you entertained." Banner stepped in and lunged.

Nan pivoted and slashed down at Banner's blade arm. The blade skipped off his armor.

Banner made a grab for Nan's knife. She saw an opening and caught him in the nose with her elbow. Banner staggered back, barely avoiding Nan's vicious follow-on kick.

Nan bounced back and prepared for the next rush. She could see the wheels turning in Banner's head. *He is going to a grapple game next. Can't let him get me into a ground contest.*

As if on cue, the big man abandoned finesse, and rushed forward arms wide. Nan tried to sidestep. Banner grabbed her arm and yanked hard. Nan felt something tear in her shoulder as she twisted loose. Her arm hung awkwardly.

"Looks like you got a bum wing there, Gunner," Banner said.

"I only need one arm to finish you," Nan replied.

Banner laughed and moved in for the kill.

Nan lowered her guard slightly, and Banner darted in. She dropped to her back and slashed upward. She felt her blade connect, and Nan kicked up with both legs and felt her boots sink into his diaphragm. Banner spiraled over her and landed on his back. A growing bloodstain spread along the inside of his pants.

Nan scrambled to her feet and resumed her fighting stance.

Banner lay on his back, trying to catch his breath.

Nan said, "I told you I would take your ball sack."

Banner rolled to all fours. His severed femoral artery pumped his life away with each passing second. He coughed, fumbled with a pouch at his belt, and pulled out a med patch.

Nan walked over and kicked his knife away. "I'm saving you just to see your humiliation at the prisoner exchange." She grabbed the patch and pushed him onto his back just as he lost consciousness.

# CHAPTER FIFTY-ONE

One month later, as the sun set on the plains outside the walls of Themyscira, preparations for a delayed Beltane finished up. It promised to be the largest gathering in decades, both a victory celebration and the traditional welcome of Spring.

Gus and his crew lounged in Chief Consul Sidra's pavilion at the center of the action. Admiral McGowan, Dame Constance Stillwell and her aide Harry Beston, and Mitzi Grey and her aunt Sadie had also joined them.

"So, someone needs to tell me what's so special about Beltane," Nyrkki said.

Sadie said, "Beltane is a celebration of Spring's promise of new life. Of course, there is the feasting, dancing, and the bonfire, but some couples choose to pledge to each other with a handfasting to formalize their commitments. Many others will find a partner for the evening and part at the morning light. Nine months from now, we will reap the fruits of tonight's celebration."

Zia Forte looked over at Admiral McGowan. "Well, *Corvus* much appreciates the fruits of his labor in the wake of the battle,

Admiral. Remember, you owe us standard salvage rates by tonnage for rescue of *Jishin* and the other Dellan ships we towed after the battle. And that is *a lot* of tonnage!"

Falkirk McGowan raised his glass reluctantly. "Perhaps, you would negotiate a volume discount?"

"Sorry, any discounts must be negotiated before services are executed," Zia said. "As per Governance maritime law."

Nyrkki leaned in. "Amore, enough business for tonight, enjoy!"

"Dear, besting an opponent at business *is my joy*."

"Look, the party is getting started," Gus said as a large procession of drummers entered the area.

A couple dressed as the Green Man and Maiden Goddess led the procession. Sidra and Jill Tower followed. The ladies were flanked by Jess and his lancers shining in their polished parade armor. Torch bearers sang and drummers kept the line in step. The ladies both wore a long snow-white cloak of fine-spun wool clasped at the throat with a Consul's badge of office. A wreath of laurel and holly crowned Jill's head. The Houses followed, escorted by Guildmen from the Trades.

Drake pointed and said, "Oh, I see Pela!" He stood and waved. He noted that she was the only member of Customs that was not escorted. Pela tried to ignore him but couldn't suppress a smile.

The procession rounded the area and came to a halt in front of the bonfire stack. Jill stepped forward, took a torch, and held it high. The Green Man and Goddess danced around her, writhing and entwining. The drumming became faster and louder as the dancers increased their efforts. At the climax, the drums stopped, and Jill screamed, tossing the torch high onto the stack. The pile caught instantly, and fire climbed into the sky.

Bonfires flared to life across the plain as the celebration spread. Shouts rose from the crowd.

Gus leaned toward Nan and said, "I guess the Matriarchs go all in for the dramatic."

Nan shot him a dirty look and shushed him.

Nyrkki laughed, and Zia caught him in the ribs with a sharp elbow.

"You need to lighten up, woman," he said, rubbing his bruised side.

"You need to show some respect, man," Zia replied, with a grin.

The procession broke up as each House retired to their respective pavilions. Sidra, Jill, and Pela wound their way through the bowing and congratulating crowd to join their friends.

Admiral McGowan rose and walked to greet Sidra as she made her way to her central seat at the table. "Chief Consul, that was quite the ceremony."

"Yes, I believe we have raised the bar this year," Sidra replied as she offered her hand. "Is this your first Beltane, Admiral?"

McGowan took her hand and led her to her chair. "I have attended once before. I met my late wife at a Beltane many years ago."

"I knew your wife well when we were girls," Sidra said. She patted the seat next to hers. "Please join me."

The Admiral bowed and took the seat. His daughter Mitzi and sister-in-law Sadie looked at each other and nodded.

"Will you look at that randy old coot?" Gus said.

Nan leaned over. "Be nice. Besides, Lenore would be highly displeased if she caught you cozying up to Sidra."

Gus waved her comment away. "No, it's not like that, I'm the Captain, and Lenore is just protective."

Nan snorted a laugh. "Yeah, right, you men really are oblivious."

Zia said, "They all need a good woman to set them straight."

"Maybe you are right, you know any?" Nyrkki said.

Zia's eyes flashed at him.

"Just kidding, amore mio."

"I was told these are the war heroes' seats," Faolin Flannery said as he walked up with a woman on his arm. "Everybody, this is Essa."

The woman nodded a greeting to the party. She looked at Drake and said, "Mr. Sheridan, Kio sends her regards."

Drake blushed and looked at Pela. She narrowed her eyes and shook her head slightly.

Flannery said, "Oh Zia, I think I found something that belongs to you." He reached into a pouch hanging from his shoulder and pulled out a squirming, chittering ball of gray fur.

"Ophelia!" Zia screamed and ran to snatch her up. "How? Where? You and HAM went down."

"Excuse me, pardon me, so sorry," HAM's polite voice drifted from the crowd as he tried to negotiate through. He burst into the pavilion and spun on his skates. "Greetings, friends! Captain Flannery was performing rescue patrols during the battle and heard my plea for help. I am most grateful for his assistance."

"You can have him back, Johansson," Flannery said. "The bugger never shuts up."

Gus laughed. "HAM, I should book you for being AWOL all this time and scaring us all to death. However, I think the EO's maintenance list will be punishment enough."

Nyrkki grabbed HAM in a bear hug that strained HAM's seams. "Ya blasted spinning whirligig, I'm gonna work ya till your rivets lose purchase."

HAM tried to speak past the massive arms engulfing him. "I am most pleased to see you again also, EO."

Admiral McGowan said, "Chief Consul, I believe it is customary for you to start the first dance. If you would do me the honor?"

"Only if you will call me, Sidra. We can't keep calling each other Admiral and Chief Consul all evening." She rose and led him away.

"Is this the target's table?" a loud voice called from behind the group.

They turned to see two Governance officers in full dress uniforms headed toward their table. The woman was tall and blonde and the man dark and stocky.

"Silky, Plug, how did you two rate liberty?" Drake asked as he wrapped an arm around each of them.

Silky answered, "I just told the air boss that you two owed us a beer, and we're not letting you get away without paying up."

Pela grabbed Drake's arm and said, "No beer for you. I want to dance before you get lost telling stories."

Plug laughed. "You heard her, Duck, no arguing with the Princess."

"Wait, no, that's Drake, not Duck!"

A handsome dark-haired man emerged from the crowd, took Silky's hand, and bowed. She looked at Drake and said, "Walks like a duck, quacks like a duck, it's a duck!" She took the man's arm and headed for the dance.

A woman pulled at Plug's arm. She was a good head taller than him and insistent. Plug said, "See ya around the system, Duck. Looks like my dance card has just filled up for the evening." He called over his shoulder, "You still owe me that beer."

Drake looked back at Gus as Pela led him away.

"Enjoy it while you can, young blood," Gus called out.

Harold Beston took Connie's hand, they stood, and walked toward the dance. Each knew the other so well, words were no longer necessary.

"I'm here to collect!" a voice called, and the group looked behind them.

Range Marshall Gems strode confidently into the pavilion and swept off his wide brim hat with a bow and pointed at Nan. "That Marine over there owes me a dance." He wore a dark green uniform with a double row of brass buttons down the front of his short jacket and snug fitting pants tucked into high-top boots. A Marshalls star flashed on his chest, and his customary knife bounced against his hip.

Nan whispered, "Aw shit." She stood and said, "Let's get this over with. One dance and we are square!"

"Ma'am, you ain't seen me dance," Gems said.

The group laughed as the pair headed away. Nan shot them a death stare and said. "Remember, what happens at Beltane."

"Stays at Beltane!" the group shouted back.

"Ms. Grey, if you please."

Mitzi turned with a start to see Jess standing next to her with his hand out. Pup sat obediently at his feet.

"It's about time you showed up. I see you took off that tin suit. Did you take the time to wash off the trail dust too?" She stood, leaned in, and inhaled. Mitzi closed her eyes and purred into his ear. "You'll do." They walked away.

"Well, that's interesting," Gus said.

Sadie slapped Gus's shoulder, "You be civil, Gus Johansson. Mitzi is a happily married woman who just likes to dance."

"What happens at Beltane." Gus made a "my lips are sealed" motion.

"What about you, Ma'am? Care to dance?"

Sadie turned at the question.

Zia said, "Desson, I didn't think I would see you here. Sadie, this is Desson. He was on the plains with us before the battle."

"Don't let her sugar coat it, I'm just an old chuck-wagon hand."

Sadie stood and took his offered hand. "I love a man that can cook, do you have any specialties?"

"A few, the boys seem to like my spring berry cobbler," Desson said. He leaned closer to Sadie and whispered into her ear. "What is that perfume? It reminds me of dew in the morning."

Sadie gathered his arm in hers. "Why, I'm not wearing perfume." She looked over her shoulder at Zia and winked. "You mentioned a dance. Let's see if you can still move, cowboy."

"Never knew what hit him," Nyrkki said, as he shook his head.

Zia punched him in the shoulder. "You behave, Nyrkki Ratuainen," she scolded. "Older folks deserve to have fun too."

Gus tried to change the subject and rescue Nyrkki. "Good thing that cowboy, Jess, showed up. Thought I was going to get stuck dancing with Mitzi all night. I'm not sure how Lenore would feel about that."

Zia gave him a side-eye. "If I were you, I wouldn't try to find out. You realize the whole 'Singing the Battle Song' naked bit was bullshit, right?"

Guss jerked his head. "*WHAT?* How do you know about that?"

"I suggested it," she said, with a grin. "Sometimes, you just gotta knock a guy over the head to get his attention," Zia hauled Nyrkki out of his chair, and dragged him toward the dance.

"Well, First Sergeant/Consul Tower, looks like we are the last two at the table," Gus said as he turned towards Jill.

"Sorry, Captain, I'm no wallflower." She dropped her cloak on the chair and laced her arm with a young Airmen's Guild flyer walking by. "What happens at Beltane." She winked at Gus and giggled. "Now, what is your name, young Sir?" she asked as they walked away.

"At least the beer is good," Gus raised his mug to Pup lying under the table. "Looks like it's just us, fella." Gus scratched the giant dog's ears.

Ophelia had climbed onto the table and was inspecting the dishes. She picked up a morsel and tasted it. The possum made a face and tossed the bit to Pup. He snatched it out of the air and swallowed it in one gulp and wagged his tail. Ophelia hissed at him but relented and threw him another bite before waddling away to find something she liked better. Pup followed her with his enormous tail thumping the table.

"Sorry I was delayed; did I miss anything?"

Gus spun at the sound of Lenore's voice. "XO, I didn't think you were coming." He caught his breath at the sight of her.

Lenore wore an emerald green chiffon dress with sheer side panels that showcased her perfect legs. Gus thrilled at the memory of the beautifully naked and shimmering Valkyrie that led his fleet into battle.

Lenore said, "I see HAM has made his entrance. He made me promise to keep it a secret."

"Thank you, Ms. Lenore. I believe my surprise was a resounding success," HAM said.

Lenore continued. "I am pleased to see you waited for me, Captain." She offered him her hand. "I was afraid Ms. Grey would have spirited you away by now."

"A pale comparison to you, my dear. I believe we know this song." Gus rose and led her away. "I wanted to talk to you about your battle song."

"If you are lucky, Captain, you might hear it again," she said and smiled as they walked toward the dance.

"I shall remain here and reserve your table," HAM called. "Besides, someone needs to keep Ophelia in line."

Ophelia looked up at the mention of her name and hissed at HAM. Pup whined and she continued sampling tidbits and tossing him the ones she didn't like.

"Thank you, HAM," Gus said, over his shoulder. "We might be awhile."

# EPILOGUE

Faber lounged in his office back in Ultima Shipyard. His brother, Caber, sat across from him in the android "suit" Faber had made to correct his malfunctioning leg.

Brother dear it was so kind,
    This new body suit for me to find.

Faber waved his smoking cigar. "It was nothing. I just took a standard battle bot chassis and mashed it together with an enhanced cognitive processor," he said. "You're not as cute as Lenore, but it suits you."

Familiar form is fitting sleeve
    My lack of beauty I do not grieve.

. . .

"Well, I've got plenty to keep me busy now and I could use the help," Faber said. "I've got to replace the star fighters we lost and repair all the damage those ham-handed pirates did to the place."

These tasks we must complete with haste,
    I fear a coming peril waits.

"Peril?" Faber sat up in his chair. "What are you talking about?"

I cast my eye throughout the sky
    Always seeking terrors nigh.

Caber waved his hand and the scene behind Faber's desk changed. It showed a starfield with the twin suns of Iz and Ix surrounded by their planets. The scene accelerated past the solar system into space toward a bright light.

A blueshift item travels now,
    Its pulsing light precedes its bow.

"Looks like we're getting visitors." Faber asked. "You got any idea where they are from."

The light is one I recognize,

An ancient Confederation drive.

"An Imperial Confederation drive signature? What is that doing out there?" Faber said.

Ship is from the Earth of old,
    Has journeyed long since Gate was closed.

"Hmmm, I didn't think they would actually do it," Faber said. "I really pissed those old Imperials when I slammed the Gate. Someone traveled a thousand light years to get at me. How much time do we have?"

We have about one standard year,
    Before the ship approaches near.

"Well then, we will need to work fast to replenish our stockpiles before they arrive."

Should we tell the fair Lenore,
    Of soon a knocking on our door?

"Let's keep this to ourselves for now," Faber said. "No sense interrupting her party."

## AN ADVANCE LOOK AT:
### The Murder of Harrison Grey

**A Jill Tower Mystery**

Captain Harrison "Hazy" Grey pulled his greatcoat tighter around his shoulders. The foggy night chill of Nakon City's Lift Port was soaking through the heavy wool. There were more practical options available, but Grey's vanity required he wear his Governance naval uniform. He had a date later that he wanted to impress.

He checked the time again and wondered why the delivery was late. His tablet posted the shipment landed but wasn't yet released from customs.

*I've got them this time,* he thought. *I've finally figured out the smuggler's system. I just need to catch them in the act.*

"This should show the Admiral I deserve more responsibility," Grey said to himself. "Exposing corruption on this scale should finally net me that Admiral's promotion. If I can get Mitzi to stop spending so much money, I might be able to retire before I die." Grey slipped a flask from his coat and took a drink. The fiery liquid warmed him on the way down.

Harrison looked around the docks again. An automated baggage cart moved through the mist towards him. "About damn time you showed up! I don't appreciate being left in the rain," Grey called to the bot operated carrier. "Stop here. I want to inspect the cargo before it goes into the warehouse."

The low-grade constructed intelligence built into the carrier didn't bother to answer. It stopped in front of Grey and he stomped up to the wagon and waved his customs clearance chip over the seal. He grunted as he struggled with the locking bars and raised the door. Rows of neatly stacked containers filled the cart. Only one box had it's door facing Grey's side of the cart. He popped the latch and opened the box.

A shot rang out and Grey collapsed. The cart door slid shut and the CI continued to the warehouse.

# ABOUT THE AUTHOR

Dale Sale

I found myself adrift after a thirty-year career in the U.S. Coast Guard. Over twenty of them as a Chief Warrant Officer, so I got a soft spot for CWOs.

Casting about for something to do I thought, "I'll write a book. How hard could it be."

Turns out it is damn hard!

I guess I'm a glutton for punishment because, I keep doing it.

# WAIT THERE'S MORE!

## WANT FREE STUFF?

So you got to the end of the book and would like more adventures from the Corvus Universe.

You, my friend, are in luck! Head over to:

www.DaleSaleBooks.com

There, for the low, low price of zero dollars, you can get some free content. All you need to do is provide your email address and I will send you some goodies.